Casting Pearls Before Swine . . .

Marianne never let him finish. She attacked, the knife free of her pocket now. A savage slash at his eyes sent Carstairs stumbling back. He caught his foot on the box filled with the silver chunks and fell hard. His head snapped back as he collided with a big rock. Wary of a trick, Marianne edged forward, the knife handle turning damp in her sweaty grip. She made a few tentative stabs at him, but Carstairs lay still. Blood oozed from the belly wound, which was only a shallow scratch and not the disemboweling stroke she had intended.

"Hey, Carstairs, where are you? We heard a commotion. Where'd you git off to?"

From the argument between the men coming from the camp, she faced three or four miners. Marianne stood over Carstairs, who moaned and tried to sit up. A single quick thrust would end all her problems.

She could kill a man. But she couldn't murder one, not even a lowlife like Carstairs.

She almost panicked when the miners came toward her. Marianne bent and grabbed the box that had downed Carstairs, opened the lid, and then emptied it onto the man's chest. The silver gleamed in the starlight.

She threw down the box and ran as if a pack of rabid dogs were coming after her . . .

DON'T MISS THESE
ALL-ACTION WESTERN SERIES
FROM THE BERKLEY PUBLISHING GROUP

THE GUNSMITH by J. R. Roberts

Clint Adams was a legend among lawmen, outlaws, and ladies. They called him . . . the Gunsmith.

LONGARM by Tabor Evans

The popular long-running series about Deputy U.S. Marshal Custis Long—his life, his loves, his fight for justice.

SLOCUM by Jake Logan

Today's longest-running action Western. John Slocum rides a deadly trail of hot blood and cold steel.

BUSHWHACKERS by B. J. Lanagan

An action-packed series by the creators of Longarm! The rousing adventures of the most brutal gang of cutthroats ever assembled—Quantrill's Raiders.

DIAMONDBACK by Guy Brewer

Dex Yancey is Diamondback, a Southern gentleman turned con man when his brother cheats him out of the family fortune. Ladies love him. Gamblers hate him. But nobody pulls one over on Dex . . .

WILDGUN by Jack Hanson

The blazing adventures of mountain man Will Barlow—from the creators of Longarm!

TEXAS TRACKER by Tom Calhoun

J.T. Law: the most relentless—and dangerous—manhunter in all Texas. Where sheriffs and posses fail, he's the best man to bring in the most vicious outlaws—for a price.

JAKE LOGAN

SLOCUM
AND THE
SILVER CITY HARLOT

Pomeroy Public
Library

THE BERKLEY PUBLISHING GROUP
Published by the Penguin Group
Penguin Group (USA) Inc.
375 Hudson Street, New York, New York 10014, USA

Penguin Group (Canada), 90 Eglinton Avenue East, Suite 700, Toronto, Ontario M4P 2Y3, Canada
(a division of Pearson Penguin Canada Inc.) • Penguin Books Ltd., 80 Strand, London WC2R 0RL,
England • Penguin Group Ireland, 25 St. Stephen's Green, Dublin 2, Ireland (a division of Penguin
Books Ltd.) • Penguin Group (Australia), 707 Collins Street, Melbourne, Victoria 3008, Australia
(a division of Pearson Australia Group Pty. Ltd.) • Penguin Books India Pvt. Ltd., 11 Community
Centre, Panchsheel Park, New Delhi—110 017, India • Penguin Group (NZ), 67 Apollo Drive,
Rosedale, Auckland 0632, New Zealand (a division of Pearson New Zealand Ltd.) • Penguin Books
(South Africa) (Pty.) Ltd., Rosebank Office Park, 181 Jan Smuts Avenue, Parktown North 2193,
South Africa • Penguin China, B7 Jiaming Center, 27 East Third Ring Road North,
Chaoyang District, Beijing 100020, China

Penguin Books Ltd., Registered Offices: 80 Strand, London WC2R 0RL, England

SLOCUM AND THE SILVER CITY HARLOT

A Jove Book / published by arrangement with the author

PUBLISHING HISTORY
Jove edition / March 2013

ISBN: 978-0-515-15354-5

JOVE®
Jove Books are published by The Berkley Publishing Group,
a division of Penguin Group (USA) Inc.,
375 Hudson Street, New York, New York 10014.
JOVE® is a registered trademark of Penguin Group (USA) Inc.
The "J" design is a trademark of Penguin Group (USA) Inc.

PRINTED IN THE UNITED STATES OF AMERICA

10 9 8 7 6 5 4 3 2 1

1

Marianne Lomax smiled sweetly as she tugged down her bodice to reveal more than a little of her swelling white bosom. With a deliberate shake of her shoulders, she set her breasts to jiggling—and captured the miner's full attention. He swallowed hard and spilled some of the drink she had fixed for him.

The auburn beauty wished he would drink more. She had a few customers who got so knee-walking drunk that she didn't have to do a thing but assure them they had been superior in bed and that she would never forget how expert their lovemaking had been. More than once she had dropped hints about this around Silver City to bolster the men's reputations. Salesmanship went a long way in keeping the best customers.

In her mind that meant ones who never caused trouble and who paid her what was more than the going rate for sexual favors in the larger cathouses.

"I never 'spected to find a filly as fine and frisky as you, Miz Marianne," the miner said. He spilled more of his whiskey on her sofa.

1

She came close to rushing to him and clawing out his eyes. That sofa had come all the way from Georgia and had belonged to her mama, rest her soul. The furniture was about all she had left to remind her of better days in the green hills with the gentle breezes and . . .

"Let me freshen up that there drink, Clem," she said, knowing she had to tend to this disagreeable business so she could get it over fast. Marianne rose gracefully, being sure to show enough ankle to keep the man's interest focused on her and what was going to occur. So much of what she did was showmanship. Most of the silver miners were done, otherwise, in a minute or two, and often felt cheated. A slow buildup, a bit of tease, a flash of forbidden flesh, and they were more than happy to pay her.

She almost laughed at that. She could hit him between the eyes with an ax handle and never break his concentration on her. He worked a claim out at the edge of Chloride Flats, where the richest silver strike in New Mexico still brought in prospectors and others itching to get rich. The town struggled to put up enough buildings to house them all. Most of the miners lived in tents, and the largest of the structures in town were adobe or two-story wood frame saloons and bawdy houses.

Just sitting in her parlor was a treat for a man who camped with sand fleas and biting gnats in a tent that likely leaked like a sieve when it rained.

"Why, thank you kindly, Miz Marianne," he said. Clem held out his glass in such a way that she had to bend over to refill it.

Marianne played the game well. She enjoyed this, bending so her rump was in the air just a little so she could shake it. Her bodice slid down a little more, giving Clem a decent view of the deep, shadowy canyon between her breasts.

"Oh, my, I am being so bold. Will you forgive me?" She pulled up her blouse in such a way that it tightened across her breasts, showing her penny-sized nipples through the cloth.

The miner didn't miss this part of the show either. She sank down beside him on her mama's sofa and considered ways of moving him to the only other item of furniture in the room where he could spill all the tarantula juice he wanted. She had taken the fainting couch in payment from the Silver City carpenter rather than take his last silver dollar. For a town where silver flowed like a river, too many were living on the edge of poverty.

As she was.

"Oh, I am suddenly dizzy," she said, taking two exact steps back, being sure the fainting couch was under her and then flopping back. She theatrically lifted her arm to cover her eyes even as she flapped her skirt.

"Are you all right, Miz Marianne?"

"I am taken faint and need to be revived," she said, drawing up her skirt even more until she exposed her leg past the knee.

"You want some of this here whiskey?"

"I need more than that, Clem. I need a man who can massage me so the circulation returns to my limbs."

"I don't rightly know how to do that."

"It'll come naturally to a *man* like you." She hiked her skirts even more to reveal snowy white thighs and the fact that she wasn't wearing any undergarments. Flapping the cloth a bit caused a small breeze across her privates. To her surprise, she was getting wet.

It wasn't because of Clem. She enjoyed the buildup to the actual act of the miner being on top of her, pumping furiously until he was done. Too few men she had ever found took the time to be certain she was enjoying the sex as much as they were.

Too damned few, but there had been some.

Clem wiped off his dirty hands on his flannel shirt and then knocked back all the whiskey to get some Dutch courage. This was a man who risked his life mining silver, would wrestle a grizzly and win, and he was afraid of a slip of a girl like her. Marianne needed the money he had to offer for her favors, but she also reveled in the power over the socially inexperienced and how she controlled them.

The miner dropped to his knees beside the fainting couch and hesitantly touched her calves. Marianne recoiled.

"Did I hurt you? I didn't mean no—"

"You sent a shiver of anticipation throughout my entire quivering body, Clem. More. Do it some more." She lounged back and hiked her feet up to the edge of the fainting couch, then spread her knees lewdly to give him a sight he wasn't likely to find again anywhere else.

He licked his lips, rubbed at his bushy mustache, and moved closer. His callused hands made her shiver as he parted her thighs even more. His mustache tickled as his face came closer. And then all hell broke loose.

The front door crashed open and slammed so hard against the wall it rebounded.

Marianne struggled to get her feet under her, but Clem was in the way.

"Git yer face away from her pussy or I'll thrash you good and proper!" The threat came just before a deep-throated roar like a mountain lion ready to attack.

"What's goin' on?" Clem flopped back and sat heavily on the floor to the side of the fainting couch, giving Marianne a chance to pull down her skirts and try to stand.

A hand more like a ham hock shoved her back. Marianne's arms windmilled as she struggled to keep her balance. She lost the fight and sat heavily on the couch, staring up at Lester Carstairs.

"You can't bull your way into a lady's house like this!"

"Lady?" Carstairs spat. The dark, viscous gob hit Clem on the shoulder and spattered onto his cheek.

This infuriated the miner. He surged to his feet, hands balled into fists.

"You cain't talk to her like that. You think you can bully ever'body in town, but it's time somebody stood up to you!"

"Clem, no!"

Marianne's warning came an instant too late. While the miner was declaring his intentions, Carstairs reared back and unloaded a punch that came from a mile off. His huge left fist crashed into Clem's belly. The miner grunted. But Carstairs was already delivering an uppercut with his right. This connected solidly. Clem's eyes rolled up in his head, and he crashed backward, falling stiff as a board.

"You have no right!"

"I got a right. I'm layin' claim to you, whore. You're the purtiest in town, and you're mine now. Mine and nobody else's 'cuz you got what I want!" He stepped forward, hands reaching for her.

He froze at the sound of twin hammers cocking on a double-barreled shotgun.

"You touch my ma and I swear I'll kill you where you stand."

"You don't want to get my blood all over your ma, now do you, boy?" Carstairs turned to face his diminutive attacker.

"Run, Randolph, go!" Marianne cried to her twelve-year-old son.

But the boy pressed his lips together in grim determination and aimed the shotgun straight at Lester Carstairs's chest. The shotgun was almost too heavy for him to heft and the barrels swung about in tiny circles. Marianne saw what was happening but her son didn't. Carstairs wasn't a man who scared easily. More than one man in Silver City had pointed a six-shooter at him and lived to regret it—or had even died because of such folly. He wouldn't have any more compunction about killing a boy than he would a gunfighter.

The shotgun strayed the barest amount from dead center on his torso, giving Carstairs the chance to step up and bat it away. His powerful fingers closed around the blued barrel of the ten-gauge and yanked. Randolph couldn't hold on.

"I ought to turn you over my knee and whup your ass, boy," Carstairs said. He grabbed for Randolph, but the boy had gotten over the surprise of losing his shotgun.

As Carstairs immediately found out, this wasn't the boy's only weapon. As he grabbed for the boy, Carstairs let out a howl of pain and jerked away. Blood gushed from his hand. Randolph had cut him with a small knife. Waving around the short-bladed knife made Marianne think of David and Goliath. But outside of Biblical stories, might made right. Carstairs would take any amount of punishment to get the boy now.

Marianne drove forward, her shoulders crashing into the backs of Carstairs's knees. The man cried out and fell over her. By the time he got himself upright, she had the shotgun trained on him. It didn't waver in her grip.

"I don't know what my son's loaded this with. I hope it's buckshot since that'll tear a hole the size of my fist in your belly and make you beg for dying," she said.

"You wouldn't—" Carstairs screeched in fear as Marianne pulled the first trigger. The fainting couch exploded in a welter of wood splinters and cotton stuffing.

"Damn, I missed. I won't this time," she said.

"I'm goin'," Carstairs said. "But you remember this. You're *my* whore. I take what I want."

Randolph lunged and tried to cut Carstairs again, but Marianne held him back. She followed the man all the way out the door. Only when she heard a horse trotting off did she sag down, shaking.

"You shoulda killed him, Ma. I would have, but he—"

"You're twelve years old," she said sternly. "You don't go killing grown-ups. And where'd you get that knife?"

"Billy gave it to me. It was a gift."

"He show you how to cut a man, too? Don't answer that." Tears ran down her cheeks, but she wiped them away. "Fetch some water and see if you can't wake up Clem. He got more 'n he bargained for tonight."

"Do it yourself. I don't want anything to do with your johns." Randolph ran off, sobbing.

"Randolph! Wait!" But it was too late. The boy had disappeared into the darkness, probably to spend the night with that friend of his, William McCarty.

She leaned against the shotgun and decided it was probably for the best. She didn't like having to sell her body to keep her son fed and clothed, but she'd do whatever it took to raise him right. It was a shame he had to see her with any of her customers.

Marianne picked up the whiskey bottle and dabbed some of it on her fingers. Waving this under Clem's nose caused the miner to twitch. When he opened his lips, she poured a little of the potent liquor in. He choked, gasped, and his eyelids shot wide open.

"It's all right, Clem. He's gone."

"Did he—"

"No, he ran off 'fore he could get around to that."

"You and him, you his woman like he said?"

"Never." The vehemence of her denial convinced Clem.

"I'm feelin' kinda woozy, Miz Marianne."

"You go on, Clem, and get some rest. I'll be here for you when you're ready."

"All I got's a greenback dollar," he said, fumbling in his shirt pocket. She pressed her slender fingers against his.

"Nothing happened. You keep it. Or go buy yourself a half bottle of rotgut with it."

"I took up your time, Miz Marianne. Don't seem fair not to pay you somethin'."

"What's not fair is Lester Carstairs," she said, guiding the miner to the door. She closed it behind him, seeing that it had to be repaired. Carstairs had kicked it in and broken off the latch.

Marianne found herself so angry she paced, then wanted to scream. Carstairs had taken it into his head that he could have her anytime he wanted because she sold herself. Not many of the girls in the cribs in Silver City wanted anything to do with Les Carstairs. He had a reputation of beating up whoever he was with, and rumors had it more than one girl had disappeared, probably murdered at his hand and buried up in the mountains, never to be found.

"How am I going to fix that door?" She stopped and stared at the broken wood, then decided she might as well clean up now and worry on it in the morning.

She had a powerful lot to worry on. The mortgage payment on the house was due in another week, and she was still four dollars shy. What she would have gotten from Clem would have helped, but she was afraid she'd have to ask the banker for more time. He wasn't likely to give it since houses, like any building in Silver City, were in short supply. He could foreclose and sell it for ten times what Marianne had paid for it only a year earlier. There hadn't been the silver find then and not more than a hundred people had made Silver City their home.

Now that many came in a week, seeking their fortunes.

She dropped the shotgun onto what remained of the fainting couch, then went to the small kitchen to fetch a broom and dust pan. Cleaning up the debris was about all she was capable of doing at the moment. As she rummaged in the small closet to get the broom out, she heard a muffled voice coming from the front of the house.

"Randolph, get on in here. We need to talk."

She returned to the front room, intending to have him help her clean up. But her son wasn't anywhere to be seen. Marianne started to tug open the front door when the window to her right broke. Her mouth dropped open as she saw the whiskey bottle with the flaming rag stuck into the neck.

Then the bomb exploded, sending broken glass and fire straight at her.

2

John Slocum cursed as the heavily loaded wagon hit a rock and sent him flying up off the hard wooden bench. He landed askew on the edge and almost tumbled to the ground. Only by dint of will did he stay in the driver's box. The leather reins turned slippery in his grip, but he drove his boot heels into the wagon's side and recovered.

The mules brayed in protest at the steep climb. He had been whipping them along for the past four days to keep his cargo intact. A quick glance over his shoulder made him curse anew. Sawdust had leaked out from under the canvas covering large blocks of ice enclosed in wood crates. Moving the ice from Santa Fe, New Mexico, down to Tombstone in Arizona Territory was one of the most lucrative cargoes possible. The miners paid top dollar for a sliver of ice in their drinks. All he had to do was get the heavy load there before it melted.

"Shaddup," he bellowed to the mules. They ignored him, continuing their noisy protests at such abuse. With a quick spin, he secured the reins around the wheel brake and vaulted to the ground.

Legs a bit shaky from driving so long, he braced himself against the side of the wagon as he went to the rear. As he had feared, one crate had cracked open from too much jostling along the rough road. He was a hundred miles outside of Tombstone, still on the New Mexico side of the Continental Divide. All he had to do was reach the southern pass.

Pulling back the heavy canvas protecting the crate from the sun, Slocum tugged at the loose board. A new river of soggy sawdust dribbled out.

Replacing the sawdust as insulation wasn't going to happen, but he might stuff in dirt or leaves to replace what had leaked out. Looking around, he decided pine needles were his best chance of keeping the ice from melting and ruining this freight run.

He grabbed a hammer and whacked at the loose nails, securing the crate. The holes in the top of the crate would let him stuff in pine needles or whatever else he could find. He wasn't exactly sure where he was but close to Steeple Rock assured him there wouldn't be much more of this mountain road to traverse. From Steeple Rock he would turn west through the broad pass and into the Sonoran Desert until he reached Tombstone.

As he gathered brittle pine needles by the handful, he hesitated. Slocum put his hand down flat against the rocky ground and felt vibration. The pine needles fluttered down as he slid his Colt Navy from his cross-draw holster and stood. A rider came mighty fast on his back trail. With the grade this steep, there was no cause to kill a horse by galloping unless circumstances warranted it.

Dire circumstances.

The rider came around a bend in the road and slowed when he spotted Slocum holding his six-shooter. Then he drew rein, stood in the stirrups, and waved.

"You John Slocum? Holst sent me."

Slocum lowered his six-shooter to his side and motioned with his left hand for the rider to approach. It didn't make a lick of sense that his boss would send a rider out since there was nothing Holst needed to tell him. He didn't give two hoots and a holler if Slocum died on the trail as long as he delivered every cold cubic inch of ice to Arizona. Loss of profit, loss of the wagon and team—those mattered to Holst, and he had no reason to think anything jeopardized them. Slocum had driven this route three times in the past two months without any trouble.

The rider came closer, keeping his hands in sight.

"Glad I caught up with you. Holst sent me to give you a hand. Looks like you're needin' it. Break down?"

"Crate broke open," Slocum said, not giving anything away. With the canvas pulled back and sawdust all over the wagon bed, any fool could see what had happened.

"Damn. You expose the ice?"

"Holst is a cheap bastard. He told me over and over how this route didn't need but one driver. What does he expect you to do?"

"Prices are way up over in Arizona. He reckons to sell this load for ten times what he has before. Been burnin' up the telegraph lines to make it happen."

Slocum said nothing. He sized up the rider. Short, slender, red hair, and fair complexion. He wore his six-gun high on his right hip, where it would be hard to draw astride the horse and damned near impossible to draw with any speed even if he stood with both boots on the ground. This wasn't a gunfighter. From his clothing, he might be a miner rather than a freighter.

"You want me to help?" The man rode closer, then dismounted when Slocum remained quiet. "I've worked as a carpenter, and looks like you was stuffin' leaves and shit into the box to keep the ice from meltin' any more. It melted much?" His bright blue eyes worked to see if the wagon bed was wet from vanishing ice.

"Not much gone. The crate only busted open a mile or two back, at the foot of this hill."

"Do you think pine needles will work better than leaves?"

"There're more of 'em around here," Slocum said, glancing at the ponderosa all around. It was early enough in the spring that the oak, aspen, and other trees that shed their leaves every fall still clung to their new bright greenery. Winter snow had rotted last autumn's crop of leaves, but the pine needles were eternal.

"Good point," the man said, dropping to his knees and sweeping the needles up the way Slocum had before being interrupted.

"You my assistant? You're not my boss."

The redhead laughed easily and said, "From what Holst says, you don't even look at him as your boss and he pays you, tells you what to do. You're free as the wind, that's what Holst said 'fore he sent me along."

Slocum stepped away as the man jumped into the wagon, examined the crates for sturdiness, then began stuffing stacks of the dead brown pine needles into the holes. For all his industry, the man seemed distracted. Slocum knew it might be that he hadn't holstered his six-shooter, but the man's interest focused more on the ice. The notion that a single man would steal the cargo entered Slocum's mind.

"You got a name?"

The redhead looked up, pushed his hat up to expose a pale forehead, then grinned. Slocum figured that smile melted the ladies' hearts. It did not affect him.

"Frank's the name."

"You supposed to ride with me all the way to Tombstone?"

"That's what Holst told me."

"You finish replacing the insulation, then mount up, ride back to Santa Fe, and tell Holst I don't need help."

"I don't get paid."

"Then go over to Silver City. It's not more 'n ten miles to the east. Find a saloon and drink until it seems about time for me to drive back. You can tell Holst you did what he said, and I won't gainsay that."

"But I can *help!* There's no point in coolin' my heels. I'm an honest fellow. I don't get paid for work I don't do."

That argument appealed to Slocum since he felt the same way, but something about Frank didn't set well with him. The youngster was open and was quick with his smile, maybe too quick. He was personable and no gunman from the way he wore his pistol. If he went for that smoke wagon, it'd be a week from Thursday before he hauled it free of the holster.

There wasn't anything to worry on about Frank, other than nothing he'd said about Holst and why the owner of the freight company would have sent him made any sense.

"Go on and hammer in the last of the nails," Slocum said, still watching Frank like a hawk.

The man held the hammer, considered the job, then set to driving the nails back in with a vengeance. He dropped the hammer, pulled up the canvas, and snugged it under the edges of the crate before jumping to the ground.

"See? I'm real handy to have around."

"You got a newspaper?"

"What's that?" Frank looked hard at Slocum, then nodded. "I got one in Santa Fe a couple days ago." He went to his saddlebags and fumbled around.

Slocum held his six-shooter ready in case the stranger came out with a hideout pistol, but Frank turned and held out the *Santa Fe New Mexican*, the leading northern New Mexico newspaper.

A quick glance at the date convinced Slocum that Frank was telling the truth about being in Santa Fe when he said, but that proved nothing about his claim that Holst had sent him. Slocum took the front page of the paper.

"Be right back. You watch the wagon."

"As if anyone out here'd steal it," Frank said. Something in his words rang hollow.

Slocum headed for the bushes as if seeking privacy to do his business, found a thick-boled oak, and stepped behind it. He waited a few seconds, about as long as it would take to drop his pants, then peered around to spy on Frank. The man had climbed back into the wagon and leaned against the crate as if he wanted the cold ice to chill him. What came next startled Slocum.

Frank went to the driver's bench and dropped down, reaching for the reins wrapped around the brake. Slocum's hand went to his six-gun, then he froze. Tipping his head to one side, he heard riders approaching fast and hard.

The redhead yanked the reins off the brake and snapped them, but the mules were too stubborn to obey another driver. It had taken Slocum several hours to get them to obey him, and he couldn't say they trusted him one little bit. He had simply shown them not obeying him was worse than pulling the heavy ice-laden wagon up the steep mountain grades. Frank didn't have time enough to establish that kind of bond.

The riders struggled up the slope both Slocum and Frank had conquered already. Two had six-shooters out and a third galloped forward, his horse's flanks lathered from the exertion.

"You can't have the wagon!" Frank cried. He started to draw his six-gun.

Slocum had been right about the man's ability to use the pistol. Frank stood, got his hand way up to the butt, and fought to get the barrel clear of the holster. The rider on the lathered horse never slowed. As he raced by Frank, he grabbed out. His hand slipped from Frank's shirt, but the impact on his chest sent Frank falling from the driver's box, tumbling ass over teakettle.

The other two riders came up on either side of the wagon, guns pointed at Frank. The redhead struggled on the ground. The blow had stunned him. The fall had knocked the air from his lungs. He made tiny gasping sounds and kicked feebly like a newborn baby. It would take him long minutes to recover.

"Kill him?"

"Naw, don't waste the bullet," answered another road agent. "We got what we want. You drive this rig, Jericho?"

The one called Jericho had knocked Frank out. He trotted back, studying the mule team, and nodded brusquely.

Slocum tried to get a better look at the trio. They wore dusters with the back flaps pulled up to hide their faces from anything other than a direct look. With them clustered around the wagon studying it, Slocum had no chance to identify the outlaws.

The one named Jericho stepped off his horse and over into the driver's box. It took him a bit of fishing to capture the reins Frank had dropped, then he snapped them and convinced the balky mules to pull. Slocum stepped out, intending to bushwhack the thieves, but Jericho was a better driver than he had any right to be and already had the wagon over the summit and on its way down the far side of the hill. The other two flanked him. Slocum might have made a superb shot and winged one. There wasn't any way in hell he could have shot all three to stop the robbery.

From the way they had ridden and the way they'd talked, they weren't likely to give up their icy loot easily.

Slocum went to where Frank still made tiny mewling noises. There wasn't anything he could do but wait for the man's lungs to work right again. He sat on a stump and looked after the road agents.

"Why the hell would they go to all that effort to steal a block of ice, even if it's worth ten times what Holst told me?"

"S-Slocum, stop them. You can't let 'em get away."

"I'm not getting killed over a wagon loaded with ice," he said. "Did Holst really send you?"

He hoped the unexpected question would give an answer different from the one the red-haired man had made before. Slocum had waited too late—or Frank hadn't lied.

Recovering, Frank sat up and clutched his ribs.

"Nothing's broken," he said at length. He had pretty well covered when he said, "Of course Holst sent me. Who else?"

Slocum looked at the empty air where the wagon had been parked. He had no doubt his cargo was ice from the way it had begun to melt. It wasn't as if Holst had spare gold he wanted to ship secretly to Tombstone. The money flowed in the other direction, from Arizona to Santa Fe. The ice was valuable, at ten times the going rate or not, but the trio of robbers had worked together well. They could have robbed a stagecoach or a bank and gotten actual specie or greenbacks that wouldn't melt on them.

"You reckon they have a buyer for that ice?"

"We got to get it back, Slocum. Where's my horse?"

Slocum jerked his thumb over his shoulder at a grassy patch where the horse contentedly nibbled at the spring grass. If he moved fast enough, he could be on the horse chasing down the road agents rather than Frank. Again, Slocum waited too long.

Frank fetched his six-shooter and held it so that he could lift and fire before Slocum could get his own Colt into action.

"I'm goin' after 'em," the redhead declared.

"You against the three of them didn't play out too well before. Can your horse take the pair of us on its back?" Slocum deciphered the unspoken curse. Frank's plans didn't include the legitimate employee of the New Mexico Ice and Coal Company. Then it was the redhead's turn to be a tad too slow on the uptake. Slocum had his pistol out and moving to center on the man's chest.

"We can ride double," Frank said, bowing to the inevitable.

Slocum let Frank drag his horse away from the tempting, juicy grass and mount. He caught the cantle and pulled himself into an uncomfortable spot behind.

"Let's ride. They can't travel too fast without wrecking the wagon," Slocum said.

"That's not goin' to stop 'em," Frank said.

"What's so all fired important about a block of ice that they'd steal it?" Slocum felt Frank tense at the question.

"I told you what Holst told me. Prices have gone through the roof. They ought to get more for that ice than if they robbed a train."

Slocum doubted that, and the road agents had been veteran thieves. They worked well together and instinctively hid their faces, as if they had experience. Having both Frank and a gang of robbers show up at the same time to steal the ice made him mighty suspicious. What else had Holst slipped into the cargo? Knowing the ice magnate as he did, Slocum couldn't guess. Holst was a sharp businessman, but the Panic of '73 had left its scars even though more than a year had passed. Ice and coal were necessities, but Holst was hardly the only one able to furnish those commodities.

"Think Holst has some competition that wants to drive him out of business?" Slocum asked, thinking aloud and not expecting Frank to answer.

"Could be, yeah, could be. Good reason to send me out to be sure the shipment arrived."

"Slow down," Slocum said sharply. He pointed off the road—hardly more than twin ruts through this stretch of mountains—where the road agents had driven the wagon. "We want to take them by surprise. That's the only way to get the ice back."

In a small meadow two men worked on the crate, trying to pry off a side of the crate holding the ice block. Slocum shifted to draw his pistol when Frank swung about and landed a heavy elbow to his chest. Lifted away from the horse by the blow, Slocum landed hard, then scrambled to keep the horse from kicking him with his rear hooves.

Frank pulled out his six-shooter and charged. He got off two shots before the road agents noticed they weren't alone. One dropped to his knee and pulled up a rifle he'd laid in the wagon bed. The other went for his six-gun with a well-oiled speed and ease that convinced Slocum they were true desperadoes.

In his headlong attack Frank had neglected to find the third outlaw. Slocum spotted the man on the ground behind the wagon, rifle in his grip. He had snugged the rifle to his shoulder and calmly took aim. Opening fire on the outlaw, Slocum shouted and ran forward. He fanned off all six rounds. None came close to the rifleman but did disturb his aim.

The single round the road agent fired missed Frank but struck his horse squarely in the chest. The horse never stopped galloping as it put its head down and somersaulted, sending its rider flying through the air to land with a dull thud. Again Frank had the wind knocked from him. This time, his horse lay a few yards away, dead.

Slocum was exposed and didn't have time to reload. He knew he was a dead man if he tried to run. The trio of owlhoots could take their time chasing him down. Since death appeared his bounty no matter what he did, he kept running forward, screaming at the top of his lungs.

The frontal assault unnerved the outlaws. The one on the ground began firing as fast as he could lever in a new round. The other robber with the rifle in the wagon took up firing, too. The air filled with lead all around Slocum. He kept running until his toe caught the edge of a marmot hole. Stumbling, he lurched forward. Lead tore at his sleeves and his hat, sending it flying. He crashed to the ground with more bullets kicking up dirt all around.

And then there was only silence. He lay on his belly, expecting one of the road agents to finish him off with an easy shot. Instead, they began arguing. He tried to follow the disputation but a roaring in his ears made his usually sensitive hearing a joke. They had to think they had killed him, but his curiosity got the better of him. He turned his head slightly toward the wagon to see what they were up to.

Two had mounted and one held the reins of the third road agent's horse. The man in the driver's box got the mules pulling again. Chains clanked and leather harness creaked. The lead mule brayed in protest, but the rig began pulling away. Slocum wanted to leap to his feet and chase after them but common sense held him where he was until the wagon and the men who had stolen it disappeared at the far side of the mountain meadow.

He sat up, every bone in his body aching from the fight. Before he stood, he reloaded his six-shooter. And then he went to see to his unwanted comrade in arms.

As Slocum nudged him with his boot toe, Frank rolled over, shoved the gun up so Slocum saw only the huge muzzle, then pulled the trigger.

3

"It had to be that son of a bitch Carstairs," Marianne said, her lips pulled back into a razor slash of anger. She clenched her hands until her broken fingernails cut into her palms. Warm blood dripped to the thirsty ground.

She had fought the fire as long as she could before exhaustion settled in, and she'd collapsed near the well. Randolph had found her soon after, but she hadn't allowed him to fuss over her. Keeping him safe was the only thought in her head when she'd sent him to fetch the sheriff. Grant County covered a huge part of southwestern New Mexico, but Harvey Whitehill made Silver City his home. More than likely, he'd be at home and able to help.

Marianne had been right. The sheriff returned with Randolph in hardly more than a half hour. From the way he worked to keep his shirt tucked into his trousers and how his gun belt wasn't fastened properly, she knew her son had awakened the lawman from a sound sleep. Whitehill still rubbed at his eyes and grumbled.

In the midst of the burned-out house, Marianne poked

through embers to find what she could salvage. There was precious little.

"You knock over a lamp?" Whitehill asked. "No point gettin' the volunteer firemen out. The damage is all done."

"You didn't hear me, Sheriff," she said, not even trying to hold back her anger. "Carstairs filled a whiskey bottle with kerosene, stuck a rag in the neck, lit it, and heaved it through my window." She rubbed at the scorch marks on her clothes where she had been caught in the initial explosion.

Bits of glass tinkled to the ground as she dislodged them from her skirts. All she could think was that no amount of washing or mending would ever make this blouse or skirt right again. That was something else to chalk up against Carstairs. This had been her favorite outfit.

"I was talkin' to your boy. Randolph here didn't see it. You actually witness Carstairs throw the bomb?"

She considered lying and saying that she had seen the despicable snake do the deed, but she couldn't. Marianne shook her head. Ash and ember cascaded to join their cousins on the house floor.

"Clem reported to me what happened when he was, uh, courtin' you," the sheriff said carefully. "Can't do squat about that either. Carstairs might have roughed Clem up, but he's not about to press charges."

"I don't blame him, but I'll bring charges. He attacked me. Clem might fear for his life from Carstairs and his cronies, but I want to see him punished. Sheriff, I lost *everything.*"

"Looks that way," Whitehill said, nodding as he stroked his mustache in thought. "You might reconsider, Marianne. Not even Texas Jack Bedrich can protect you from him."

"They hardly know each other," she said firmly. "Jack and Carstairs weren't friends, but there wasn't bad blood between them either."

"When you and Texas Jack started cozying up to each

other," Whitehill said. "You got to know how Carstairs feels about you. He never made a secret of that."

"I am not chattel. I made my decision, and it's with Texas Jack!"

"Ain't seen hide nor hair of him for weeks. Where'd he get off to?"

"He had business in Santa Fe. Maybe Las Vegas, too. He was kind of vague where he was going."

"Surely would have been better for everyone if you'd married him when he asked."

"That's my business, Sheriff Whitehill." She looked past the lawman to her son, sifting through the soot and ashes where his tiny room had been. Any belongings that survived this fire were on the boy's back or in his pocket. Marianne had the irrational urge to demand that Randolph give her the knife he had flashed.

She would use it to finish the chore of giving Carstairs a second mouth to grin from. That seemed fitting.

Whitehill looked over his shoulder toward Randolph, then back. She read it on his face. He knew why she'd been so reluctant to marry Texas Jack Bedrich when he had asked her. The miner hadn't been too keen about having an immediate family, preferring to start his own brood with her. She had been through too much raising Randolph to split her love between him and a husband. If her husband didn't accept them both as a package, she had to balk like an old jenny mule.

But Bedrich was handsome and likely rich, though he had never come out and said as much. The change in his demeanor had been obvious. Before he'd asked her to marry him, he had been anxious. Then ebullience followed, along with the proposal. She knew Jack well enough to think that he wanted her to marry him for what he had to offer as a man, not as a rich man. She simply wished he had seen how she needed a husband *and* a father for her son.

They were both wary about any kind of relationship but

for different reasons. If Jack rode up right now, she'd yell "Yes!" to the star-filled black night sky and mean it. If the sheriff couldn't take care of Carstairs, Texas Jack Bedrich could and would.

"You got any idea when he'll be back?"

"Soon, I hope," she said so earnestly that Randolph looked up. He hadn't taken to Jack.

"I want this matter settled before he rides into town again. I don't need the streets runnin' with blood, either his or Carstairs's or Carstairs's henchmen."

"Then you clap Carstairs into jail."

"I'll talk to him, but we both know he'll deny everything. His boys'll back him up, the lyin' sacks o'—" Whitehill cut off his denunciation when Randolph came over, holding the charred pages of a book in his hands.

"This is all that's left, Ma," he said. She took the diary from him. Ever since leaving Georgia, she had kept a journal. Like all her possessions, the memories it contained had gone up in flames.

"Thank you, Randolph." She clutched the book to her chest. Brittle pages broke and fluttered to the ground.

"I can help gather your belongings," Whitehill said, looking around. "Or is that all you, uh, need."

She nodded, shock wearing off and a desolation entering her soul unlike anything she had experienced in years.

"I'll make certain sure Miz Gruhlkey finds a room for you at the hotel. Damned shame losing a wood building like this when most of Silver City is still livin' in tents. Too damn many prospectors comin' to town every week to keep up with them."

They started walking the mile into town, Marianne not feeling like talking much. Randolph was sullen, but Harvey Whitehill proved a real chatterbox. She wondered if he intended it to keep her mind off her problems. Or maybe to divert her from the idea that kept popping into her head of taking care of Carstairs once and for all. She didn't need

Jack's help. She could drive her son's knife through Carstairs's black heart and no one need be the wiser.

"You won't mind stayin' at the hotel, will you, boy?"

"Naw," Randolph said.

"That's because his best friend lives there, too," Marianne said with more venom in her words than she intended.

"Billy's an all right guy!"

"He—"

"Listen to your son on this one, Marianne," the sheriff said. "William has lived through some hard times this past year, his ma dyin' of consumption and not havin' a pa anywhere to be seen. Gettin' the job sweepin' up and doin' odd jobs for Miz Gruhlkey is exactly what he needed."

"He's a bad influence," she said.

"Is not! Billy knows 'bout everything," Randolph said. "He—"

"Enough. I won't argue with you. It's not good that you two will be under one roof."

"A boy Randolph's age needs friends. He can do a lot worse than William. Now, that Dunleavy boy's a caution. I swear he'll be hanged in another year if he doesn't straighten up. Worst part of it, I'm goin' be the one who has to arrest him. Caught him stealin' twice already and what he tried to do to the Wilson girl, well." Whitehill looked at the back of Randolph's head as he ran ahead. "You don't want to know."

"I probably do already, Sheriff."

"Marianne, it ain't my place to say this, but I will anyway. Especially considerin' what happened tonight."

"I do what I have to," she said. "Making ends meet, even in a boomtown like this, is difficult."

"Men'll be men, but you can find other ways to take their money without, well, without—"

"Without fucking them?" she said harshly. "Don't think it doesn't pain me. Randolph knows what I have to do. If the other boys in school torment him about it, he's never said." She let out a deep sigh. "That's one thing I'll say for Billy.

He's always polite, and I could never see him calling me a whore around town."

"There're other jobs. Might not pay as good, but I'll see what I can do."

"There's no need for you to put yourself out, Sheriff. Just do your duty, and put Carstairs behind bars."

"I'll try to do that, but he has powerful friends. It'd be a help if Texas Jack got back soon."

"I can handle my own problems, thank you," she said sharply. Marianne immediately regretted it. "I'm sorry. That was impolite. I know you're only trying to help." She wondered if it was because she was a pretty woman or because of what Jack could do for him. Texas Jack Bedrich might not be the heir apparent to Captain Bullard and his fabulous find in Chloride Flats, but he carried a considerable amount of influence.

Marianne trudged along the quiet streets laid out by Bullard more than four years earlier, just before he was killed by Apaches. The town had grown since then, but the men living here hadn't changed. There were only more of them.

"Your son's already passed along word of the fire," Whitehill said, pointing to the hotel's front porch. Randolph and Billy stood off to one side, heads together, whispering their mutual confidences.

Marianne saw how much alike the two were, at least in physical size. Billy was two years older but almost frail. When he wasn't looking downtrodden, he was defiant. Of late, defiant was all Randolph showed the world—and her. It was his age, of course, but also had a great deal to do with Jack. Randolph didn't want a stepfather, probably because of the tales Billy had told him about his. Being abandoned had to affect a boy. Marianne wanted to be sure Jack wasn't that kind before she accepted his proposal. She could work out trouble with Randolph afterward, with Jack's help.

"There's Miz Gruhlkey. Billy's rousted 'bout everyone in the hotel from the look of it."

Marianne canted her head back and saw lights in most windows.

"Burned out, were you?" Mrs. Gruhlkey said, sniffing in derision. "Bound to happen, I suppose, the way you carry on." The woman pulled her nightgown closer to her frail body and took a step toward Marianne. "You and your boy can stay here. The sheriff vouches for you. So does Billy. But you won't ply your Cyprian ways under my roof. I run a respectable hotel."

"Respectable? Is that what you call it now, Ruth?" Sheriff Whitehill chuckled. "I seem to remember that a still blew up in your kitchen last month."

"I only wanted to prepare medicine. Dr. Fuller charges an arm and a leg for his potions."

"Doc gets it from the Last Oasis Saloon, straight out of Ben's back room. That's trade whiskey you call a potion."

"It helps my rheumatism, and I feel my joints getting all sticky standing out here in the nighttime cold. You," she said, her bony finger stabbing at Whitehill, "are responsible for her behavior while under my roof."

With that, Mrs. Gruhlkey swept back into the hotel, slamming the door behind her.

"That puts me in my place," Marianne said, having to smile.

"But you won't turn tricks? Not if I get you a job?"

"Don't know what I'm able to do," Marianne said truthfully. "I took in wash, but most of the miners are so poor they don't have anything more than the clothes on their back. Peeling it off to wash, well . . ." She shrugged. Whitehill knew what she meant. This was how she had started doing more than laundry for the miners. If they were naked anyway, why not when they paid extra?

"I'll let you know in the morning. If I don't get some sleep, I'm gonna fall over right here in the street. Too many folks would find that downright risible." Whitehill touched the brim of his hat and said, "Night, Marianne."

She watched the sheriff until he disappeared around the corner at Third Street. It was time to find a bed and sleep in it. More likely, she would cry herself to sleep. Marianne called for her son, but he and Billy had vanished.

With every footstep seeming as if she were mounting the gallows, she went up to the hotel's front door and inside. It had been a long night. In spite of her exhaustion, she doubted she'd get a wink of sleep.

She was right.

4

Slocum stared down the barrel of the pistol. He hardly flinched when the hammer fell on an empty chamber.

For a moment, he did nothing, realizing his own six-shooter was empty, too. Then he moved with the speed of a striking snake. His Colt Navy whipped around so the barrel caught Frank's wrist. Slocum felt bone yield, but he doubted anything broke. It didn't have to. Frank let out a yelp of pain as his six-gun went flying from his grip.

"Why'd you go and do that?" Frank grated out, clutching his right wrist.

"You tried to cut me down."

"It was reflex, Slocum, reflex and nuthin' else. I got all het up in the heat of the fight and got confused."

Slocum said nothing, considering what to do. His six-shooter was empty, but he held the high ground, towering over the supine redhead. Frank's six-gun might be empty or the hammer might have fallen on a dud, with the next round live and deadly. Slocum hadn't followed the man's fight against the trio of road agents, being too busy staying alive himself.

He scooped up the pistol, opened the gate, and spun the cylinder. All the rounds had been fired. A backhand toss dropped the gun beside Frank.

"It could have been that way. I ain't used to fights. Not like you, Slocum. Not like you." The man's bright blue eyes fixed on the Colt's worn ebony handles and the well-used gun itself.

"I'm no shootist," Slocum said. He backed away, reloaded, and then went to where Frank's horse lay still.

It already drew flies, and in the distance he heard howling coyotes exchanging dinner requests. Before long, every scavenger in the mountain forest would circle, waiting for the chance to grab an easy meal.

"You'd better get what gear you want. We have a long walk ahead of us." Slocum tried to get his bearings. "Silver City is that way, at least ten miles, maybe twelve. It's as close as we can get to the law."

"The law! What? Why?"

"Outlaws stole my cargo. They shot your horse, left us for dead. If I don't report this to Holst, he'll think I made off with his ice, his wagon, and his team."

"That makes sense," Frank said, but Slocum heard no conviction in the man's voice. Other than not letting Frank get behind him, Slocum wanted nothing more to do with the red-haired man.

Slocum waited for Frank to strip the saddle from his horse and heave it up onto his shoulder. He staggered a little. Slocum waited for him to ask for help, but Frank held his tongue. That was just fine. Walking wasn't something Slocum took kindly to, and reaching Silver City might take a day or longer with this rugged terrain slowing him.

"If we follow the wagon tracks, we might overtake them," Frank ventured.

"You still hot to recover the cargo?" Slocum wondered at the man's determination. Holst might have found himself a real bulldog. Once Frank got something in his head, he refused to let it die.

It struck Slocum as odd how Holst hadn't sent Frank along with him rather than setting him on his trail, but the ice company owner was cantankerous and did things in his own way. A persuasive argument might have been enough for Holst to send Frank along. Or the redhead could have convinced Holst that the cargo was too valuable to trust to Slocum alone. If that were true, Holst's fears had been realized.

After an hour walking, Frank dropped his gear, mopped his forehead with his blue kerchief, and pointed off at an angle.

"The wagon went that way."

"And a half-dozen riders joined them," Slocum said. He stared at the ground, then dropped to his knees to get a better read. Looking up, he said, "Apaches. These ponies weren't shod."

"Indians wouldn't want the ice. They might just scalp those mangy sons of bitches so we can claim the wagon and ice again."

Slocum rolled the idea over in his head. What Frank said had merit. Apaches would strip the outlaws and leave the rest. They had no use for a wagon and even less for ice. But if they made any mistake while trailing the Apaches, he and Frank would find themselves in a world of trouble. Even if they didn't, the chance of discovery by the Indians was great. Slocum had been told several war parties had slipped away from their reservations dotted around the New Mexico and Arizona borders.

"The Apaches had a camp at one time where Silver City got built," Slocum said. "Might be they're heading there."

"Going home?"

"Something like that," Slocum said. "This used to be their hunting grounds. More likely, they're trying to avoid the cavalry and aren't anything more than a raiding party."

The words hardly left his lips when distant gunfire came rolling toward them from farther down the mountain. He

touched his six-gun and wished he had the Henry rifle he'd
left in the driver's box. Firepower counted whether they went
against either the outlaws or the Indians. Taking on both
sides required more guns than either he or Frank could bring
to bear. The smartest thing he could do was let the outlaws
and Apaches shoot it out, then go pick up the pieces.

"Come on, Slocum. We got to get down there," Frank
said.

"Hold your horses. Let me scout ahead before we bull
our way into a fight we can't win."

"But the ice!"

Slocum stared at him. Frank was single-minded about
the ice, and that made no sense. Even if Holst paid the man
a bonus to deliver the ice—or withheld payment for not
delivering it—the devotion to duty made no sense when bal-
anced against the man's life. If Slocum hadn't seen the melting ice during the trip, he would have thought Holst was
shipping something else to Tombstone.

"You that good a scout?"

"Not too bad," Slocum said simply. He studied the forest
around them, choosing how he would approach the fight.

The reports from a half-dozen different weapons rolled
like thunder. With that fierce a fight going on, all attention
would be directed at anyone in front of a muzzle. Slocum
could creep in behind, get a notion what was going on, then
make his plans.

"I don't like it," Frank said.

"No reason you should. I'm the teamster, the cargo's my
responsibility, no matter what Holst said to you."

Frank bristled, then subsided. From the storm cloud of
anger lingering on his face, Frank was about ready to try
plugging Slocum again. This time his six-shooter was
loaded. Turning his back on him would require an act of
faith that Slocum didn't have.

His only other option was to gun down Frank first.

He took the one that didn't require him wasting a bullet

when he said, "You skirt the fight in that direction. I'll go this way. Just be sure you know who's in your sights before pulling the trigger." Slocum watched the redhead's reaction. To Frank, it wouldn't matter who he aimed at. Everyone counted as an enemy.

That suited Slocum. He could handle drunks and back-shooters. What he couldn't handle was uncertainty as to a man's intentions.

He motioned for Frank to head out, waited until he no longer saw the man's hat or the thatch of red hair poking out from under the brim, then started in the same direction, tracking with all the skill he had. What Frank did was more important than who was still filling the air with lead.

Frank moved quietly, but Slocum's step came softer than a gentle breeze. He avoided bushes that might spring back and give him away. Where he stepped hardly bent the blades of grass. He placed his boots in the imprints already left by the redhead. This was pure caution on his part. There might never be anyone backtracking Frank, but if there was, he would find only one set of footprints unless he was one damned fine tracker.

The redhead blundered through a thick clump of under-growth, then flopped forward onto his belly. Slocum took his time approaching to make sure Frank didn't catch sight of him. Ahead, through the edge of a copse, he saw one of the road agents clutching his arm and hopping around. He'd been hit several times, but what chilled Slocum was why the man limped.

He hadn't taken a bullet in his leg. An Apache arrow with its distinctive fletching had driven itself halfway into his thigh.

Slocum slid his Colt back into the holster, then began climbing an oak tree to get a better look at the battle still raging. Not rustling the leaves proved difficult but neces-sary. Frank stirred uneasily not ten yards ahead and below him. The redhead fingered his six-gun but made no effort to add his fire to the skirmish. For that, Slocum was glad. Frank finally showed some common sense.

He edged out on a thick limb and clung to it with his knees and reared up. Using one hand, he pushed smaller limbs out of the way. From this vantage, he had a complete view of the battle. The road agents had pulled the wagon up not twenty yards away and had exposed the crate. From the condition of the wood panel in Slocum's field of view, they had tried to rip off the slates and hadn't succeeded. The hammer he had carried might have bounced out as they made their breakneck descent this far on the mountainside, or they might have been in such a hurry to cool their hands that they didn't see it in the wagon bed.

They had been caught flatfooted by the Apaches and hadn't a chance to do more than return fire. Now that the battle was stretching on, the road agents were finding better cover and doing a credible job holding off the Indians.

Slocum counted the places where the Indians attacked from and knew there were no fewer than five in the band. Holst hadn't warned him of any Apaches slipping away from their reservation, but such a small band might not have been noticed by the cavalry.

The outlaws certainly noticed them, however.

The one with the arrow in his leg rolled under the wagon where his partner fired methodically to hold the Apaches at bay. The sound of his rifle told Slocum his Henry was being put to good use. If he'd held it in his hands, the fight would have been over in a few seconds. During the war he had been a sniper for the CSA and had turned the tide of more than one battle by sighting in on a federal officer's braid, then robbing the Yankees of their commanding officer. From his perch in the tree he saw which of the Apaches ordered the others about.

Killing the war chief wouldn't make the Indians run away, but it would throw them into disarray. They would have to palaver and agree on a new war chief, which bought time.

The outlaw with the arrow in his leg screeched when his partner rammed it through so the arrowhead came out the back of his leg, then snapped off the shaft before pulling back. Slocum couldn't see the arrowhead clearly but it likely was a broadhead. Yanking it out rather than shoving it through would have caused an even worse wound. Again, he developed some respect for the road agents and their fighting experience.

They weren't fools. So why did they risk their lives for a hunk of ice?

A sudden lull in the gunfire caused Slocum to tense. The silence hurt his ears after all the loud reports. Clouds of white gun smoke drifted through the meadow, making it difficult for either side in the fight to see the other. If even one Apache had had Slocum's vantage, the fight would have been over in a flash.

The three outlaws lay still on the ground under the wagon. This trick lured out two braves, both armed with bows and arrows. The other Apaches with rifles remained in hiding. Step by step they made their way through the smoke until they were only a few yards away.

The Indians saw they had fallen for a trap and dived to the ground as they loosed their arrows. One road agent's slug hit a warrior. From the way he remained facedown on the ground, Slocum thought he had died instantly. The other brave rolled over, firing arrows as he tried to find cover from the road agents' new fusillade.

The Apache jerked as at least one slug tore into him, but he kept fighting, kept moving, let the remaining three warriors offer covering fire so he could escape.

For their part, the Apaches likely wanted nothing more than the mules still hitched to the wagon. Slocum couldn't guess what the road agents wanted. One of them moved from under the wagon and climbed into the bed to use the ice in its crate as cover. For whatever reason, Frank took this as a sterling opportunity to join the battle. He got off three rounds before the outlaws figured they had been flanked and turned their guns on him.

The redhead jumped to his feet and tried to replicate the frontal assault Slocum had tried. It didn't work out for him. He jerked upright, clutched his side, then was spun around again as another round drilled through his hide.

"They're comin' back!"

Slocum didn't know which of the outlaws shouted the warning, but they turned their guns once more on the Apaches. Mounted now, the Indians galloped forward, the wounded man with the bow and arrow trailing a second horse. They circled the fallen brave and tried to get him belly down across his horse. The outlaws fired with the precision of a military unit and drove them away.

The riderless horse reared and pawed at the Apache on the ground, forcing him to release the bridle and return to his own horse. The four surviving Indians beat a retreat.

"Think they'll come back?"

Slocum couldn't tell which of the outlaws asked the question. It didn't matter. They helped their wounded partner into the driver's box and shoved the reins into his hand. Although twice wounded, once by bullet and the second time with an arrow through his leg, the man did a credible job of motivating the mules into pulling. The wagon rattled away toward the far side of the small clearing where the battle had occurred.

The wagon and two outlaws on their horses disappeared through a cut in the woods, possibly an old logging trail.

Slocum lay prone on the tree limb, waiting to see if anything stirred in the clearing. He didn't want the Apaches coming back for their fallen companion, but he wanted that dead man's horse. Without it, he had a long walk to Silver City.

After waiting a respectable time when no one showed his face, Slocum slid over the limb, dangled, and then dropped to the ground. He remained in a crouch, hand on his six-shooter as he listened for anything out of the ordinary. The forest had returned to its natural sounds now that the gunfire had stopped.

He walked toward Frank, then spun when movement at the edge of his eye caught his attention. The Indian pony had tangled itself up in the thick undergrowth. Bridle wrapped around a thornbush, it reared but could not pull free.

Slocum went to help it. Gentling the horse took a few minutes. White still showed around its eyes, and it tried to toss its head and lash out with its front hooves, but Slocum eventually won it over, yanked the bridle free, and had himself a mount. It had been a spell since he'd ridden bareback, but there wasn't a horse alive that could throw him if he put his mind to it. Try as it might, the Indian pony sunfished and bucked and eventually decided it was the lesser of two evils having a white man astride it than fighting further.

A slow walk back to where the ice wagon had stopped completed the conquest. Slocum had himself a new horse.

He looked down at Frank, wondering if he owed the man a burial. Then he cursed. Frank moaned, stirred, and tried to roll onto his back. The effort proved too great, but it didn't kill him either.

Unless Slocum wanted to use that bullet to put the man out of his misery, he had a companion all the way to town. He dismounted, got his shoulder under Frank's gut, then heaved. Without rope, he couldn't lash the weakly stirring man to the horse, but when he mounted, Frank in front of him, he could hang on to keep him from sliding to the ground.

It would be a long, slow ride to Silver City.

5

"I don't know what all they're asking me to fix," Marianne Lomax said, frowning. She looked out over the crowd gathered in the Lonely Cuss Cantina and Drinking Emporium and began to despair. "You did what you said, Sheriff, and there's no way I can repay you, but this is too much." She started to take off the leather apron, but Harvey Whitehill reached over the bar and caught her wrist. She started to pull away but couldn't. His grip was too strong.

"There's plenty of time to learn, Marianne. Look at these yahoos. So what if one asked for a Mississippi Peach Fizz and you didn't know how to fix it? He was just funnin' you. You can draw beer and pour shots of whiskey. Not much else bein' served here or anywhere else in Silver City that ain't those or some combination of 'em."

She reached over and used her left hand to pry loose his grip. It made her uneasy having him touch her—having anyone but Texas Jack touch her, actually. How she missed him!

"I'll stick," she said. "I need the money."

"Tom Gallifrey is a skinflint and doesn't pay his barkeeps

too good. That's why he has such a hard time keepin' help, but you can make tips. Just talk to the men."

"And?"

"And nothin' more. Just listen. Most of these galoots want to brag on how good they are at minin', how rich they're goin' to become, and have a pretty lady pay them some attention. You don't have to do anything more than listen."

"Unless I want to?" She saw the disappointment on his face an instant before a poker mask dropped down.

"Do what you please on your own time."

"I won't, Sheriff. That wasn't the real me taking men to my bed for money, no matter what the other womenfolk in town say. Letting my son starve wasn't going to happen."

"You have any trouble, call me. Or I just hired me a new deputy who'll stick close to Silver City. His name's Tucker, but he goes by the moniker of Dangerous Dan. He's a real character, but he comes well recommended."

"Tucker," she said. "I'll remember that. If I ever have to holler for help. Excuse me a second, Sheriff." She scooped up a bung starter and hurried to the end of the bar where two men stood, faces inches from each other, knives in their hands as they shouted.

Marianne never hesitated as she swung the wood mallet. The flat head connected with the nearest man's forehead, staggering him back a pace before he collided with another patron and both fell to the sawdust-covered floor. The other man looked startled, then laughed and pointed the tip of his knife in the fallen man's direction. Marianne strained to swing the mallet backhanded. She knocked him out with the blow to the side of his head.

"A drink to whoever drags both of them outside," she said. Without even raising her voice, she got four men scampering to do her bidding.

Marianne looked over her shoulder. Sheriff Whitehill smiled ear to ear.

"You're gonna do just fine," he said. He stepped over a chair that had been knocked on its side and went into the cold night air.

Marianne caught her breath. She liked the sheriff and didn't want him to go, but he had a way of meddling in her affairs. Whether he was sweet on her or just determined to be helpful to someone in need presented a question she couldn't answer.

"Hey, bartender, can you fix me up one of them fancy drinks like the rich folks back East drink?" The grizzled miner looked first left and then right to be sure he had an audience. The hubbub in Lonely Cuss died down to see if the miner could stump her.

"What'll it be? But you got to be willing to pay double for anything really fancy."

"I kin pay!" The miner dropped a leather sack on the bar. From the melodious tinkle, Marianne knew it held silver coins. "Give me a Silver Salud!"

Marianne nodded as if she knew exactly what he meant. For all she knew, he'd made up the drink on the spot to see what she'd do.

"I got the fixings back here," she said, looking at the rows of bottles on the back bar. "Before I fix it, are you a gambling man?"

"What's that? Well, I done set in on a poker game or two in my day."

"And he danged near lost his eyeteeth, too! He's a terrible gambler!"

"So, bet or not?" she asked.

He looked at her suspiciously and asked, "What's the nature of this here bet?"

"Your friends will blindfold you. You'll sample two drinks and you got to tell me which is the Silver Salud. You guess right, the drinks are on the house. You guess wrong, you pay for a round for everyone in the Lonely Cuss."

Marianne stood back and let the arguments and laughter

ripple through the dozen men crowded close to the bar. If the miner had intended to back down, he couldn't now with the others pressing him into the bar.

"I'll do it, but you got to make the best goddamn Silver Salud you ever did make."

"I'll let everyone else watch," she said. "You boys blindfold him. You got a lot riding on him not seeing."

"Hal ain't never bought a drink for no one before. I want to see this."

Willing hands whipped a couple sweaty, dirty bandannas around the miner's eyes. Marianne waved her hand in front of Hal's face to be sure he couldn't see, then she stepped back.

"All right, everyone, you watch real close. And watch him so he can't see how I'm fixing the drinks."

She rattled bottles, clinked shot glasses together, and ended up pouring two shots of whiskey from the same bottle. The notion that a fancy drink would be served like a shot worried her, so she rattled more glassware, found a pair of champagne glasses, and poured the shots into them. With a dramatic clink, she touched the two rims together.

Many of the miners laughed themselves sick, holding their bellies and whispering among themselves, but they were in on the joke. The two closest to Hal shouted at him and shoved him back and forth to keep him from overhearing.

"The two drinks are in front of you. Pick the Silver Salud and you don't pay."

"Them varmints know which is which?"

Marianne didn't have to answer. The roar of assent went up and rattled the vigas in the adobe bar's ceiling.

"All right. Stand back and let a master do his work." Marianne reached down and guided Hal's hand to the first champagne glass. She ran her fingers up and down his wrist just enough to encourage him, then held up her hand for silence.

"Got to be fair. Nobody give him any hints," she called. Marianne smiled as the miner tentatively sniffed at the drink, then flicked out his tongue to taste it.

"Got a kick to it," he said, "jist like a real Silver Salud."

"You have to try the other one, remember. You have to decide between the pair of them.

"Both might be Silver Saluds," Marianne said, egging them all on. This produced a round of new jokes. "Let me put the other one in your hand, Hal." Again she took his brawny wrist and stroked over it as he slid the stemware crystal glass between his fingers.

He repeated the same ceremony he had before. Then Hal went to sipping first one, then the other, until both were drained. He finally held one glass high above his head.

"This is the Silver Salud. This is it!"

Marianne thought the roof would come off from the laughter.

"You danged fool," someone called out. "Them's both nuthin' but whiskey."

"Good whiskey, though," Marianne said. "The best you'll find anywhere in Silver City. Which of you boys wants a 'Silver Salud'? Or should I say, 'Hal's Silver Salud'?" She held up the bottle of trade whiskey to a roar of approval.

Three bottles later, most of the customers were either passed out or moaning about getting back to their claims. Hal clung to the bar to remain upright. After he'd bought a round for everyone, he found the tide of tarantula juice flowing like a river back in his direction. He hadn't paid for a drink afterward.

"Gotta ask," Hal said, leaning forward as if to share a confidence with her. He didn't quite shout. "What the hell's a Silver Salud? I heard of 'em in a dive along the Barbary Coast o'er in Frisco."

Marianne fished about under the bar and dropped a copy of *The Yorkshire Bar Guide* in front of the miner.

"Look it up."

"I cain't read too good. Need my readin' glasses, you know."

Marianne flipped through the book. Most of the pages were stuck together or so faded from having liquor and beer spilled on them that they were unreadable. She pressed the book flat and pointed.

"You got a good memory, Hal. This is what goes into a Silver Salud. Equal parts of schnapps, nitric acid, beer, and apple brandy."

"Sounds tasty," he said. "You mix me up one of 'em next time I'm in?"

"Sure thing, partner," she said. "Right now, I got to close the cantina." She looked to the door where Tom Gallifrey, the owner, stood surveying the interior.

He came over, looking like he had eaten something that didn't agree with him.

"How'd it go?"

"Good," Marianne told him. "I don't have much experience, but I'd say real good." She pushed the cash box across to him.

His eyes widened at little at the stacks of silver coins mingled with a few gold disks and the piles of greenbacks.

"I did all right for myself, too," she said, patting her skirt pocket.

"How's that? You took money? That's skimming, cheating! Gimme."

"They were tips. For me," she said.

"I don't allow no such thing. All the money's mine. You get a salary at the end of the month, nothing more."

Marianne began to fume, then pulled out the wad of money and laid it on the bar as she decided what to do or say. This was hers!

"You be back tomorrow night?" Hal asked.

"Don't think so," she said. Tom looked at her.

"You fixing to quit already?" the Lonely Cuss's owner asked.

"You're firing me. This is all mine. The customers gave it to me." She scooped up the money—pretty near ten dollars—and stuffed it back into her pocket.

"Firin' her? You can't do that, Tom. Tonight's the most fun any of us from out at Chloride Flats have had in a month o' Sundays."

"Might be the fun can continue in some other saloon," she said, watching Gallifrey closely. "I'm sure I can get a job building Silver Saluds for you elsewhere."

"That there's 'Hal's Silver Salud,' " the miner said, grinning from ear to ear.

"Never heard of such a thing," Gallifrey said.

"She has, and that's what matters to me and my boys. No reason to come to the Lonely Cuss if Marianne's workin' somewhere else in town."

"Might be there was a misunderstanding," Gallifrey said, his eyes going back to the cash box filled with the evening's revenue. "Might be you can keep whatever tips you're paid if you keep deliverin' like this." He tapped the metal box with his forefinger.

"Can't promise that, but I can promise to try."

"I'll buy another round for the house if you stay, Marianne," Hal said.

"Old-timer, go home. Come back tomorrow when there're customers in the Lonely Cuss and make the offer then." She reached across the bar and patted his shoulder. Again she received the broken-toothed smile.

"See ya then, Marianne. G'nite, Tom, you clenched-up asshole, you!" Laughing, Hal barely made it through the door. Outside he began serenading the night.

"You made a friend there," Gallifrey said uneasily. "He's foreman at the Work Whistle Mine. Got a dozen men beholden to him."

"Do tell," she said, slipping her shawl around her shoulders. "If you don't mind, I want to get some sleep. This about wore me out."

Tom Gallifrey looked down into the cash box again and nodded his head once. Feeling vindicated, Marianne followed Hal into the cold New Mexico night. Thin clouds worked their way across the face of an almost full moon casting light as silver as the metal pulled from the ground. The cold mountain air invigorated her. Step quick and stride long, she headed toward the hotel down the street.

Halfway there she got the uneasy feeling of someone watching her. Marianne looked over her shoulder, then started to run. A shadowy figure bolted into the street and chased after her.

She reached the hotel steps, tripped, and fell. Pushing herself up off the steps only got her in more trouble. She slid into her pursuer's arms. Like bands of steel, he circled her waist with one arm and clamped a calloused hand over her mouth. He spun her around so her feet left the ground, robbing her of any leverage at all. In his grip she was helpless.

"You got the pistol we stole?" came a child's voice.

"I want to shoot him. You promised."

"You can cut him up. You got a knife."

The curious argument caused Marianne's captor to spin back around so she faced the hotel. At the top of the steps stood Randolph and Billy McCarty. Randolph had his knife out. In the bright moonlight the blade glinted like pure silver. He slashed at the air, causing it to turn to liquid and leave deadly trails behind. Billy held something small and dark in his hand.

"Dang it, I can't get this thumb buster cocked!"

"I'll stab him then!" Randolph took a step forward as a metallic click cut through the stillness of the night.

Marianne watched in horror as Billy stepped out beside her son and aimed whatever he held in his hand.

As suddenly as she had been seized, she was dropped. Marianne sat heavily in the street, gasping for breath. She looked up and called to Billy, "Give me that gun! I'll shoot him!"

The boys laughed.

"Did you see the way he lit out like a scalded dog!" Randolph laughed even harder.

"He surely did run like a dog with his tail 'tween his legs," Billy said. "What a lily-livered coward!"

"Give me the gun!" She fought to her feet and grabbed for the gun, only to find herself holding a kitchen knife wrapped in black paper. He had struck the blade with a small rock to produce the clicking sound that had run off her attacker.

"We don't have a gun," Billy said. "We bluffed him!"

"You could have been killed. *I* could have been killed." The impact of what she said hit her. Marianne sat on the hotel steps, too shocked to cry or say another word. She had been rescued from robbery and probably worse by two young boys carrying out a bluff.

6

It was past sunup when Slocum tugged back on the reins and stopped the Indian pony. The horse nickered, glad to stand rather than walk with its double load. Down below the rise spread Silver City in a broad, shallow bowl, tents scattered willy-nilly amid dozens of more permanent buildings. The sound of hammers driving nails came to him, giving the impression of a growing town.

Slocum put his hand on the middle of Frank's back to keep the man from sliding off the horse again. How he had stayed alive gave Slocum pause, but this wasn't anything he wanted to dwell on. Frank either lived or died. If the long miles to Silver City hadn't killed him, chances were good the town's doctor would. Finding a vet might be better, but Slocum didn't care. Frank had put himself in the line of fire for no good reason.

"Giddyup," Slocum said, tapping his heels against the pony's flanks. The horse hesitated, then finally agreed to enter the white man's town. Its reluctance told Slocum it hadn't been stolen from some rancher. It was an Apache horse born and bred.

He attracted scant attention as he rode with Frank slung in front of him. The inhabitants of Silver City likely saw more curious things in the course of their day. This was a boomtown and drew men both outrageous and dangerous. Slocum and Frank were neither.

"Where can I find the doctor?" Slocum called to a man struggling to load a sack of flour into a buggy parked in front of the general store.

"All the way across town, over near the sheriff's office."

"I'll need to talk to him, too," Slocum said.

"You a bounty hunter? Got yourself a desperado?"

"Nothing like it," Slocum answered. "Highwaymen bushwhacked us."

"That there's an Indian horse."

"So it is," Slocum said, urging the horse into motion. "Much obliged."

He rode past several saloons, his thirst increasing with every scent of beer wafting out into the street. There'd be time to wet his whistle when he dropped off Frank and talked some with the law. The goal came into view as Dr. Fuller's shingle swayed in the morning wind as if beckoning him onward.

"We're almost there," Slocum said. Whether he directed the words to the horse or Frank didn't matter. Neither was likely to understand.

Slocum swung his leg up and over the moaning body and dropped to the ground in time to catch Frank as he slid down, too. Grunting, Slocum got the man over his shoulder and stumbled the few steps to the doctor's door. He kicked at it with his boot until a youngish blond man with muttonchops and pince-nez glasses opened it.

"You don't have to kick it down," the man said irritably. He adjusted the glasses, squinted, and then motioned Slocum inside.

Slocum dropped Frank onto an examining table.

"So what happened? You a bounty hunter?"

"That seems a popular question. Nope, he got shot by road agents."

"Not you? No, you'd have no reason to bring him in if you shot him. What are you to him?"

"We might work for the same man up in Santa Fe."

"That's a strange way to say it," the doctor said, slipping into a white linen coat. "Do you or don't you work for the same man?"

"I was driving a wagon to Tombstone from Santa Fe and this one, name of Frank he says, overtook me west of town and said Holst sent him along to keep me company."

"So this Holst didn't send him?"

Slocum shrugged. He had no evidence other than what Frank said about that.

"You paying for his care? He's not shot up too badly, but getting bounced around did more to lay him up than anything else."

"Contact Holst, New Mexico Ice and Coal Company up in Santa Fe."

"Yeah, as if anyone out of my sight will pay a dime, even if this gent does work for the company." The doctor rummaged through Frank's pockets. His eyebrows rose when he discovered a few greenbacks.

"I'm not a thief," Slocum said. "I'll be over at the marshal's office."

"Sheriff Whitehill. This is the county seat of Grant County."

"Thanks," Slocum said, slipping out into the dusty air that settled on Silver City. Inside the office the doctor's antiseptic made his nose twitch. Out here the pollution was more in keeping with what he accepted as normal. The smell of horse dung in the streets, outhouses, and rotting garbage all assailed him along with the purity of the sky and the gentle wind keeping the smells from becoming overwhelming.

He walked a dozen yards over to the jailhouse, hesitated a moment, then lifted the latch and entered. It had been a spell since he'd had a run-in with a federal judge back in Calhoun, Georgia, that hadn't ended well—for the carpetbagger judge. Slocum had been gutshot by Bloody Bill Anderson on William Quantrill's orders for protesting the guerrilla raid on Lawrence, Kansas. By the time he had recuperated, the war was over and Reconstruction in full bloom.

The judge had forged documents saying taxes had gone unpaid on Slocum's Stand and had ridden out with a hired gunman to seize the property. He had won the property, but not the way he expected. Slocum had buried him and his henchman by the springhouse and had ridden west, never looking back. For this, wanted posters dogged his steps and made him leery of dealing with any lawman. All it took was one who spent too much time pawing through musty piles of old wanted posters to ruin his day.

A whippet of a man looked up. He pushed back from his desk where a newspaper had been spread open. From the ink smudges on his fingers, he had been reading it running his finger along under each line.

"What can I do for you?"

Slocum closed the door behind him and looked around. The three cells were simple and likely hard to get out of unless you had a key. Iron bars had been well tended, and the dirt floor in each cell might be harder than the adobe in the foot-thick walls. Slocum vowed to stay out of those cells, but from the sheriff's cordial greeting and the lack of wanted posters put up anywhere around the small building, there shouldn't be a reason to worry.

"I work as a teamster for an ice company up in Santa Fe," he said.

"Holst? I know the varmint." The sheriff tipped back in his chair, hooked his thumbs in the armholes of his brocade vest, and fixed Slocum with a steely look.

"Hope he didn't rook you," Slocum said, "because I need a lawman to help recover the wagon I was driving." He explained what had happened. The longer he talked, the more the sheriff scowled.

"You got a name?" the lawman finally asked.

"Slocum."

"I'll get a telegram off to Holst about this. I'm Harvey Whitehill."

Slocum had never heard Holst mention him. He took that as a good thing since Holst could go on about his political and business rivals until a man's ears fell off.

"Will the man over at Doc Fuller back up what you said?"

"Don't know if he's in any shape to. The doctor thought the trip here took more out of him than getting shot."

"Three outlaws, eh? And Apaches? Them I heard about. A courier from over at Fort Bayard brought around the news a small band of Warm Springs Apaches had left the reservation. Thought they might end up annoyin' us here in Silver City since this was one of their old campgrounds."

"I'd heard that," Slocum said. "But the Indians attacked the road agents more to get the mules hitched to the wagon than what was in it."

"Only ice?" Sheriff Whitehill shook his head. "Can't say I wouldn't mind a chip or two of ice in my whiskey, but these gents were mighty insistent on stealin' the whole danged block. You got to wonder on that. Where'd they sell it?"

"That thought occurred to me, too," Slocum said. "It's likely too late to salvage the ice, but Holst wouldn't mind seeing the wagon and mules back."

"Can't blame him overmuch," Whitehill said. "Let's you and me go for a ride."

"You know the road agents?"

"Can't say I do, but from where you said they robbed you, there's only a couple places they could drive a wagon."

"Along the road over to Tombstone," Slocum said, "where I was headed."

"No point in them showing up with the ice if you'd ever challenge them. Might be the only place they could sell the ice, but more 'n likely, they went here." Whitehill unrolled a map and stabbed down on it. "That's not more 'n a couple miles south of here."

"Why there?"

Whitehill stroked his mustache and pursed his lips as he thought. Then he shrugged.

"'Cuz they have to go somewhere. No idea why they'd take ice if they didn't have a use for it. The road to Tombstone is mighty lonely. From here they might go on over to Shakespeare. Those owlhoots runnin' the way station there might sell the ice to stagecoach passengers with some luck."

Slocum saw the town Whitehill pointed out was about thirty miles to the southwest. He had no way of knowing if the sheriff guessed right, but it was better than anything Slocum could come up with.

"All I've got is the Indian pony. No gear."

"You rode here just fine. Won't hurt you none to ride bareback a day or two longer."

Slocum went to fetch his horse and waited impatiently as Whitehill ducked into Dr. Fuller's surgery. The sheriff returned, frowning.

"I got myself the makin's of a real mystery here, Slocum. The man you brung in let the doctor pull out a bullet, then snuck out when Fuller turned his back."

"He must be around town somewhere. He didn't have a horse and wasn't strong enough to walk too far."

"I got me a new deputy. He can take care of our refugee."

"But the doctor told you everything I said was right?"

Whitehill looked hard at Slocum and nodded once. Slocum saw he wasn't a man to take anything for granted and had questioned the doctor.

"As much as he could. Saddle up." Whitehill hesitated, grinned crookedly, then amended, "Mount up. We got a hard ride ahead of us."

Slocum found himself hard-pressed to maintain the pace

set by the sheriff. His pony was tired from hauling two men into Silver City and hadn't been given time enough to rest or eat its fill. Still, the Apaches had trained the horse well, and it lagged behind only a few times.

After four hours of riding, the sheriff motioned for Slocum to pull up.

"See those tracks?"

Slocum didn't have to dismount to know they had come across the wagon tracks. From the way the right side tracks were intermittently wider, he knew this was the ice wagon. The wheels on that side wobbled a mite, causing it to track poorly. He had complained to Holst about this but all the satisfaction he'd gotten was a wrench, a spare axle nut, and the promise to repair the wagon when Slocum drove back from Tombstone.

"Took 'em longer to get here than it ought to have, from what you said about the robbery and the skirmish with the Indians."

"They likely wanted to put some distance between the Apaches—and me." Slocum explained about the right wheels.

"They can't be too far ahead." Sheriff Whitehill looked at Slocum's six-gun. "Don't be too quick to use that hogleg, but don't be too slow neither."

With that, the sheriff motioned Slocum to ride some distance to his left, then slowly worked his way along the rocky path down a steep slope. Slocum spotted the wagon before the lawman. He imitated a quail to get Whitehill's attention, then pointed. The sheriff slid his rifle from the sheath and started ahead. Slocum mirrored his approach.

They didn't immediately go to the wagon sitting forlornly in the middle of a rocky clearing. The mules tugged on their harnesses, trying to reach some grass nearby. The canvas had been ripped away from the crate. The road agents had worried open the side of the crate. From the puddle of water beneath the wagon, Slocum knew the ice had been exposed to the sun and had melted away.

"Now don't that beat all," Whitehill said. He cocked his rifle.

Slocum perked up and looked around. Seeing nothing that threatened them, he rode to the far side of the wagon so he could get the same look at the crate that the sheriff already had.

He caught his breath.

"Pass over that Colt, Slocum. I got some questions to ask, and you're goin' to give me the answers."

Slocum stared at the damage done to the crate, the sawdust insulation all caked and lying in wet lumps—and at the body that had been frozen into the ice he had been shipping.

7

"You can't think I had anything to do with killing him," Slocum protested.

"Shut yer tater trap and drive. I'll get to the bottom of this, but it surely does look as if you are the one who killed . . . him."

Slocum looked sharply at the sheriff. From the way Whitehill spoke, he knew the identity of the dead man. How that was possible posed as big a question as to how the body got into the cake of ice Slocum was driving to Tombstone. A quick look at the body had shown a bullet had ended the man's life, going into his chest just above his heart. The ice and melting water had partially erased the blood from the man's coat, but the expression on his face had been frozen. He hadn't died easy.

Snapping the reins, Slocum maneuvered the mule team along a steep ravine. He considered his chances of letting the wagon tumble down the embankment and trying to escape. Whitehill had taken his six-shooter and rode at some distance so he could get the drop on him if necessary. The sheriff hadn't formally arrested him, but Slocum had been in custody enough times to know how it felt.

Riding out had been a trip of mutual caution. Whitehill didn't quite trust him, and Slocum was wary of the lawman. Driving the wagon back to Silver City was a different can of worms. He might not be under arrest, but the way the sheriff treated him was no different.

"Who is he?" Slocum asked after another mile. "Your expression when you saw him tells me you know him."

"Ain't sayin' more 'til I find your partner. The one what sashayed away from Doc Fuller."

Slocum fell silent. Had Frank known they were going after the wagon and what they'd find? If the redhead had plugged the man bouncing around in the rear of the wagon, how'd the body end up in a block of ice and why would Frank chase it halfway to Tombstone? Better to let Slocum deliver the body while heading in the opposite direction. Frank could have been in Kansas by now rather than all shot up and hiding out in Silver City.

The one thing Slocum knew was that Frank had the answers Sheriff Whitehill thought he had.

They rattled and rumbled along and finally rolled into Silver City after midnight.

"You set right there. Don't move a muscle 'less I say," Whitehill warned. He cocked his rifle, dismounted, and let Slocum tie the reins around the brake before climbing down. "Head for the calaboose."

"I didn't kill him."

"Never said you did, but you know more 'bout this than you're sayin'. It's time for you to let me hear the whole story."

"I told you all I know."

Whitehill laughed harshly, then poked Slocum with the rifle muzzle to get him moving along the darkened street. Gaiety in the saloons called to Slocum. He badly needed a drink to ease the pain of driving most of the day. More than this, he wanted to be surrounded by men not inclined to shatter his spine with a bullet if he moved in the wrong direction.

He went into the jail. Whitehill dropped his Colt on the desk, then said, "That back cell looks to be a good fit, Slocum."

Slocum closed his eyes and shivered as the sheriff closed and locked the door. He had thought he'd avoid getting locked up. Bringing Frank to town had been a mistake. After fighting the road agents and the Indians, he should have kept riding in any direction that wasn't Silver City.

He sank to the straw pallet that passed for a mattress on the cot and drew up his legs. Stiff all over, he stretched and tried to work out the kinks from the long drive into town. A muscle spasm in his leg brought home the reality of his problem. The sheriff thought he'd murdered the man in the ice.

"Don't go anywhere, Slocum. I'll see to . . . him. Ain't a chore I much cotton to, but it's got to be done."

Left alone in the cell, Slocum began hunting for a way out. His first impression had been right. The dirt floor was sunbaked. An inch down he hit a hard white layer. Caliche. It would take dynamite to dig through the hardened clay, and if he had a stick or two, blowing a hole in the adobe wall was a quicker way to freedom. The bars and the lock on the door were as secure as he had feared. Above he saw no way to scrape through the wire mesh between him and the roof. Disheartened, he sank back to the pallet.

When feeding time came—breakfast, most likely—this would be his only chance to get away. But Whitehill was a cautious man and unlikely to make a mistake that would let Slocum get free. Time worked against him, and he couldn't go anywhere or do anything.

He looked up when Whitehill returned. The lawman put his rifle back in a wall rack and sank to the desk chair. It creaked under his weight. From his expression, a load of worry was added to that weight.

"I got the body over to Doc Fuller. Couldn't find the town undertaker. He's probably out on a bender. Never seen a man drink like Rafe Olney. Suppose it keeps him from laughin' durin' the funerals. Looks like it was his dog what died, but I know he thinks all the dyin' is funny and makin' him rich."

"Burying that body going to make Rafe Olney rich?"

"Could be, could be," Whitehill said.

The sheriff reached for his six-gun when the door creaked open an inch, then crashed back against the wall. Filling the doorway was a man about as broad as he was tall.

"You shouldn't have waited up for me, Sheriff," the man said, coming in.

Whitehill relaxed.

"Didn't know when you was fixin' on doin' your duty, Deputy."

"I had a squabble to deal with east of town. Two gents decided the same cow belonged to each of them."

"So you shot and ate it yourself," Slocum piped up.

The deputy took a couple steps toward the cell, his hand going to his six-shooter.

"Who's that?"

"A fellow what needs to answer some questions," said Whitehill.

"Don't expect the truth out of that lyin' son of a bitch's mouth," the deputy said.

"You'll never admit I saved your hide, will you, Tucker?" Slocum stood and leaned against the bars.

"Whatever he's in for, Harvey, I'll stand bail for him," the deputy said. "I owe him that and a bit more. Might even owe him a drink, 'less he's in for rowdiness and public drunkenness."

"That's not a crime," Whitehill said. "How do you know him, Dan?"

Dangerous Dan Tucker walked over and stuck his face within an inch of Slocum's.

"I had some trouble up in Durango. You know my boast how I can whip an entire room of drunk cowboys? I was doin' a damned good job of it but—"

"But he didn't know there was a muleskinner in the room," Slocum finished.

"Damned 'skinner woulda kilt me dead if Slocum hadn't stopped him." Tucker spat. "I took that man's own knife and used it on him. The rest of them boys quieted down right away, but I'd'a had a knife 'tween my ribs if Slocum hadn't stopped him for me."

"You think Slocum could kill a man?"

"Know he could. Saw him do it not a minute later."

"Saved your hide a second time that night. The muleskinner had a partner with a shotgun."

"Small world," Whitehill said. He ran his fingers around the metal ring holding the cell keys. "All right, Slocum. One question. Did you kill Texas Jack Bedrich?"

Slocum looked from Tucker to the sheriff.

"I don't know anyone named Bedrich. Was that the muleskinner's partner?"

"Muleskinners don't have names," Tucker said. "Just poor bathin' habits." He sniffed. "Smells like you're one of 'em now."

"So you don't know Jack Bedrich?" Sheriff Whitehill came over.

"*I* don't know Bedrich," Tucker said. "How's Slocum supposed to? You just got to town, right, Slocum?"

Whitehill unlocked the cell door.

"Don't make me regret this, either of you."

"Hell, Sheriff, I'm already regretting it!" Tucker clasped Slocum hard, pushed him away, and shook hands.

"So am I," grumbled Whitehill. He threw the ring of keys to the desk and sat. "You really don't know Bedrich?"

"Never heard of him in all my born days," Slocum said.

"Yet you brought in his most recent partner, more dead than alive. If I hadn't seen proof that Bedrich was in that block of ice with my own eyes, I'd figure you killed Texas Jack and tried to gun down Frank."

Slocum tried to make sense from it and couldn't.

"You reckon Frank knew his partner was inside the ice?" Slocum asked.

"Must have, from the way you tell it. But Frank wasn't really Bedrich's partner," the sheriff said. "Former partner is more like it. They had a big bust-up a couple months back. Texas Jack was always doin' that with his partners. He could be real ornery and not above usin' men for his own gain." He took a deep breath, then added, "Then again, the split might have been over Bedrich's woman. I think Frank was sweet on her, too."

Slocum perked up. The way Whitehill said it, he might be sweet on the same woman.

"If Frank killed Bedrich and stuffed him in the ice, why'd he come so all fired fast on Slocum's heels?" Tucker perched his butt on the edge of the sheriff's desk and let a short leg swing back and forth nervously.

"Doesn't make a lick of sense," Whitehill admitted. "You keep a sharp eye out for Frank. From what the doc said, he's not gettin' out of Silver City walkin'. Might be the only way he'll get out of town is in Rafe's hearse."

"Hearse? The town digger's got a hearse?" Tucker looked skeptical.

"More like a wagon with a canvas top on it. Painted all black, has black horses to pull it. Rafe's got quite a business goin'."

"With the ice gone, I suppose I ought to fix up the wagon and go back to Santa Fe. Holst will have a fit," Slocum said.

"Cain't let you do that, Slocum, not 'til this matter of a bullet in Bedrich's chest is cleared up. You might be tellin' the truth—"

"He is," cut in Tucker. "If he ain't, I'll cut his tongue out and roast it on an open fire."

"I might have your tongue, too, Dan," said the sheriff. "As I was sayin', until this gets cleared up, you can work on your wagon all you want but don't go headin' them mules northward or tryin' to ride that Apache pony out of here in any direction."

"Apache pony?" Dangerous Dan Tucker shook his head. "You can't do things like an ordinary fellow, can you, Slocum? How'd you come by an Indian mount?"

"You can catch up on all this on your own time. Get out there on patrol, Tucker. Saloons will be closin' up in another hour or so."

"You owe me a drink, at least, Slocum," Tucker said. With that he melted into the black night.

"Tell me one thing, Sheriff."

"You can sleep in one of the cells if you're short some cash money," Whitehill said.

The last thing Slocum wanted was to spend another night in a jail. He had endured that too many times to be comfortable, even if the cell door wasn't locked this time.

"I'll make do," he said. "What I wanted to know was about this Texas Jack Bedrich. You made it sound like him and Frank squabbled over more than a woman."

"Don't know they fought over her, but they might have. Bedrich and Frank made a decent strike on the edge of Chloride Flats where all the silver is mined. Frank's the sort who is never satisfied with what he has. Always wants more. You know the type?"

Slocum nodded. He did.

"Well, sir, I think Bedrich gave Frank the claim. Don't rightly know what he got in return, but Bedrich had a nose for blue dirt. He could sniff out silver chloride a mile off, and might have."

"That still doesn't explain how Bedrich ended up dead in a block of ice being hauled to Tombstone," Slocum said.

"Nope, it don't," said Whitehill. "Now you skedaddle.

I got the other end of town to patrol. Dan's a good deputy, but he can't do it all."

Slocum stepped into the cold mountain night and saw the stars being blotted out by thin clouds. This time of year brought torrential rains, but it would take an hour or two to build. That'd give him plenty of time to wheedle the livery stable owner for a place to stay in exchange for some work and maybe even get the mules fed and watered. Repairing the wagon could wait 'til sunup.

But as he walked down the middle of the Silver City street, noise from the saloons appealed to him. He had ridden in thinking how good a taste of whiskey would be. With almost a dollar in change rubbing together in his vest pocket, he could afford a shot or maybe do with only a beer. A smile crossed his lips as he thought how ice could have given him cold beer.

The smile vanished when he remembered there'd been a body encased in it.

He stopped and peered into one smoky cantina. The Lonely Cuss was mostly empty, a couple customers sprawled over tables. One snored loudly, and the other made curious hiccuping sounds. A faro table stood lonely on one side of the door, and what might have been a piano at the rear lay cloaked in darkness. No one seemed inclined to play it, which was fine with Slocum. He wasn't in the mood for music.

No one stood at the bar. He thought the place might be closed, then saw movement as the barkeep heaved a tray of beer mugs onto the bar with a loud clanking.

Slocum went in, worked his fingers around in his pocket, and found a dime. As good as whiskey would taste, a couple beers would do him as well.

"Beer," he called to the barkeep.

"Just a second," she answered, bent over to lift another tray. Slocum appreciated the view. He might even be talked into a third beer if she would lean over like that again. The trail got mighty lonely, and the real thing in flesh and blood was better than his imagination ever could be.

She dropped the second tray and turned to him. Their eyes locked, then she said, "Hello, John. It's been a long time since Georgia and that dead carpetbagger judge."

8

"Hell, Marianne," he said. "It has been a while."

"You want some whiskey? You always had a fondness for Kentucky bourbon."

"Beer's all I can afford."

"I don't own the Lonely Cuss," Marianne said, brushing back her auburn hair and never looking away from him, "but Tom doesn't watch over my shoulder much after the first night or two I worked here." She rummaged about, found a shot glass that sparkled in the dim light of the coal oil lamp over the bar, and poured two fingers. "Not Billy Taylor's Finest but good enough."

He sipped, then let the bourbon wet his lips and roll across his tongue. His mouth watered at the unfamiliar taste of good whiskey. With a quick motion, he downed it. The fire seared its way down to his belly, where it pooled. After a few seconds the warmth spread and eased some of the aches he'd accumulated from working the mule team on a wobbly wheeled wagon.

"That's the second best thing that's happened to me today."

"Only the second?" Marianne asked.

"Seeing you again. That has to be the best."

She snorted and snatched the shot glass from in front of him, running her rag over it to give it a good cleaning.

"That's a fine thing to say when you didn't even have the decency to bid me farewell."

"You know the reason why. After I killed the judge and his henchman, I couldn't stay in Calhoun."

"They did search for you, that I'll grant. Had a squad of soldiers from the Yankee garrison hunting for you nigh on a week. By then they decided you'd hightailed it where they'd never find you."

"Never knew that. I rode due west."

"I tore down all the wanted posters I could. They must have nailed a hundred to trees and posts in town. Most of the folks were too timid to defy the blue bellies."

"You wouldn't have been. You were never timid in anything you did."

"Not with you, John."

"Nope," he said. His mouth still tingled from the whiskey, but asking for another, even if he paid, didn't seem right.

"What brings you to Silver City?"

He hesitated. Telling Marianne the entire story would take forever. Instead he said, "I'm working as a teamster hauling from Santa Fe to Tombstone. Got robbed out on the trail, came to town, and the sheriff rode back with me to salvage the wagon."

"Sheriff Whitehill's a fine man," she said. "Sometimes, though, he seems to love his job more than he does the people. Glad you got the wagon back. Did you recover any of the cargo?"

Again he hesitated, then shook his head.

"I've got to close up. You want to roust those two and get them outside? They're both harmless. Lum and Abel."

"Long as it's not Cain and Abel," he said. This caused Marianne to smile just a little bit. It was real and not forced.

"You always could make me smile, John, when you weren't breaking my damnfool heart."

"I didn't want to lead the law to you. That's why I left so quick."

"Get them out. I'm about finished here." She pulled out a tin box and snapped the lid shut.

Slocum wondered how much money was in that box. Then he had his hands full getting first one, then the other man to his feet and wobbling out the door.

"Come on back tomorrow," he told them.

"Shure thin," slurred one. "Love watchin' that purty li'l filly 'hind the bar. Love watchin' her hiney. Love . . ." He wandered into the night, telling the stars alone why he came to the Lonely Cuss. Slocum didn't doubt Marianne drew in more than this fellow because of her beauty and good humor.

"Gimme the box," said a rough voice.

Slocum turned and had his six-shooter out, cocked, and aimed in a smooth motion.

"Wait, John, no, it's all right. He's not robbing me. This is Tom Gallifrey, the owner."

"You got yourself a bodyguard?" Gallifrey snatched the box and opened it a crack, peering inside to assure himself it contained the night's money. He was short and looked like a weasel, his thin gray-skinned face, deep-set pale eyes, and curled lip giving him a sly look.

"Sorry about that, Mr. Gallifrey," Slocum said. "You came up unexpected and—"

"Good to know you're not gonna get yourself robbed of my money," the cantina owner said, clutching the box to his chest. He grunted and headed off into the night, disappearing around a building. In seconds Slocum couldn't even hear his shoes against the gravel on the ground.

"You can see what I have to put up with," she said. Marianne linked her arm with Slocum's. "Walk me home. To the hotel."

They started down the boardwalk, the clicking of their steps loud in the still night.

"It's good to see you again," she said. "I never thought I would."

"Not out in New Mexico, this far from home."

Marianne laughed and said, "So you still think of Georgia as home? I do, as well."

"Why'd you leave?"

"I—" Marianne tensed and pulled away from him. He felt the tension in her grip on his arm and could almost hear her brain grinding to a halt. She finally said, "There were reasons. Like you, I had reasons."

"You killed a judge?"

"Nothing like that, but as serious. I don't think I can ever go back any more than you can, John. When I left right after you did, I drifted about for a while, then stayed in New Orleans for a year or more. The Crescent City didn't suit me then, and I moved on to Houston."

"You drift up here from Texas?"

"Something like that. I lived in Eagle Pass, then decided the constant raids from across the border and by the Indians made life too dangerous for me and . . ."

"And?" Slocum heard her hesitation to speak what she thought. Her reasons for moving or not were her own. If he had to give her a list of reasons he had become a drifter, it would been difficult. Why had he left Colorado to go to Santa Fe? Because he had left Denver City to go to Durango? And before that he had gotten tired of working on a Wyoming ranch? The winters in Wyoming were fierce. But he had gone there from Kansas because those summers were humid and crushing hot.

Were any of those reasons? Along with such superficial reasons came more important ones. In Kansas the cavalry hunted him down for a robbery gone wrong outside Salinas. The work in Wyoming had been good, but he had left Denver after an altercation with a gambler who had mistakenly thought he had a better hand and a faster draw. He'd been wrong on both counts, but he had powerful friends. Moving on had been an easy decision for Slocum since it kept him a mile ahead of a lynch mob.

He could hardly expect Marianne to have worse reasons for her slow migration from Calhoun. He only hoped her reasons were better.

"I like new scenery in my life from time to time. This is lovely country. Mountains but with a touch of desert. Not much snow in the winter and folks say the summers are mild."

"You have a fellow?" Again he felt her tense and drift away from him even more. She barely had her hand in the crook of his arm, which was all the answer he needed. "He's a lucky man."

"You ever marry, John?"

His silence provided all the answer she needed.

"I didn't think so. You were always the wild wind. A woman who made you settle down would have to know how to lasso a prairie tornado."

"You came close."

"I would have gone with you, if you'd asked."

"The carpetbaggers would have burned down your family's house if they so much as thought you were with me."

"I suppose. I would have risked it. Then."

"Then," Slocum said, a touch of sadness in his voice. "Twelve years is a long time."

"Nigh on thirteen," she corrected. "But who's counting?"

She had been. And so had Slocum. Marianne Lomax was a hard woman to get out of his head—and his life. She had been his first love, and like so much else, the war and its aftermath had ruined his plans. He knew, even if Marianne denied it just a little, that retribution would have been great against her family if she had left with him. More than this, Marianne riding with him would have slowed his escape just enough to get caught. As it was, federal troops and more than one marshal had come close to snaring Slocum as he rode through Georgia and into Tennessee. From there he had barely made his way to the Ohio River and down to Saint Louis. Two bounty hunters had left him shot up, but he had ridden west from there and their bodies had drifted down the Big Muddy.

The peace following the war had been as brutal as the war itself. He snorted at this idea. The war had been as cruel as any human could imagine. It just never got better afterward.

"Here we are, John. Thank you for walking me home." Marianne looked up at the hotel. "It's not much, but I got burned out of my house."

"Apaches?"

"It would be understandable if it had been redskins. No, it was a white man with difficulty taking no for an answer."

She looked hard at him, making him wonder what he should say—or do. For a moment he thought to kiss her, then a crash from inside the hotel broke the spell.

"Good night, John." She gave him a chaste hug and spun away from the circle of his arms. At the door she hesitated, looked back at him, then slipped inside.

Slocum sat on the steps and looked around Silver City without seeing the town at all. His gaze was fixed on a time long past, back in Georgia when he and Marianne had been lovers. He tried not to regret much in his life. Living day to day helped, but a few things still gnawed away at him. The death of his brother, Robert, during Pickett's Charge. How the judge had tried to steal property that had been deeded to the Slocum family by King George II. And leaving Marianne behind.

Other than that, Slocum had evened the score as he rode through life. Some men had died; others had been rewarded for their friendship. He carried damned few grudges, but he discovered he still carried one big torch. She had just gone into the hotel.

And she was taken by another man. Whatever chance he once had with Marianne Lomax was passed. They had been young and reckless and in love, but the love was as real as the dirt under his feet or the clean, crisp air he breathed.

Slocum began his slow walk to the stables. As much as he would have preferred to share Marianne's bed after all these years, he had to be satisfied that he had clean straw— and that he wasn't locked up in the town jail.

As he started to turn down a cross street on his way to the stables, movement caught his eye. He stopped and looked over his shoulder. A shadow moved fast, back toward the hotel. He shrugged it off. The saloons were closed now, and the hotel probably filled every night with all the new prospectors on their way to find fortune in the silver fields.

But something caused him to reverse his path and return to the hotel in time to see the dark figure dart behind the hotel. Slocum slipped the leather thong off the hammer of his six-shooter and went to the back of the hotel. A quick look around failed to reveal whoever had just come here. Then he looked up. Like a fly, a man worked up a drainpipe to the second floor where a window blossomed with pale yellow light.

Any number of people could be trimming the wick and lighting their lamps, but the only one Slocum could be certain had just entered the hotel was Marianne. He started to call out to the man clinging to the drainpipe, then whipped out his Colt Navy when the window opened and he caught sight of Marianne letting in night air.

The man jumped from the drainpipe to the windowsill and shoved Marianne back into her room. Slocum started to fire, but his target had disappeared into the room. Sounds of a ruckus came down to him.

If the intruder could make it up the pipe, Slocum reckoned he was agile enough to, also. He slid his six-shooter back into his holster, tested the drainpipe, and wondered if it might not be better to go around front and rouse the night clerk. But the muffled sounds from the room started him up the pipe, no matter how rickety it was under his weight.

Ignoring the sound of nails pulling free from the wooden walls, he kept climbing until he could peer into the room. He might have misjudged the situation. This could be Marianne's beau and their way of spending the night together.

A single glance saw that the dark figure held her wrists in one hand and had stretched her facedown across the bed so her screams were muffled by the comforter. From the way she kicked and tried to get free, she wasn't enjoying this. Slocum had seen enough rape in his day to know what was sex play and what was violence.

"Show me where it is," the man gritted out between clenched teeth. "Give it to me. Now! Do it or you're gonna regret it!"

As the drainpipe tore free of the wall, Slocum jumped, caught the window ledge, and shinnied up so he was halfway into the room. The noise of the pipe falling to the alley below and his scrabbling to pull himself in distracted the rapist.

The man twisted about. Slocum didn't get a good look at his face but caught enough in the lamplight to identify a scar on his cheek. The diversion of Slocum pulling himself into the room gave Marianne the chance to kick back like a mule, jerk hard, and roll off the bed, half pinned between the wall and the mattress.

Like a striking snake, the intruder drew his pistol and fired. The window glass about Slocum's head shattered. Most of the glass fell against his hat brim, but one shard cut his cheek, about where the other man sported that permanent scar. The gunman would have fired again and ended Slocum's life if it hadn't been for Marianne grabbing up the comforter and spinning it out like a fisherman's net. It descended to block the man's view and ruin his aim.

This slug went through the blanket and into the wall

beside the window. By this time, Slocum had kicked hard enough against the outer wall to find purchase so he could shove himself into the room. He landed with a thud on the bare floor. Rolling, he got out his pistol and fired from beneath the bed. Although flat on his back when he fired, his aim was better than the still-draped intruder.

The man grunted and turned. Slocum had winged him in the left arm. Then a hail of bullets kept Slocum under the bed and Marianne crouched down next to the wall. The gunman fanned off the rounds remaining in his pistol. The room filled with choking gun smoke.

Slocum heard a door slam and heavy footfalls out in the hall. He rolled back and got to his knees. The smoke vented from the room through the open window, but Slocum had no chance to stand. He was bowled over as Marianne hit him.

They struggled for a moment, then she reared up and recognized him.

"John!"

"I saw that owlhoot climbing the drainpipe, then you poked your head out the window. Did I interrupt anything?"

"You idiot!" Marianne raged. "Of course you did. He was trying to rape me!"

"Then I'm glad I stopped him."

"You didn't think I'd do that with Jack!"

Slocum took that to be her lover.

"Are you hurt?"

"No, thanks to you. But you're bleeding." She touched his cheek.

"I need to go after him. I don't want to lose him in the dark."

"Wait, don't," she said, clinging to his arm. "He's a dangerous man."

"He's going to be a dead man when I catch him." Slocum saw the expression on her face. "You know him, don't you?"

"That's the man who burned down my house."

"He has a scar on his cheek."

"His name's Carstairs."

"Have you told the sheriff?"

"There's not much he can do." Marianne clung to him and began sobbing. Wetness from her tears spread on his shirt. "I've missed you so terribly all these years."

He heard the sound of a horse galloping away into the night. That had to be Carstairs heading west. Slocum wanted to get on the trail right away, but Marianne held him too tight to easily leave. And the truth was, he'd rather have her arms around him than face down this Carstairs.

But that would come soon enough. Even if her lover Jack or the sheriff weren't up to it, he wasn't going to let Carstairs get away with his crimes.

9

"I can't ask you to fight my battles, John." Marianne shuddered in his arms as they sat on the bed, thighs pressed together. The cold wind blowing through the shattered window might have caused part of her reaction, but Slocum knew better.

"It's my fight now," he said. "This Carstairs owlhoot took a shot at me. I can't let him get by with that."

"You should tell Sheriff Whitehill and let him chase him down. The two of us can swear out a warrant for him."

"From the sound of it, Carstairs would be out of the cell and on the trail again before we could spit."

"He's got powerful friends. He's foreman of a big mine out in Chloride Flats."

Slocum knew what this meant. If Carstairs said the word, a dozen miners would come to town with blood in their eye. Whitehill wouldn't want that, even with Dangerous Dan Tucker to back him on any play. Keeping the peace in a boomtown like Silver City depended as much on placating the rowdy elements as it did on throwing them in jail. Only Carstairs had gone past hurrahing the town or getting drunk and beating up another saloon patron. Burning down a woman's house and then trying to rape her went far beyond simple misdemeanors.

"He was alone when he came in. He might not have let his men know what he was up to. They wouldn't cotton to raping a woman any more than I do."

"I'm too confused to know what to think right now."

"Ma, what happened? There was gunfire."

Slocum released Marianne, guilty about holding her the way he had been with two young boys looking on.

"It's all right. Mr. Slocum saved me from . . . from being robbed of something very valuable."

"Carstairs," the taller boy said, almost spitting it out. Slocum sat a little straighter on the bed. Something about his voice reminded him of his brother, Robert.

When the boy stepped into the room and the lamplight caught his face, Slocum almost blurted something better kept penned up. The boy might sound like his brother but he was the spitting image of . . . John Slocum.

"John, this is my son, Randolph."

"Randolph was my pa's name," Slocum said, more to himself than to Marianne.

"I know."

He looked sharply at her, but she pointedly refused to meet his gaze. Randolph had the same lank dark hair Slocum did, and if he could tell in the dim light, his green eyes matched perfectly.

"How old are you, Randolph?"

"John, don't—" Marianne was cut off by her son's reply.

"I'm almost thirteen. Will be in six months, at least. This here's my best friend, Billy."

"I should introduce you properly," Marianne said. "William McCarty, Randolph Lomax, this is my friend from Georgia, Mr. Slocum."

Randolph fingered a knife he held behind his back, thinking Slocum didn't see it. From where he stood, the boy had his back to a mirror set into a dresser at the corner of the room that allowed Slocum to see everything. The other boy, Billy, might have a small pistol in his pocket. Slocum couldn't tell, but the heft and size of the lump was about right for a derringer. They were a dangerous pair, Randolph and Billy.

"Who shot out the window?" Billy asked.

"Bet it was that son of a bitch Carstairs," Randolph said.

"You go wash your mouth out with soap, Randolph Robert Lomax! You will *never* use such language in my presence."

"Aww, Ma."

Slocum felt as if his guts had been turned inside out and then tied into knots. Randolph had been his pa's name and Robert was his brother. And how had the boy come to use his ma's maiden name?

"It's all right," Slocum said, "because I'm thinking on what he's saying. We should get Whitehill on his trail."

"We've been over this, John. He won't do it."

"Naw," Randolph said, "he's as scared of Carstairs as everyone else is in this town. Everyone except Jack. He ain't afraid of no man, including the likes of Lester Carstairs."

"He's gonna marry Randolph's ma," Billy piped up. The boy was slight and pale. His hands moved nervously, but something in his eyes spoke to Slocum. He sounded older than Randolph, although he looked to be the same age or even younger because of his size.

"She told me," Slocum said. "When's Jack due back?"

"He's overdue by a couple days," Billy said, again assuming the role of spokesman for the Lomax family. "That don't mean much. He's a prospector and a damned fine one, too. He promised me a job in a new mine."

"When? When did he do that?" demanded Randolph. "He never said nuthin' 'bout a new mine. He—"

"Boys," Marianne said sharply enough to silence their bickering. "I need to get some sleep. Why don't you show Mr. Slocum out?"

"Can't he figure it out on his own?" Randolph looked irritated.

"Your ma wants us to show some manners," Billy said. "You don't want to go out through the lobby. Miz Gruhlkey is a stickler for propriety. You'd never answer enough of her questions to keep from her whackin' you with her broom, the old witch."

"We can go through the cellar. Then . . ." Randolph and Billy put their heads together, plotting the sneakiest departure.

"You can trust them to get you out past Mrs. Gruhlkey, no matter how sharp her eyes are for such things."

"What do you want to do about Carstairs?" Slocum asked.

"He won't dare try anything again."

"I'll make sure of that."

"John, please, don't get involved."

He already was. Slocum let the boys lead him down a laundry chute to the cellar, then crawl out a narrow window into the alley where he had pulled down the drainpipe in his climb up to Marianne's window. The boys disappeared like ghosts, leaving him to stare at the window.

After a few minutes the light went out, but Slocum heard the sobbing for some time. He went to the building immediately behind the hotel, sank down, drew up his knees, and rested his forehead there. He slept fitfully until sunrise, but Carstairs never returned.

And with the rising sun warming his face, Slocum remembered what he had heard Carstairs saying in the room to Marianne.

"This isn't something the sheriff'd take care of, Slocum," Dangerous Dan Tucker said as he sipped a cup of coffee strong enough to clean the gunpowder out of a rifle barrel.

Slocum stared out the café window into Silver City's main street. Commerce had begun early, and the bustling trade told him how much money there was to be made in a boomtown. The miners would mostly go bust, with a very few hitting it rich. Those who made the real money sold the miners picks and dynamite, wheelbarrows and overalls. Without flour for biscuits and oatmeal and beans, a prospector starved. Slocum had never seen one of them who'd take the time to hunt or forage. That stole away precious time better spent hunting for the elusive precious metal, whether it was gold or silver.

"Carstairs is that important?"

"Don't know the ins and outs yet of the town, but yeah, I'd say so from what I've heard," Tucker admitted. "The Argent Mine is one of the biggest. Without its metal flowing into the banks, the saloons, and all the rest, Silver City would be a shadow of itself."

"Where could that silver go, if not here?"

"Shakespeare's a day or two ride off. You been there with the sheriff?"

"Almost there," Slocum said.

"The stagecoach route runs through Shakespeare. Put the silver on the stage and it goes to banks in Mesilla or El Paso."

"I 'spect Whitehill is more worried about Carstairs turning his crew loose on the town."

"That would be a consideration, too, Slocum." Tucker drained the coffee. "If I was you, well, you can finish that thought all by your lonesome. Have never taken you for a dull boy."

Slocum could figure out what the deputy meant with no trouble at all. Dan Tucker might wear a deputy's badge, but he was more outlaw than lawman at heart. He was saying Slocum should handle the problem with Carstairs rather than waiting for Whitehill to get around to it.

"How pissed will the sheriff be if he finds I've left town? He is still sitting on a body I was carting around in a block of ice."

"About that, Slocum. You know Marianne Lomax real well, from the way you have been goin' on about her."

"We both come from the same town in Georgia."

"I—never mind. Got to go." Tucker stood and started from the café so fast Slocum thought somebody had lit his ass on fire. He had never seen Tucker so edgy.

The deputy stopped at the doorway but didn't turn as he said, "You might tell Marianne to go on by the jailhouse to talk to Whitehill. Not sure you want to be with her when she goes."

"Wait, Dan." But Slocum spoke to thin air. Tucker almost ran off, leaving Slocum to scratch his head, wondering what it all meant.

He finished his breakfast and was on his way out when he bumped into Marianne, looking radiant in the morning sun.

"I hoped to find you here, John. This is about the only restaurant in Silver City that doesn't poison its customers and then bury the bodies out back."

"Good food. The deputy paid for my breakfast."

"You're short on funds," she said, nodding. He watched her pensive mood turn into something harder, more determined. "Come out to the house with me."

"The one Carstairs burned?"

"I don't know if you can find anything that'll prove he was the culprit, but you know more about what to look for than I do, I'm sure."

"Because I killed a judge?"

Marianne turned somber.

"Because you have experience far beyond that, unless I miss my guess. What I've had to do to stay alive and keep Randolph fed went down a different road."

"What do you mean by that?"

She looked up at him, her bright blue eyes boring into his soul. Her auburn hair gleamed in the sun, and shadows cast on her cheekbones gave her a gaunt, haunted look.

"You know what I mean."

And he did. Selling her body to keep food on the table didn't set well with him, but he had done things more criminal. Killing men was the least of it, though he had never hired out to murder anyone. That didn't hold down the number of corpses he'd put into early graves, but there were worse things than what Marianne had done.

"This man you're going to marry, Jack. Doesn't he—"

"Don't talk about him, John. Texas Jack is a fine man, but he isn't above a swindle or two if it suits him. He loves me, and I love him."

For a moment Slocum missed what she had said. Then it hit him like a ton of bricks falling on his head.

"Texas Jack Bedrich?"

"Why, yes, you've heard of him?"

Slocum stared at her, not sure what to say. Marianne started to say something more, then her eyes went wide and she covered her mouth with her hand. Shaking her head, she backed from him. The wildness in her expression came rushing out as she cried, "No, John, don't say it. Don't tell me something's happened to him!"

"He's dead," Slocum said. More than once as an officer in the army and after, he had delivered such bad news to wives and lovers, mothers and children. As much as he wanted, there were not words to soften the blow. Easing into the news never worked. Quick, brutal, get it over with. That was for the best.

"You? You killed him?"

"No, but I brought his body in to the sheriff."

"What happened?" She had gone pale, and her hands shook, but the steely determination he had seen in Marianne before held her together now.

"I don't know how he died. A bullet. But who killed him?" Slocum shook his head. "I was attacked by road agents and fought off an Apache war party. A man named Frank was—"

"Frank? He killed Jack?"

"Don't know that, but it's possible," he said. No matter how much he, Whitehill, and Tucker hashed out everything that had happened on the trail, Bedrich's killer could never be determined that way alone. They needed more than palaver. They needed evidence.

"He and Jack had a falling-out months ago."

"Over you?"

"I don't think so. Frank fancied himself a ladies' man, but he hardly gave me a second look when he was with Jack. I heard him muttering about me being a whore and how he'd never sully his organ by—"

"The sheriff thinks they broke off their partnership over a claim."

"He and Jack had a decent strike. It produces enough for one man to get along, but not two. Jack talked about selling out his share, but then he stopped all mention of it because something else occupied his every thought."

"Other than you?" Slocum asked.

This brought a tiny smile to her lips that faded quickly.

"He was a driven man, completely consumed by whatever interested him at any given time. Oh, he loved me, but he also loved other things." Marianne smiled ruefully. "That's why I thought I'd found a real man. Finding silver was as important to him as I was."

Slocum heard more in her words that wasn't stated. He hesitated to ask how Texas Jack and Randolph got along. Marianne doted on her son, but too often stepchildren were ignored when a woman remarried.

"Frank is somewhere in the area," Slocum said. "He didn't wait for the sheriff to question him, but I can't figure how he had a chance to kill Bedrich. Carstairs, though, is another matter."

"Carstairs," she said. "I had almost forgotten about him." She took a step toward the livery stable, then shifted and started in the other direction before turning and stumbling into Slocum. "I'm sorry. I'm so confused, so shocked." She fixed him with her steady gaze. Tears had welled in her eyes. "The truth, John. Did you kill Jack?"

"No." He didn't hesitate, he didn't waver. "But I'll find out who did."

"For me?"

"For justice," he said. He saw her accept his promise and that he meant he'd find who killed her fiancé or die trying.

10

"He was going to be gone for a week," Marianne said listlessly. "Only a week. It had been more than two, but Jack never was good at knowing what day it was if the passion caught him."

Slocum had nothing to say. Marianne rode behind him on the horse, arms circling around his waist, as they both rode bareback out to where the house had been burned to the ground.

"I don't know what's going on anymore, John. I don't. How can I tell Randolph about Jack's death?"

"Boys take news better than you think. Randolph will, too. How'd he get on with Jack?"

"Not that well. There was an immediate fire between them, but Randolph is like that with everyone. Always locking horns. Just his age." She paused, then added, "His age and Billy. Billy's a bad influence, but there aren't many boys in town around Randolph's age."

"He'll be all right," Slocum said. "He probably knew before you did that Jack was dead."

"Or Billy did. I swear, that boy must live with his ear to

82

the ground. He knows everyone and everything that happens in town. He ought to work for the newspaper as a reporter."

Slocum's nose wrinkled as he approached the house. The stench of burned wood and belongings would take weeks to disappear. A few good rains might erase the smell, but it had been dry so far this year. He drew rein and looked down at the charred frame, the sofa burned down to its springs, the items that had been Marianne's world and history.

"That the front door? Or where it used to be?" He pointed to the far side of the ruins.

"I reckon Carstairs came from the trees and heaved the bottle of kerosene in with the burning rag stuffed into it, then hightailed it back to the woods."

Marianne slid off the back of the horse and walked around. Slocum remained mounted as she began poking through the debris. He urged his horse toward the stand of trees, studying the ground for tracks. It had been too long for him to get any proof anyone had come this way, much less Carstairs. Just thinking on the man brought back the vivid image of Carstairs holding Marianne pinned to the bed, about to rape her.

He sucked in his breath and stared into the undergrowth, not really seeing anything. He heard Carstairs's words again. He had wanted Marianne to give him something—but had he meant sex? Holding her in such a compromising position had led Slocum to believe Carstairs wanted to rape her, but there might be other explanations.

" 'Give it to me,' " Slocum repeated. Why had Carstairs burned her out and run away when he could have raped her as she fled the house?

"John, can you give me a hand with this? It's my cedar chest."

He rode back slowly, then dismounted and went to where Marianne struggled to pull a blackened box from under a mound of cinders. Fumbling around for a moment, he found the handle and tugged. It came off in his hand, forcing him to burrow down farther and get under the chest. A quick heave brought it out.

"I hope nothing inside is too burned." Marianne pried open the lid and smiled almost shyly. "It's got most of the things I brought from Calhoun," she said. She dug through the seared clothing as Slocum began searching the house.

"Tell me what happened the night Carstairs burned you out," he said, standing by the front door. The fire had destroyed the frame entirely, but the door panels were intact. He used one of the fallen panels as a scoop to find the melted bit of glass from the bottle that had ignited the fire.

"Well, it's a bit embarrassing," she said, never looking up as she pulled out baby clothing that must have been Randolph's. Marianne carefully laid it aside and continued her hunt. "I was with, well, I was with Clem, who was going to pay me for my favors. The bank had warned me I couldn't miss another payment or the house would be taken away."

"Clem a miner?"

"A moderately successful one, and a nice man."

"You ever with Carstairs?"

"No! Jack warned me about Carstairs, not that he had to. I saw how Carstairs acted around women and heard how he treated the soiled doves in town."

Slocum felt a pang that Marianne had been selling herself—that she'd had to.

"Was this the first time he'd barged in? Carstairs?"

"He always circled around like a vulture, but he'd never said more than a dozen words to me. I think he was afraid of what Jack would do if he did."

"Carstairs is foreman of a big mine. He and Texas Jack have any business dealings?"

"None that I know of. Jack's only partner was Jim Frank. You know about their falling-out."

"Jack never gave you any money, to keep the bank from foreclosing on your house?"

"There wasn't any need. I kept the payments current until

Jack went out on business, then he didn't have any more spare cash than I did."

Slocum stopped and stared at her.

"You mean the bank told you to pay up or get out after missing only one payment?"

"Two," she said.

Even in a boomtown, the bank wouldn't try to foreclose that fast.

"Did Texas Jack piss off the bank president?"

"He pissed off damned near everyone," Marianne said, a small smile curling her lips now. "Including me, but I loved him for it. Damn him for leaving me." She forced back tears and turned from Slocum.

He kept kicking through the debris, not sure what he hunted. After a half hour, he knew he wasn't going to find it, whatever it was.

"You have anything you want to sling in a blanket so you can take it back to town?"

"Some things from the cedar chest. My dowry," she said softly. "There wasn't much, but it was enough for Jack. We were—"

Slocum dug his toes into the burned debris and dived forward, arms outstretched. He grabbed Marianne in a steely grip and carried her backward until her heel caught a burned, curled-up floorboard, sending them both crashing to the ground amid a flurry of soot and black cinders.

"What's got into you, John?"

He stayed atop her long enough for the second bullet to sail past. From the corner of his eye he'd seen movement, then the bright spark of sunlight off the front sight of a rifle. His quick tackle had saved them from getting ventilated.

"Stay down," he said, scrambling about in the ashes and coming to a kneeling position behind the cedar chest with his six-shooter drawn.

Bracing his hand against the wooden chest, he squeezed off a round. He was rewarded with a string of curses from the underbrush where he'd spotted the rifle barrel. Another quick shot didn't bring any new cursing. From all his time in the army as a sniper, he had learned to trust his instincts. The first shot might have winged their attacker. The second missed.

"They tried to kill you!" Marianne's outrage caused her to stand. Slocum tackled her again.

This time she didn't flop onto her back but sat hard. Her blue eyes flashed angrily, then widened in horror.

"The gunman is still out there. He could have shot me!"

Slocum wanted to find the sniper to learn who had been the target. The slug had passed between them, so either could have been the intended target. Or the rifleman's intent might have been to run them off. Something in the burned remnants might have been the shooter's goal, rather than killing them. Somehow, Slocum had the itchy feeling between his shoulders that he had been the target, not Marianne. That didn't make her any safer if he left her alone, but he had no choice.

"You have a hidey-hole?" He kept his keen eyes fixed on the woods for any sign of movement.

"I, uh, yeah, I guess so."

"Crawl in there and wait for me."

"John, no, you can't!"

She reached for him, but he had already dashed halfway to his horse. Slocum threw his arms around the pony's neck, kicked hard, and mounted as the horse ran a few tentative strides. Staying low, his head down near the horse's neck, he galloped for the woods and then burst through the curtain of brush into a cool dimness. He gave the pony its head as he hunted for his attacker.

He saw nothing, but ahead along the game trail the horse instinctively found, he heard pounding hooves. Slocum kept low to prevent the rapidly passing tree limbs from knocking him off or cutting his face. Fear of another ambush evaporated. He was the hunter now, and his quarry ran for his life.

The Indian pony was stronger and slowly closed the distance. The man he chased kept shooting back over his shoulder with the rifle, wasting ammo. Not a single round came close to Slocum, and the noise only spurred on the racing pony. When they were within a half-dozen yards, Slocum lifted his six-gun and fired.

The man's hat went flying. He grabbed for it. As he turned, Slocum got a good look at his face. Lester Carstairs. He fired again, but Carstairs was already off balance and fell from horseback to land with a loud thud.

Slocum lacked stirrups to give more control. All he could do was draw back on the reins and use his knees to convince the running horse to slow. By the time the pony swung about, Carstairs had vanished into the forest on foot.

Without hesitation, Slocum slid from the pony and hit the ground running. Carstairs's rifle lay on the ground where he had dropped it. Slocum didn't bother to check. The magazine was likely empty. That meant all the firepower Carstairs had rode in his six-gun. Slocum slowed when he reached a tangle of brush, then dropped to his knees to get a better look ahead.

Carstairs either underestimated Slocum or had panicked and thought of nothing but a clumsy ambush. Hiding behind a tree, his hand braced against the bole, he waited for Slocum to blunder forward. Slocum slipped his pistol back into its holster and cut off to his left, making a wide circle to come up on Carstairs from the man's rear.

Carstairs nervously shifted his weight from foot to foot. Even if Slocum had popped into view where the miner thought, his aim would have been off. Slocum stepped forward on cat's feet, not making a sound. His shadow betrayed him as it swept across the tree Carstairs used for refuge. The man whipped around, but Slocum leapt like a mountain lion. His left hand closed around Carstairs's wrist and his right drove straight for the man's neck. Grease and dirt made the throat slippery, but Slocum's strong fingers bore in to choke his enemy.

Carstairs made gasping sounds. He squeezed off a round and then dropped his weapon as air was denied his lungs. Slocum bent forward and put his weight behind the choke. Carstairs dropped to his knees. Both hands tried to pry loose the fingers killing him, but his strength had already left him.

Slocum followed the man to the ground, then through force of will stopped choking before he took a life. For what Carstairs had done to Marianne, he deserved to die. She was sure he had burned down her house after barging in on her and a client. Slocum knew this was the man who had tried to rape her the night before. The identifying scar on his cheek stood out, livid and ragged.

He released his strangling fingers and rocked back, gasping from exertion. As Carstairs slowly recovered, rubbing his tortured neck, he found himself staring down the bore of Slocum's Colt Navy.

"Any reason I shouldn't kill you and leave your worthless carcass for the coyotes?"

"I don't know you from Adam. Why'd you chase me? You tryin' to rob me? Take it. Take ever'thing. I—" Carstairs blanched when Slocum cocked his pistol.

"You burned out a friend of mine, then you tried to rape her last night. Or did you? Was it rape or was it something else?"

Carstairs's mouth opened and closed like a fish flopping on a riverbank. Then he recovered some of his sand when Slocum didn't pull the trigger.

"She's got something I want. The whore won't give it to me."

Slocum hit him. The Colt's barrel left a dent on the side of Carstairs's head but didn't knock him out.

"Keep a civil tongue in your head. If you don't, I might cut it out."

"You ain't gettin' any part of it. You and the whore"— Carstairs cringed when Slocum reared back to pistol-whip him again—"you don't deserve it."

"What're you talking about?" Slocum saw the suddenly sly expression and knew he wouldn't learn any more from this man unless he had plenty of time and a sharp knife. There wasn't much the Apaches knew about torturing a man that Slocum didn't know, also. Some of it had come first-hand.

"You don't know what I'm talkin' 'bout, do you?" Carstairs spat blood from a cut lip. "Go to hell."

"You'll be there to greet me," Slocum said, drawing a bead between the man's eyes. Carstairs blanched again but didn't say a word. Considering that questions still had to be answered, and Sheriff Whitehill had only let Slocum out for the killing of Texas Jack Bedrich because of his deputy's vouchsafe, it wouldn't do to have another killing over his head.

Somehow, someway it would get back to Silver City that he had plugged this worthless snake. More than this, Slocum found it irresistible that Carstairs was willing to die rather than spill his guts about what he wanted from Marianne. That was the only explanation Slocum could come up with. Marianne had something, some item or tidbit of information, Carstairs was willing to rape and kill for.

"On your feet," Slocum said, his gun hand never twitching. Carstairs understood he was a goner if he tried anything now.

They walked to where Slocum's pony nibbled at grass. It took the better part of an hour to track down Carstairs's horse and ride back to the burned-out house. As they approached, Slocum looked for Marianne. He had told her to go to ground, and she had. She was nowhere to be found.

He called for her, then started when debris not ten feet from where he sat astride his horse slipped away from a door. She poked her auburn head out, smiled when she saw Slocum, and then hissed like a cat when she saw his prisoner.

"Root cellar?" Slocum asked.

"Give me your gun, and I'll kill him. I swear it!"

"Settle down," Slocum cautioned. "We're going to turn him over to the sheriff. Whitehill might get some answers from him."

"I don't want answers, I want to get even."

"I ought to let her claw your eyes out after what you did last night," Slocum said.

"I didn't do a damn thing to her. Nuthin' she don't collect money for from any poxy miner out in the silver fields anyway."

"Off your horse," Slocum said. "Get down, or I'll plug you where you sit."

Grumbling, Carstairs dismounted.

"Climb aboard, Marianne," Slocum said. "It's a ways back to town, and one of us is going to be on foot."

"That's my horse. You can't steal it!"

"Might be we can lasso him around the neck and drag him some," Marianne said.

When Slocum looked favorably on that, Carstairs started hoofing it toward distant Silver City. It took until sundown for them to return and get their prisoner to the jailhouse.

"Go on in. You're going to spend a considerable amount of time here," Slocum said, his six-shooter waving around to point out the entire jailhouse.

Carstairs cursed under his breath, lifted the latch, and went in, Slocum and Marianne close behind. Sheriff Whitehill looked up from a newspaper spread on the desk in front of him. His eyes darted from Carstairs to Slocum and then back before he let out a gusty sigh, made a big production of folding the paper and then tipping back in his chair. He eyed them, covered in dirt and soot, and shook his head sadly.

"Spit it out. What's goin' on?"

"They tried to gun me down, Whitehill. They—"

Slocum jammed his six-shooter into Carstairs's spine to shut him up.

"He tried to bushwhack us out at Miss Lomax's house," Slocum said.

"Then he ran off, John chased him down, and we brought him back. And last night he—"

Slocum reached over and caught Marianne's arm to quiet her. Even a whore could be raped, but adding this charge to trying to kill them both only muddied the waters. Slocum doubted Whitehill would take kindly to locking up Carstairs on a rape charge, and the jury would be even less inclined to convict. The trial would be a circus, not a way to achieve justice.

Whitehill had them go over the story several times, then let Carstairs speak his piece.

"I was out there, all right, Sheriff, but I never tried to shoot them. Slocum came chargin' after me while I was out in the woods. I heard a shot, sure, but it wasn't me who fired on them. And he charged like a wild Injun. I ran."

"And he caught you," finished Whitehill. He gusted another sigh. "You brung his rifle in, Slocum?"

"Wouldn't prove a thing, Whitehill. I fired it at him tryin' to escape his evil clutches," Carstairs said. "After he started chasin' me."

"Slocum, did you actually see Les here shoot at you?"

"No, but he was the only one in the woods."

"The only one you found, you mean!" cried Carstairs. "There was someone else who tried to gun them down."

"Marianne, you see Carstairs doin' any shootin' at you?"

"No, Sheriff, but he—"

"So neither of you can swear on a Bible that Carstairs shot at you. But you ran him down in the woods when there might have been somebody else out there you didn't see. That sum it all up?"

Slocum said nothing. He gripped Marianne's arm harder when she tried to add to the charges by describing what had happened the night before in her hotel room. The time for such incrimination was past, Slocum saw, as the sheriff

listened to her. Whitehill would think they had tried to kill
Carstairs as retribution, or at least frame him for attempted
murder. The lawman would never throw any Silver City
citizen into the lockup simply for soliciting a soiled dove,
and Marianne had the reputation.

On the other hand, the sheriff seemed to have hidden
feelings for her, and Slocum sensed that Whitehill was itching to show off and even protect her in some way.

"You see anybody else out there in them woods, Les?"
The sheriff's eyes bored into Carstairs.

"Well, no, but I—"

"And what were you doing over by Miz Marianne's
place?"

Carstairs glared at him. "Mindin' my own business."

The sheriff chewed his bottom lip as if thinking things
over. "Well, it's been right quiet in town so far, and I don't
want anything complicatin' my evening. Les, I'm gonna
hold you 'til I can get to the bottom of this."

"You can't do that!"

"You've been accused of some serious things. I can hold
you till I look at all the evidence."

"My rifle's still out in the woods. I gotta go get it."

"I'll send Dan out to find it. For now, you stay put."

When the sheriff turned to get his key ring, Carstairs
sneered and whispered to Marianne, "This ain't the end of
it. I'm gonna find out where it is."

"You take Marianne on back to the hotel, Slocum," the
sheriff said. "I'd run you out of town, but there's still the
question of how Texas Jack died."

Slocum took Marianne by the elbow and steered her out
of the jail. She sagged against him, exhausted after the day's
events.

11

"He didn't believe me," Marianne Lomax said, her lip quivering from emotion. She wrapped her arms around herself as if she could keep out the night cold that way, but Slocum knew it wasn't the mountain air that caused her to shake.

It was barely suppressed anger.

"The sheriff's afraid," Slocum said. "He doesn't want to have Carstairs's entire crew hurrahing the town."

"They'd lie to get their boss out of jail," Marianne said. "I should have lied. Then it would have been my word against theirs!"

Slocum walked beside her as they made their way to the hotel. It was late, and the day had been a long one. At least the sheriff had agreed to consider the possibility that Carstairs had taken a shot at them. Slocum didn't doubt that the mine foreman had done that very thing. But who had he been aiming at?

As much as he hated to admit it, he was the likelier target. Carstairs wanted something from Marianne, and anyone who got in the way was a problem to be solved, a man to be ambushed. The more he thought about what he had seen the night before, the less he thought Carstairs had tried to rape Marianne. He had been demanding that she tell him where something was. But what?

"That's no good," she said, breaking his train of thought.

"What do you mean?"

"Even if I lied, no one would believe me. They think I'm a harlot, a Cyprian who has a grudge against Carstairs." Marianne laughed harshly. "The Silver City harlot. That's me. I sell my body and that's all a jury would remember. Evidence against Carstairs—my testimony!—wouldn't be credible."

"You're too hard on yourself," Slocum said. They stood on the front steps of the hotel. Slocum saw the curtains in the sitting room flutter. Someone was watching them.

It might be her son or his friend. More likely the hotel owner was spying on them.

"John, you can't imagine how hard I am on myself for all I've done, for all I *haven't* done. Raising a boy like Randolph is a full-time chore, and I just can't spend the time with him I should."

"It's not easy earning a living, no matter how you do it."

"Why don't you come up, John?" Marianne looked up at him, her eyes bright with tears. Her lip still quivered. "I don't think I can sleep. I'm too wound up, and I want to talk. I need to."

Slocum glanced at the curtains, but they hung still now.

"What about Mrs. Gruhlkey? She wouldn't take kindly to me going to your room, especially after shooting out the window last night."

"You're right. She warned me about that and how she'd throw Randolph and me into the street if I tried to sneak any man into my room," Marianne said. She reached out and ran her fingers up and down the lapels of his coat. A light tap sent up a tiny cloud of soot and left her fingers greasy black. She kept running her fingers over his chest, then said, "I owe you a bath."

"It's late," he said.

"Old man Higgins never locks up his barber shop. If you can heat the water, I'll . . . wash your back."

He hesitated, but then his resolve faded as memories of Georgia and the time he and Marianne had spent there rushed back. He tried to brush off his coat and only produced a new dust storm. He smiled ruefully before saying, "Reckon you have a point about me needing a bath."

"Just like we did before," she said, nudging still other memories.

The first time he and Marianne had gone off together in the piney woods had seemed innocent enough, but she had fallen off a log crossing a stream and drenched herself. She had sputtered and then shaken all over like a wet dog. He had laughed so hard he had fallen into the stream, too.

From there, assuring each other they were only going to dry their clothes, the inevitable attraction of youth had brought them together in the cottony warm summer sun on a patch of grass.

"The grass probably never recovered," Marianne said.

Slocum's eyes widened in surprise. She might have read his mind.

"It's not that hard, John," she said. "We got to know each other pretty well, and even got to the point of finishing each other's sentences."

"We did," he said, "but you're wrong on one thing."

"What's that?" She looked up at him, blue eyes shining in the dark.

"It *is* that hard."

"Umm, so it is," she said, her hand moving down his chest, past his belt buckle to his crotch. Her fingers squeezed lightly and traced the outline of his growing erection. He squirmed as she gripped more firmly. "We do need to get you out of those filthy duds."

Pressed together hip to hip, shoulder to shoulder, and her hand never leaving his crotch, they walked slowly toward the barber shop in the middle of a long row of buildings fetched up against one another like sheep in a flock. Marianne proved she knew the people of Silver City well. The front door opened on well-oiled hinges. Slocum guided her in ahead of him, his hand pressing into the roundness at the rear of her dress.

He kicked the door shut with his heel so he didn't have to turn. He spun her about. She came into his arms easily. Slocum experienced an instant of giddiness. It was as if the past thirteen years had never happened, and they were youngsters exploring the mysteries of sex for the first time.

Their kiss started out passionately and grew in intensity until both were gasping. He pulled her close, hard enough to crush her breasts against his chest. As his hands began roving up and down her back, he found laces and hooks that came undone. When she pushed away from him, her upper garments fell to her waist, leaving her clothed only in a thin shift that hid nothing from his lusting gaze.

Her firm breasts pressed insistently against that gossamer fabric so her nipples were outlined clearly. As he watched, they grew along with her arousal.

"I want you, John. I want you now!"

She came against him again, kissing his lips and stubbled chin and dirty cheeks. This gave him the chance to return the lavish kiss on her slender neck and nibble at her earlobes, moving from one to the other, leaving a trail of kisses across her forehead, on her closed eyes, against her cheeks and lips, as he went.

Marianne sagged a little.

"You still have the power over me," she said, "to turn me into a damp dishrag."

He supported her, one arm around her waist. With a scooping move, he swept her up into his arms. This way they kissed more as he went to the back room, where a galvanized bathtub stood to one side and a stove with a water pump beside it in a shallow pit filled with rocks on the other.

"Get the water. I'll start the fire," she said.

"No fair. You've already started my fire."

"And you've started a forest fire in me," she said. They kissed a little longer, then Slocum lowered her to the planked floor.

He watched as she dropped to her knees in front of the stove and bent over, her rear end presenting such a delectable sight as she added wood to the iron belly. Slocum heaved a sigh, turned his attention to the pump, and began working the handle furiously. From deep in the guts of the earth came a choking sound followed by a deep gurgle and a rush of water. A nearby pail caught the flood.

He swung the bucket around and saw Marianne stripping off her shift. The flames cast pale light against her breasts, creating deep shadows between the snowy globes and turning the penny-sized aureolas and nipples a ruddy red. His erection strained a bit more at the sight.

"In the pan on top," she said, grinning when she saw how he stared at her. "You like what you see?"

"Every bit of it," he said. His lips met her right tit and sucked in the tip.

She moaned softly and thrust her chest forward so he took more of the pliant flesh into his mouth. He nibbled, gently at first and then greedily gobbled. His tongue swirled about the rubbery, hard bud and pressed it deep into the marshmallowy underpinnings. This caused Marianne to lose her balance and sit back heavily so that her skirts rode up, giving him a new view that made him even harder.

"Darned skirts," she said. She flopped back on the floor, lifted her behind, and wiggled sinuously to get free of the skirt. Another couple sensuous movements left her entirely naked save for her shoes.

"You're overdressed," he said, kneeling in front of her.

His hand moved along her bare calf and worked upward to the auburn thatch nestled at the juncture of her thighs.

"I remember you as a man of action. You never let anything stand in your way before."

Slocum began unfastening the shoes. As he did so, he bent forward and kissed every inch of skin as it appeared from the high-top shoes. Her ankles received his attention and then the arch of her foot. She began moaning loudly as he worked to the toes. He sucked on them until they curled under, and she began bucking about on the floor.

"That's driving me plumb crazy," she gasped out. "Do it some more."

He did.

By the time he had pulled off her shoes so she lay entirely naked before him, the water had come to a boil. He dumped this into the tub, added another bucket of cold water, then started a second bucket to boiling. As he finished pouring the water into the bowl on the stove, he felt her bare body moving against his back. Her hands reached around and unfastened his gun belt before working on the buttons at his fly. He almost came as he had that very first time in the Georgia woods when her long, slender fingers circled his freed manhood and began stroking up and down.

"Get me out of my jeans," he said, kicking off his boots.

As Marianne worked to peel off his filthy pants, he dropped his coat, vest, and shirt to the floor. By the time she had skinned him of his pants, the water boiled. Rather awkwardly, he took the water while she kept her arms around his waist, hands slipping up and down on his fleshy shaft. He dumped the water in, then added more cold.

"This will do us," Marianne said insistently.

"With you holding on to me like that, you can get me to follow you anywhere." He yelped as she jerked hard on him, turning him around so he fell backward into the water.

She swarmed after him, her knees slipping to either side of his thighs so she poised directly over his throbbing spire, wantonly spread for him. Both gasped when she lowered herself down, letting him slip fully within the tight, wet cavity.

"Time for a good scrubbing," she whispered in his ear. "Move . . . vigorously."

Slocum was pinned under her weight, but surrounded by her clinging tight sheath of female flesh, he found the strength to lift up and ram even farther into her. Her tightness about him massaged and squeezed and aroused. She lifted enough so he slipped out, only to thrust back in. The hot water sloshed all around, tickling and teasing their most sensitive flesh, but Slocum concentrated on the heat mounting in his loins. No water could heat him like her willing, wet core.

Clinging to one another, thrusting the best he could, twisting their hips, and him driving ever deeper into her pushed them both closer to the brink of ultimate desire.

Slocum reached around, cupped her bare wet ass cheeks, and began lifting and dropping her in a smoother rhythm that set them both to crying out. Faster, deeper, harder they strove together until Slocum no longer held back. He felt as if the ache in his cock would drive him crazy if he didn't get off. With a loud cry, he arched his back, clamped down firmly on her slippery ass, and drove upward like a Fourth of July rocket—with the same results.

He exploded, then she did.

More water sloshed out onto the wood planks and drained quickly between the slats. But Slocum was more aware of Marianne pressing hotly against him. He held her. Too many memories came rushing back. That first day in the woods, yes, but the other times. He had been recuperating from his war wounds, and she had nursed him to full health. Her parents would have shot him for what he and Marianne did in their bed, but Slocum didn't care. And Marianne certainly didn't. She had sought him out as eagerly as he had found her for their frequent trysts.

"I wish we could stay this way forever, John."

"We can. We should."

"No, we can't." Marianne put her hands on his shoulders and pushed back until her elbows locked. She stared down at him. "The water's too cold, what little there is left of it."

"You shouldn't have sloshed it all out," he said.

"Me? You were the one who—Oh, you!" She kissed him, then lithely stood, her feet still on either side of his legs.

He looked up at about the most delightful view he'd ever seen. If he rode the West for another thirteen years, he doubted anything would compare with this instant. Then she stepped out and began working to refill the bathtub. Reluctantly, he joined in the work, heated more water, and then they spent the next hour washing each other. It took longer than necessary but neither complained.

After they had dried themselves off on the single towel in the bathroom, Slocum said, "Suppose I ought to leave some money. What's this Higgins charge?"

"Two bits for fresh water, a nickel for used," she said.

He fished around in his vest pocket and found a dime.

"This'll have to do. We did most of the work."

"Is that what you call it?" she teased.

He swatted her rump.

"Don't get sassy."

"You liked it before."

"Yeah, I did," Slocum said. His thoughts jumbled up, unable to separate the idyllic days in Georgia with this moment. Silver City was anything but peaceable, and folks here weren't taking too kindly to Marianne.

For all that, her luck was awful. Getting burned out was the start of a bad stretch. Finding that Texas Jack Bedrich had been murdered had been about as bad as it got. This tore Slocum up inside. He hadn't known Bedrich, but the man's death opened a door into the past Slocum had thought forever closed.

"Walk me back to the hotel. I wish you could come up but—"

"Mrs. Gruhlkey would object," he said.

They looked at each other, then laughed.

"We're back to finishing each other's sentences," she said.

The short walk to the hotel could have been a thousand miles and Slocum wouldn't have objected. As it was, Marianne parted company and vanished into the darkened lobby all too soon. Slocum settled his gun belt, tugged on his hat, and headed back toward the jailhouse, feeling a world better for his bath—and confused about what to do. He had never felt the way he did toward Marianne before or after.

Slocum reached the calaboose just as the door opened and Carstairs stepped out. The man stretched mightily, then went toward a horse tethered to an iron ring set into the jail's adobe wall.

Faster than thought, Slocum had his six-shooter out, cocked, and was about to fire when Dangerous Dan Tucker called out for him to stop.

"Prisoner's getting away," Slocum said. Tucker came up from behind and grabbed his wrist, pulling the pistol out of line.

Carstairs stopped, took in the tableau, then laughed. He swung into the saddle, cockily tipped his hat, and rode away, whistling off-key.

"You can't let him go!" Slocum struggled, then subsided when Sheriff Whitehill exited the jail. Two other men followed him outside.

The sheriff pointedly refused to shake hands, which produced chuckles from the men. They sneered at Slocum, then disappeared around the jailhouse. In less than a minute both rode past, never giving him or the lawmen a second glance.

"You let Carstairs go!" Slocum raged.

"Had to," Whitehill said. "Those two men gave him an alibi. You're damn lucky I don't clap you in the clink. They said you kidnapped their boss from their mine out in Chloride Flats."

"What I told you was the truth," Slocum said.

"Don't doubt it, but it's all three of them varmints' word against yours and Marianne's. Nobody here but Dan knows you and, well, ain't no one in Silver City likely to give much credence to anything Marianne says."

"Because they think she's a cheap whore?"

"They know she ain't cheap," Whitehill said. The sheriff stepped back when he saw the dark cloud on Slocum's face. "You go get yourself some sleep. Otherwise, I might just have to put you in a cell."

The cell Carstairs has just vacated, Slocum thought bitterly. He jerked from the deputy and left them in the street. Slocum wondered how Marianne would react when she found the lawmen had released Carstairs.

He knew how he felt. She'd take it even worse. And that wasn't a good thing for anyone.

12

Marianne Lomax felt as if Slocum had punched her in the stomach. She wobbled a mite, reached out, and supported herself against a chair in the hotel lobby. She jerked away when he reached out to steady her.

"You cannot be joshing me, John Slocum. I'll rip out your heart if you are." She saw the weathered lines on his forehead and the forlorn look in his emerald eyes. He stood like a little boy in front of the schoolmarm, fingering the brim of his hat held nervously.

"I tried to stop the sheriff, but there wasn't a thing I could do. Carstairs rode out like a king last night, right after we—"

"—we were amusing ourselves in the barbershop," she said, scowling hard. Her lips pressed down into a thin line. Sucking in a deep breath, she held it for a moment, then released it with an explosive gust. "I will *not* permit this."

"Whitehill said two of Carstairs's men alibied him."

"Lied for him is more like it," she said, her voice rising. She tried to control her rampaging emotions, then abandoned the attempt entirely. "I'll cut his throat! I swear I will see him in the grave before he ever rides free after all he's done to me!"

"Hush up," Slocum said, looking around.

"I don't care who knows. He burned me out. He tried to rape me. Carstairs is not going to waltz away without paying for his crimes!"

It surprised her that Slocum cared if anyone overheard, then she saw the focus of his concern. Randolph and Billy sat on the steep stairs and listened to every word coming out of her mouth. For a moment she wished she could take it all back. Setting a poor example for her son distressed her, but Les Carstairs not paying for what he did to her made her furious.

"Randolph, come over here," she said. Her son approached, but she kept looking at Slocum, wondering if he would help her bring Carstairs to justice. Slocum seemed different from when she knew him in Georgia. He was harder, more pragmatic—and he had been hard-bitten and cynical right after he returned from the war. Principles still ruled his hand—his gun hand—but she had less idea what those ideals were now than when she had known him before.

Before . . .

"Yeah, Ma?" Randolph stood in front of her, looking so young and vulnerable and trying to be a man. He almost succeeded in that, but he would always be her little boy, no matter what.

"You have that knife?"

"The one Billy gave me? Yeah," he said with some reluctance.

"Give it to me."

"What? Why? No!"

"Do it," she said, her anger causing her cheeks to burn. "I don't want you getting any crazy ideas, not after what I just said."

"If *he* won't do anything about Carstairs, I will!" Randolph thrust out his chin and tried to look tough. He glanced at Slocum, then at her. She felt as if he had stabbed her with his still sheathed bull cook's knife. In one sentence he had rolled up everything that frightened her the most.

Slocum had killed men. She knew that all too well. But he hadn't offered to be her defender, casting doubt on whatever it was between them. Worse, she had feared Randolph would take up the challenge and go after Carstairs. The mine foreman's reputation resonated in Silver City and beyond as one of utter disregard of human life. Sending men to their death in a poorly built mineshaft bothered him as much as stepping on a bug. He had killed more than one man in a bar fight, claiming self-defense each time. With all the men in town cowed by him, no one dared step forward and testify to the truth.

Texas Jack had never feared Carstairs. The times they had clashed always saw Carstairs backing down. But the man she had loved so and intended to marry was dead. She couldn't even afford a proper burial for him.

"Give me the knife. And don't you go getting another one. You, either, William McCarty," she said loud enough for the older boy to hear, as if he wasn't following every word with the intensity of a cat at a mouse hole.

"Ma, I won't do nothing that ain't right."

"Your grammar needs improvement," she said. "And I need to see that knife passed over to me." Marianne held out her hand and tried not to shake. She felt as if she had walked onto a stage where everyone expected her to know the lines.

Randolph silently handed over the knife. She took it and slid it into the pocket amid the folds of her skirt.

"You stay out of trouble," she told her son. She tried to kiss him on the top of his head, but he pulled away and sullenly left. He and Billy spoke in low voices for a moment, then hastened out the front door.

"He wouldn't take on Carstairs by his lonesome," Slocum said.

"I don't need your opinion, John Slocum. Nor do I need your advice or your help."

"I didn't let him go. He'll run afoul of the law eventually. Tucker won't take anything off him, and I suspect Whitehill won't either, though he plays it closer to the vest and lets Carstairs hide behind the letter of the law."

"I need to go to work," she said. "Good day, sir."

"It's not even noon," Slocum said. "The Lonely Cuss won't see customers for hours yet."

He spoke to the door as she slammed it behind her and stepped into the hot noonday sun. A quick look around failed to reveal where her son had run off to. It didn't matter. She felt she had put the fear of God into him so he wouldn't do anything foolish. For her part, though, Marianne wasn't sure what she would do. She started walking and somehow ended up at the city lockup just as Sheriff Whitehill came out.

He stopped and looked at her. She had never been able to read his expression. He must make one hell of a poker player.

"Morning, Marianne," he said, politely touching the brim of his hat. "I was headin' out for some grub. Want to join me? I'll buy."

"Why did you let that snake slither off like that?"

"Suppose Slocum told you."

"Lester Carstairs deserves to have his guts strung from the telegraph pole all the way across to the lightning rod on top of the hotel."

"That's a mighty ugly picture you're paintin'," Whitehill said.

"What he did was mighty ugly, Sheriff."

"Why don't you call me Harvey? We can take this argument down a mite if it's not sheriff and citizen but Harvey and Marianne."

"I want to step it up, not bury it under your honeyed words, Sheriff Whitehill."

"You think I'm some kind of silver-tongued fox? Do tell,"

he said, nodding as if this explained everything. That made her angry all over again. She had held it in check as she stormed around town, but the embers flared again into a raging forest fire.

"I think Carstairs has you cowed, that's what I think!"

Whitehill shook his head sadly.

"Then you don't know me so good, Marianne."

"That's Miss Lomax to you, Sheriff Whitehill." She turned and flounced off, her skirts brushing the dusty street and causing small dust devils wherever she stepped.

She felt him watching her and refused to turn and glare back. When she turned the corner in the street and found a spot beside the bakery, she broke down. Tears streamed down her cheeks, leaving dirty tracks that puckered when the small wind blew across her face and dried the tears with its harsh breath. She forced herself to stop sobbing. All the men in her life had abandoned her. Not a one would stand up to Carstairs.

"Why'd you have to go and get yourself killed, Jack?" She wiped away the tears and blew her nose in a hanky she'd brought from Georgia. It had belonged to her mama and shouldn't be used for such gross cleaning. It was meant to be fluttered about daintily, not become soggy with tears and leakage from her nose.

She crumpled it up and threw it away with sudden determination. If Slocum or Whitehill wouldn't stand up for her, then she had to do it for herself. Head high and anger under control, she went to the livery stables to have a palaver with the owner.

In an hour she had ridden to the Argent Mine at the edge of Chloride Flats, where she could hear Carstairs bellowing his orders to slacking miners. Marianne watched Carstairs going around the camp, shouting and doing little to actually get the men working harder. If anything, they stopped altogether as soon as his back was turned. She knew she could cajole them into pulling every ounce of silver from the ground and never once raise her voice. All it took was knowing the individual miners. Working in the Lonely Cuss as barkeep had honed her skills dealing with these men. Some could be browbeaten, but others required sweet-talking.

The work in the mine progressed through the afternoon, but Marianne grew increasingly unsure what to do. Riding up and demanding a confession from Carstairs held no appeal. If he could lie to a lawman, he would lie to her. And what if he fessed up about everything? It would be her word against his, and she had seen how well that worked out before. In the eyes of the sheriff and most of Silver City, she was only a harlot willing to say or do anything for a dollar.

More to the point, and this caused a cold chill to pass through her, what if Carstairs took up where he left off when Slocum had run him out of her hotel room? Marianne touched Randolph's knife still in her pocket. It gave her a measure of security, but she had to be close enough for Carstairs to grab her before she could use it. A wild thought crossed her mind.

Why hadn't Billy given Randolph a six-shooter? The boy had a knack for "finding" things. Even a derringer would have stood her in better stead than a knife.

Then she realized how crazy she was becoming. Young boys and firearms were a dangerous mix. It was common enough for boys to carry knives, but not guns, at least around town.

The only thing she could do was sneak close enough to Carstairs so the knife presented a warning that held him at bay. The image of her drawing the sharp blade across the man's filthy neck both frightened her and gave her a sense of satisfaction. She could kill a man. But murder one? Even Lester Carstairs? She wasn't sure, but if anyone provoked such killer instincts in her, it had to be the mine foreman.

As the sun sank below the Mogollon Rim, she urged her horse to a game trail that skirted the tent city set up to house the miners. Finding a spot to leave the horse was easy enough. The miners were intent on nothing more than wolfing down their food and passing around a whiskey bottle until it was empty. The liquid painkiller served to put most of the men to sleep. One that wasn't intent on finding his bunk and going to sleep was her target.

Carstairs made a circuit of the camp, now mostly asleep, then headed back toward the mine. Marianne sucked in her breath. It was now or never. She made a great deal of noise trailing Carstairs, her skirts catching on bushes and her shoes crunching against gravel in the path. He either didn't hear because he was deaf or was too intent on returning to the mine.

At the edge of the clearing filled with piles of black tailings, she saw him stop and look around. She froze like a deer, not sure if he had spotted her. She trembled as he stared directly at her, then he turned away and began digging in a pile of rocks cast off from the mine. He hadn't seen her in the dark.

She made her way through the mounds of debris and saw him brushing off a box that had been buried. He opened it and fingered the contents, then closed it and stood. He saw her immediately.

His hand flashed to his side, but he wasn't wearing a six-gun. His palm smacked his thigh, then he shifted his weight, dropped the box, and took a pugilist's stance. Fists high, he called out.

"You show yourself, you son of a bitch!"

She stepped forward, still hidden by shadows and the head-high piles of exhausted silver chloride ore.

He lowered his fists when he recognized her.

"Now what brings you out here, little lady? You come to get some of me?" He grabbed his crotch, then made thrusting motions.

"You are disgusting," she said. "I want you to do the right thing and confess to the sheriff that you burned me out and tried to rape me."

"Now that's a mighty fine idea, gettin' a little action from a piece of ass so downright purty," Carstairs said. He kicked the box he had dropped. For a moment, this occupied him more than she did.

Curious, she asked, "What's in the box you'd hidden?"

"Nothin' that concerns you, bitch."

A flash of clarity staggered her. He was high-grading the ore, stealing the best hunks of ore and putting the nuggets of silver into this box to remove when none of the other miners saw.

"You are despicable," she said. "You're as crooked as a dog's hind leg. Can you ever do anything honest?"

"So I'll burn in Hell. Ain't no concern of yours."

"You burned down my house!"

"I thought I'd just run you off so I could find it, but the fire damned near destroyed everything. Still, I'll bet a silver dollar you had it hidden somewhere else."

"What are you talking about?"

"You know, dammit. Where'd Texas Jack hide it? Give it to me and we can make a deal. You'd like that, and so would I." Carstairs stepped forward.

Marianne tried to step away, but her heel caught a hunk of ore and she sat heavily.

"That's more like it, you gettin' all ready for me. We can have a little fun, then we can deal and you'll tell me what you done with it."

"What the hell are you talking about? And you keep your distance!" She spun about to hands and knees, trying to stand.

He shoved her back to the ground. She sprawled face-down and then he hit her. For a brief instant the world exploded in bright star shells, then a curtain of red pain drew across her eyes as he began pummeling her with his fists. The pain proved almost more than she could endure.

Something deep inside caused her to rebel and refuse to yield. Marianne curled up in a ball, taking the blows on her arms and not her back and head. Then she kicked out as hard as she could. She wanted to drive a foot into his balls, but she missed. The sole of her shoe landed hard on his inner thigh and rolled him away, giving her the chance to scramble to her feet.

Battered, head hurting worse than anything she had ever endured, she faced him. Gasping for breath, hands on her knees, she watched as he got to his feet. His fists looked larger than quart jars.

"I changed my mind. I don't want you. After you tell me what I want to know, I'm gonna pass you around to all my men. You'd like that, wouldn't you, whore? You do a passel of men ever' night, don't you, whore?"

Marianne recognized the tactic. He tried to anger her to improve his chances to grapple. If she made a mistake, clawing for his eyes or trying to kick him again, he would take the pain and she would be his prisoner in a flash. Her hand brushed across her torn skirt and the knife tucked away in the pocket.

"What is it you want? You have to tell me!" She played for time now, in a way different from Carstairs. Her fingers fumbled at the sheathed knife, trying to get it pulled free so she could use the wickedly sharp blade to defend herself.

Hell, she'd kill him if she got the chance!

"It ain't turned up, so Texas Jack did somethin' with it. You and him was fornicatin'. He turns up dead, so I reckon you kilt him and took it off his corpse."

Carstairs edged closer, then pounced like a mountain lion. Marianne tried to yank the knife free but it caught in her skirt. Twisting slightly so her right side was to the charging man, she braced the butt of the knife handle against her thigh an instant before he grabbed for her.

He let out a high-pitched keening and jerked away. She had opened up a cut across his belly. Carstairs reached down and pressed his fingers into the wound. The expression on his face boiled with hatred.

"You can't cut me, whore. I don't care if you got the papers or not, I'm—"

She never let him finish. She attacked, the knife free of her pocket now. A savage slash at his eyes sent him stumbling back. He caught his foot on the box filled with the silver chunks and fell hard. His head snapped back as he collided with a big rock. Wary of a trick, Marianne edged forward, the knife handle turning damp in her sweaty grip. She made a few tentative stabs at him but Carstairs lay still. Blood oozed from the belly wound, which was only a shallow scratch and not the disemboweling stroke she had intended.

"Hey, Carstairs, where are you? We heard a commotion. Where'd you git off to?"

From the argument between the men coming from the camp, she faced three or four miners. Marianne stood over Carstairs, who moaned and tried to sit up. A single quick thrust would end all her problems.

She could kill a man. She couldn't murder one, not even a lowlife like Carstairs.

She almost panicked when the miners came toward her. Marianne bent and grabbed the box that had downed Carstairs, opened the lid, and then emptied it on the man's chest. The silver gleamed in the starlight.

She threw down the box and ran as if a pack of rabid dogs came after her. Panting harshly, heart pounding, she tried to calm herself. The miners found their boss. Tracking her in the dark wouldn't be in the cards. Circling the tent camp, she found her horse and started to mount when she realized she still clutched the knife.

Her first impulse was to throw it away, but good sense prevailed. She stared at the blade and saw the thin sheen of drying blood on it. The blade slid easily back into the leather sheath jammed in her pocket. Settling the knife so it wouldn't fall out, she stepped up and tugged on the reins, getting the horse trotting away from the mining camp.

All the way back to Silver City she fumed and fussed at how Carstairs had beat her up. Her eye was swollen and moving her left arm proved almost impossible. The fight had been over fast, but she had taken more of a beating than she thought at the time. With her head threatening to split, she rode to the stables and left the horse.

Seeing a light in the front window of the hotel, she sneaked around to the back stairs and carefully mounted. Every muscle in her body ached, except for the ones that downright hurt. She winced as she touched her cheek. Her left eye had swollen shut. Fumbling, she got the door open and made her way to her room. Pausing in front of the storage room where Randolph made his bed, she started to open the door to look in on him. A moment's dizziness hit her.

"No way I could let him see me like this," she said, squinting out her blurry right eye. The decision to turn in was an easy one. She had gone through too much to stay on her feet any longer.

Marianne took a few minutes to soak a rag and press it onto her left eye, then collapsed on the bed, physically and emotionally exhausted.

She came awake with a start, sunlight slanting through the window. Marianne looked up at the bloodstained tip of a knife.

"You're under arrest," Sheriff Whitehill said, "for the murder of Lester Carstairs."

13

"Slocum," came the distant voice. "Slocum!" This time a heavy hand shook him awake. He came up, ready to fight. When he saw Dan Tucker, he sagged back to the blanket stretched out on the straw in the back stall of the livery stable.

"Go away," Slocum said.

"The sheriff arrested her, Slocum. You want to let her rot in jail or are you gonna do something?"

Slocum's eyes snapped open as he stared hard at the deputy.

"What do you mean? Who's Whitehill gone and arrested?"

"You'd sleep through the Great Flood," Tucker said. The deputy perched on a keg of nails, put his hands on his knees, and leaned forward. "The sheriff arrested your lady friend for killing Carstairs. He's got real good evidence against her, too."

Slocum knew how het up Marianne had been when he'd seen her the day before, but to kill Carstairs stretched beyond any horizon he could see. He sat up and yawned. Sleep was slow in leaving his brain.

"Is there something I can do about this?"

"Well, Slocum, you ain't the law. Whitehill's got evidence and a suspect, so there's no reason for him to stop, think on it, and then make more work for himself findin' another suspect."

"Let the jury decide," Slocum said. That would doom Marianne for sure. She hadn't been on good terms with anyone in town. He thought it went beyond her hooking on the side, too. The other soiled doves working in town didn't cause such disdain and even outright hatred.

It had to be something else, and Slocum had decided it was Texas Jack Bedrich. The prospector had ruffled feathers, and being linked in everyone's mind with him worked against Marianne.

"That's about the size of it," Tucker said. "I'd help you out since I don't think she done the deed either, but Whitehill's got me doin' a dozen different things. I let them slide, he fires me. 'Tween you and me, I need this job. Been too long since I did anything respectable."

Slocum pulled on his boots, got to his feet, brushed off the straw, and finally strapped on his gun.

"You watch yourself, Slocum. If she didn't kill Carstairs, somebody else did and they won't cotton much to anyone pokin' about to find 'em."

"Thanks, Dan," Slocum said. He left the stable and stared into the sunrise. Silver City was just now beginning to stir, merchants moving goods to the boardwalk to entice miners and farmers to stop and buy, bakers putting out the bread they'd begun hours earlier, others with an eye toward making it through another day.

His thoughts drifted aimlessly like a buzzard circling above the desert, but his feet knew the way to the jailhouse. He might as well have taken up the sheriff's offer to bunk down in the cell. The way things ran, Whitehill would find more evidence against him for Bedrich's murder and let him spend more time with Marianne in the next cell than he wanted.

The sheriff looked up from a stack of papers when Slocum came in. Whitehill rocked back so his hand was closer to his holstered six-shooter.

"Figgered you'd be by sooner or later, Slocum. Dangerous Dan tell you about the new guest back there?" Whitehill jerked his thumb over his shoulder at a cell where a blanket had been strung up to give the inmate some privacy.

"Don't get many women prisoners, do you, Sheriff?"

"One's more 'n I want."

"She didn't kill him. Marianne's not capable of that."

"Dan couldn't have told you the details since he didn't know 'em. You're blowin' smoke, Slocum, 'cuz you don't have the facts. She did it. She was shootin' off her mouth all over town how she was goin' to slice up Carstairs. That's how I found him, his guts all exposed by a knife slash."

"That's a big jump from being mad to saying she killed him."

"Found her knife. Had fresh blood on it."

"That doesn't prove anything." Slocum clamped his mouth shut when he started to alibi Marianne by saying she had taken Randolph's knife from him. It didn't help anyone dragging the boy into this.

"I have enough to let a jury decide." Whitehill sounded tired beyond his years. "Doin' this doesn't make me feel the least bit good, but I took an oath to do my duty and to follow the law."

"Let me talk to her."

"Just knock," Whitehill said with a touch of irony in his tone. "And leave that six-shooter of yours here on the desk."

Slocum slipped the Colt free and softly placed it on the desk atop the papers Whitehill had been poring over. He went to the back cell and pulled the blanket aside. Marianne sat disconsolately on the cot, her hands cupping her forehead. She looked up with dull eyes.

"It took you long enough to come, John."

"News travels slow when you're bunked out in a stall. The deputy had to tell me. What happened?"

"I heard the sheriff's rendition of it." She stood and came over, her hands clutching the bars so they touched Slocum's just enough. Silently she mouthed, "Thanks for not telling on Randolph."

"You weren't shy about letting everyone know you had it in for Carstairs. How'd your knife get blood on it?"

"I told the sheriff. I rode out to the Argent Mine and spied on them, on Carstairs. He was stealing from the mine, putting big chunks of silver into a box for himself."

Slocum said nothing. This meant nothing in the woman's defense.

"I confronted him about all he'd done." Her hand went to the shiner. The vivid yellow and purple bruise half closed her left eye. "He hit me."

"So it was self-defense," Slocum said flatly. He started to go argue the matter with Whitehill when she reached through the bars and clutched at his sleeve.

"We fought and I cut him, but he fell and hit his head. When miners came, I hightailed it away from their camp, but Carstairs was alive when I left. He ordered his men to chase after me, but I had a horse and they didn't."

"It was night, too," Whitehill piped up. "Ain't many miners who're capable trackers, much less good enough to trail a horse in the dark."

"I came straight back to town and went to bed. The sheriff woke me up around sunrise. He had my knife."

"That she used to kill Carstairs," Whitehill added.

"I don't deny fighting with him." She looked down at her dress and the bloodstains. "This is his blood. On the knife, too, but he was alive when I left."

"That so, Sheriff? What'd Carstairs's men have to say about that?" Slocum asked.

"You surely do want it all ways to Sunday. You called

the same men liars when they alibied him out of jail the other night. Now you want to believe them?" Whitehill snorted, spat, then said, "They never saw Marianne, and they did talk to Carstairs after the fight near the mine. He got on his horse 'round midnight and rode out. A rancher comin' to town for flour and cornmeal saw the body smack in the middle of the road and brung it in."

Slocum studied Marianne closely as the sheriff recited the facts. He played poker and could read gamblers well, but Marianne was a closed book to him. She had cried enough to leave dirty streaks on her cheeks, but now her face presented an emotionless mask. The despair he had seen when he first spoke to her had been pushed aside, buried.

"How'd you decide she was the killer?" Slocum asked.

"She told me to my face she wanted to carve him up. I asked around. I wasn't the only one she'd said somethin' similar to, so I took it upon myself to search her room and found the murder weapon."

Slocum's mind raced. Marianne had probably returned to town by the time Carstairs got his innards all sliced up. Why had he ridden out of camp so late at night, after he'd been carved up by her earlier? Revenge? Had Carstairs found her along the road and she had killed him? It could have happened that way. Whitehill obviously thought this explained the crime.

And it had a completeness to it that bothered Slocum. Marianne had mouthed off about wanting to kill Carstairs for what he'd done to her. She was all beat up and admitted to slicing him with the knife. That nobody had seen the crime, that Carstairs acted strangely riding out of his camp after the fight, only made for more confusion.

In his gut he doubted Marianne had it in her to kill Carstairs in cold blood. From her rendition of the fight, she had the chance to kill him. If Carstairs had caught her, she could still claim self-defense—and it would have been. Even a coldhearted jury would see how a man's fists had battered her good looks. There couldn't be a single man in Silver City who wouldn't have shoved his knife into Carstairs himself if threatened in such a powerful way.

She refused to admit she had killed him. From all Slocum knew of Marianne Lomax, she wouldn't lie. And there was little reason to if the two had met up once more on the road. Carstairs would have been furious at her, making her knife work on his guts again self-defense. If she had killed him—and she said she hadn't.

The only thing that made sense to Slocum was that she told the truth. Massaging the facts just a little would bring her to another claim of self-defense, which she refused to state.

"Where's the body?"

"I had the rancher lug it on over to the undertaker's store. Olney was all drunk and passed out on his own examination table." Whitehill chuckled. "I think poor ole Rafe had drunk some of that there embalmin' fluid of his."

"Mind if I look at it?"

"Slocum, I don't care what you do to while away the hours, but there's nothin' to see. One body's same as any other, and Carstairs is very dead."

He reached through the bars and brushed his hand against Marianne's arm. She drew away as if his touch burned her. That reaction irritated him, even as he understood her reasons. The charges against her looked insurmountable, and even self-defense might not hold water if the prosecutor claimed she had been beaten up, then laid an ambush for Carstairs.

Slocum scooped up his six-shooter from the desk and headed straight for Rafe Olney's Funeral Parlor down the street. From the front door of the undertaker's, he could see the cemetery not twenty yards down the road. That made it handy for the undertaker but gave Slocum a tiny shiver of dread. Carstairs might already be buried. Digging up the body wasn't something he looked forward to, should the need arise.

Inside the small office, the heavy wine-colored velvet curtains, which might have come from a successful burlesque theater, made him stop for a moment. All sound was deadened by those curtains, so it came as a surprise when they parted and a small, thin man with a hatchet face and bloodshot eyes stepped out. Slocum's hand had already reached the butt of his Colt. He forced himself to relax and ask, "You Rafe Olney?"

"I am, sir. How may I help you in your hour of bereavement? Has a brother or parent died? A partner from the silver fields?"

"Lester Carstairs," Slocum said.

"Ah, you are in his employ. A sad thing when such a fine, upstanding citizen is cruelly dispatched."

"He was a bully and tried to rape Marianne Lomax," Slocum said. "The night he died, he beat her up."

"Ah, the woman who stabbed him to death. You a friend of hers?" Olney pulled the curtain half around him, as if he could do a magician's disappearing act using the velvet drape.

"I want to look at Carstairs's body."

"This is highly unusual. If there is to be a viewing, it ought to be arranged by someone in the deceased's family. Or a business partner."

"He in the back?"

"Sir, I can't—"

He let Slocum push past into a narrow corridor. Only two doors opened off it. Slocum saw one led to a bedroom where Olney lived. The other revealed a larger room with two waist-high tables. On one lay Lester Carstairs. Even in death a sneer marred his face, as if he knew his death would falsely indict Marianne.

"What do you want of him? Are you paying for his funeral?" Olney stood in the doorway behind Slocum, fearfully wringing his bony hands and shifting from foot to foot.

"He had plenty of silver nuggets to pay for his burying," Slocum said. He doubted any of it had been found. The miners who had saved him from Marianne at the mine likely took what the woman said had been scattered over Carstairs's chest. Even if the foreman had hidden the silver again, there wasn't any reason for him to take his ill-gotten silver with him when he rode out hours later.

Or was there? If one of the men working for him had seen the silver and Carstairs had tried to leave with it, robbery could be an explanation for his death. There'd never be any way to find his killer or prove who did it. That meant Marianne would be convicted and the real killer would get away scot-free.

A cursory look at the man's knuckles verified what Marianne had said about the fight. Carstairs had connected more than once with her face and had skinned his knuckles. The raw look and torn flesh showed these were recent injuries. Slocum peeled back the man's shirt and looked at the cut across his middle.

"This is what killed him? That scratch?"

"The sheriff thought it so," Olney said. The undertaker went to a cabinet and opened it, hands shaking. He took out a silver flask, popped out the cork, and took a long drink that settled his nerves. A second draft, consideration of a third that he finally avoided, then the flask was placed back in the cabinet.

The undertaker's voice was firmer now, as was his spine.

"You cannot be here. Illegally interfering with a corpse is a criminal offense."

"How do you properly interfere with a corpse?" Slocum asked. He peeled back more of the shirt stuck to Carstairs's belly by dried blood, hunting for a deeper wound.

Marianne had been frightened during the attack. Slocum knew how she must have felt; he had seen so many raw recruits during the war. The first shot, the first threat, their brains turned off. Their bodies might react but there'd been no telling what they would do. He had seen one youngster, hardly sixteen, fire his musket repeatedly, never once putting in a bullet. A fistfight with Carstairs would have disoriented Marianne. She had cut Carstairs enough to make him bleed like a stuck pig, but maybe there had been a deeper wound.

How Carstairs could have gotten up, dealt with the miners who had come to his rescue, and waited at his camp for hours before riding off to his death afforded Slocum more of a mystery than he cared to think on. Marianne might have stabbed him and penetrated his intestine or stomach and Carstairs had died hours later out on the road.

There wouldn't have been any way the pain wouldn't have hobbled him completely, though, if that had happened. None of his men had reported Carstairs being in such pain. He had mounted and left camp on his own. A stab wound to the gut would have prevented easy mounting, and riding would have been excruciating.

Slocum yanked back the shirt and looked at every inch of Carstairs's bloody chest. The belly cut was the only wound he saw. It had bled sluggishly but hardly amounted to an injury serious enough to kill him.

As he turned away from the table, he stopped and looked back at the body.

"You see that, Mr. Olney?"

"To what are you referring?"

"In the cut. If you bend down and look along the cut you see a bit of his guts all puckered up." Slocum spread the cut as wide as he could to allow the undertaker to see what he had by accident.

"I do not understand."

"You got a thin blade or those clamps like a doctor uses to pull out bullets?"

"I have a trocar—I use it to drain the blood."

Slocum held out his hand and waited for the undertaker

to pass it over. The thick tube had a sharp point for piercing veins. The thickness was about right, unless Slocum missed his guess.

"See that skin all puffed up."

"It appears to be pushed back and upward."

"From a bullet wound." Slocum began digging around, following the path of the slug through Carstairs's body. The sharp tip banged against the bullet. A bit of digging caused it to pop out, all mashed up and bloody. He handed it to Olney.

"I don't understand," the undertaker said.

"Carstairs died from a gunshot to the belly, not from a knife wound. It just happened the bullet went in where the knife slash had already opened him up."

"That seems incredible," Olney said, elbowing Slocum out of the way to better examine the wound. He poked and pulled, then rubbed his fingers together. "He was shot at close range. This is unburned gunpowder. I've seen this often when a man is killed by a gun barrel shoved up hard against him before the killer fires."

Slocum had seen men's clothing set on fire from the muzzle blast. The blood soaked into Carstairs's shirt hid any such evidence, but the bullet showed that Marianne hadn't stabbed him to death.

"I've got to talk to the sheriff," Slocum said. "Don't you go getting so soused you can't remember what you just saw."

Rafe Olney turned paler, if that was possible, and bobbed his head up and down as if it had been mounted on a spring. Convincing the sheriff that the man on the table had been shot to death and not killed with a knife would be easy enough. How did Slocum convince Whitehill that Marianne hadn't been the one who pulled the trigger and then hidden the pistol?

14

"I ought to hang you, Slocum," the sheriff said tiredly. He hiked his feet up to his desk and laced his fingers behind his head. He looked relaxed, but from the way he scowled, Slocum knew Whitehill was on a hair trigger. "Since you blew into town, I've had bodies pilin' up somethin' fierce. You have any reason to offer why I shouldn't clap you back in a cell for killin' Texas Jack Bedrich?"

"I didn't do it," Slocum said. "And Marianne didn't kill Carstairs either. The bullet proves that."

"It proves she didn't end his miserable life with a knife, that's all. How do I know if she had a hideout gun somewhere? Easy enough to shoot Carstairs, then toss it into a well or just bury it alongside the road."

"She wouldn't have confessed to being in the fight with him if she'd killed him," Slocum said.

"There's some logic to that, but it might be she had to explain why her eye was swole shut, and she had enough bruises to make her look like a Chinee, all yellow-like."

"Olney will confirm what I said."

"Don't doubt that for a minute. Ole Rafe's likely takin'

a pull or two on a whiskey bottle 'bout now. I go over there, and he's usually knee-walkin' drunk 'fore noon. Earlier in the day if he has a burial service."

"Let the doctor examine the body."

"Doc Fuller's got real work to do. Besides, he'd charge the county for a house visit if I did that."

"You—"

"Hold your horses, Slocum," Whitehill said, bringing his right hand around as if to caution Slocum to halt. "I'm not sayin' anything you told me's not the gospel truth. That slug came from somewhere and Rafe's likely to tell me you did pull it out of Carstairs."

"Then let her go."

"I explained that to you. I let you out because Tucker vouched for you. How Bedrich became deceased is a matter of some controversy 'tween me and my deputy. Tucker's inclined to say it don't matter much, that Bedrich wasn't liked that much so why bother? Now, I've been in Silver City longer than Dan and know Texas Jack wasn't a bad fellow. He ruffled feathers every chance he got, but he was on the up-and-up."

Slocum heard more in the sheriff's words than was spoken. Whitehill hadn't cared much for Bedrich. And there was something else he couldn't put his finger on.

"There's no way you could have known Bedrich. I got a telegram out to Santa Fe and asked the marshal there to find out what business took Bedrich that far north. So far, ain't heard back, but I will or know the reason."

Whatever had happened to Bedrich, it had been in Holst's icehouse. Slocum didn't want to muddy the water by bringing up the prospector's death, but that charge still rode mighty close behind him. Without Dangerous Dan's good words about him, Slocum knew he would be locked up beside Marianne.

"The matter of Marianne and Carstairs is something else," Whitehill went on. "She knew him, spoke ill of him, and told anyone who'd listen, includin' me, she was going to kill him."

"She's hot tempered."

"Fiery," Whitehill said, nodding in agreement. "Nothing you've told me speaks to her innocence."

"She has to look after her boy," Slocum said.

"Now that is a shame. I'll speak to Mrs. Gruhlkey about that."

"No, wait!" came Marianne's aggrieved cry. She yanked down the blanket and rattled the bars. "Don't put Randolph in her care."

"Now, Marianne, the boy needs lookin' after. Ain't gonna be a good thing lettin' him and Billy have their head. Randolph's a follower and Billy is the kind who can think up some real mischief. One day, I'll have to arrest him. It'd be a shame if Randolph joined him in a cell."

"John, you find Randolph. You look after him until I get out of here."

"What's bail?" Slocum asked. The question startled Whitehill.

"Hadn't given that any thought. Can't rightly set bail without a judge pokin' his nose in. Besides, she's likely to pull up stakes and leave before any trial. It's not like she has family or ties to Silver City."

"There aren't many who do, Sheriff," Marianne said.

"The only one in my jail for killin' a man is you, Marianne. Don't care about any of the others in town 'less they up and shoot somebody, too."

Slocum again heard something in the sheriff's tone that made him curious to find out more. It wasn't as if he denied bail for any legal reason but rather to keep her in the cell.

Where he could watch her.

"I'll see that Randolph is all right," Slocum said to Marianne. He was rewarded with a look of pure gratitude—and something more. He wished iron bars didn't separate them.

From the way Harvey Whitehill glared, he wanted there to be another set of bars. A new thought hit Slocum. The sheriff wouldn't toss him in the clink because that would put both him and Marianne together, bars or not. Slocum got the feeling Whitehill thought of him as a rival for Marianne's affections.

As much as that irritated Slocum, it made him feel a mite easier. Whitehill wouldn't let anything happen if he was sweet on her. Slocum took his leave and looked around, wondering where a young boy without any parental influence would go. He searched around the back of the hotel but found nothing. Asking after Randolph—and likely Billy, too—wouldn't get him far. Ignoring young boys unless they were up to mischief was too easy. Adults had jobs, concerns, that didn't include boys.

Slocum harkened back to when he was Randolph's age. He found himself going to the general store. Inside, out of the sun and relishing the cool interior, he looked around until he found the shelf with the stick candy.

"Help you, mister?" The clerk wiped his hands on a filthy apron. From his expression, he hoped Slocum had a great deal to order because working in the back room proved more difficult.

"Three sticks of that candy," Slocum said. "Peppermint. Striped."

"That's three cents. I'll let you have six for a nickel."

"This is fine," Slocum said. The candy lay on the counter. He reached over and took a small scrap of paper and wrapped them before tucking the candy away in his coat pocket. In this heat, they would turn sticky fast. "You catch those boys stealing your candy?"

"Boys? Oh, them," the man said in disgust. "You mean that Billy McCarty and his sidekick. Don't know the kid's name but he follows Billy around like a puppy dog. Naw, I've never caught 'em, but I know they sneak a piece or two every time they come in."

"When was the last time you chased them off? This morning?"

"Yeah, not a half hour back. I was stacking in the back room when I heard the bell ring." He pointed to a small brass bell on a spring that alerted him of new customers. "Billy was trying to stop the bell from ringing so he and the dark-haired kid could grab some food, I suspect."

"I just came from talking to Sheriff Whitehill, and he wants to know where those young'uns might hide out."

"Last time they tried to sneak off with a jar of pickles, I chased them to the stock tank at the edge of town."

"Stock tank?"

"Abandoned when Silver City started growing. This used to be free range. Don't even know what rancher built the tank, but it don't hold water worth a damn anymore. Still, there's some water in it. Might even be a fish or two, though I couldn't say."

"Much obliged," Slocum said, heading out with the candy in his pocket. He intended using it as a peace offering to get Randolph and Billy where he could watch them. Boys that age knew every hiding place there was. He might search for a month and never come close to flushing them out if they took it into their heads to avoid him.

Slocum sauntered along, not hurrying as he turned over everything that had happened. He didn't run from trouble, but he seldom sought it out. This time too much had found him. Where Marianne fit into the trouble bothered him the most. Memories of them together in Georgia spiced up everything that swirled around in Silver City. Before he had everything straight in his head, he caught sight of Billy peering over the edge of the stock tank.

The dirt walls had broken in several places, making what might have been a usual watering hole into a shallow pool. He doubted the general store's clerk was right about there being fish in the scummy water.

"How deep is it?" Slocum called. "Doesn't look to be

more than a foot or two." No answer. He edged through a small gap in the earthen wall and looked around the pond. "Doesn't look good for much more 'n breeding mosquitoes. Doubt there's any fish in it."

He found himself a spot to sit. Without looking around, he reached into his pocket and took out the candy sticks. Peeling away the paper, he made a big deal out of choosing one to suck. He twirled it in his mouth, smacking with gusto now and then as he pointedly stared across the still water.

"Ain't more 'n a foot deep 'cept in the middle. Close to six foot there. No fish, though. You're right 'bout that."

He silently held out the paper with the remaining two sticks of candy. Billy hesitantly took one.

"What 'bout the other?"

"That's for Randolph. If you'll give it to him, go on and take it."

"Naw, if I took it, I'm not sure I could hold myself back from eatin' it, too."

Billy sat a yard away and worked the peppermint stick around and around, reducing the end to a sharp tip.

"How come?" Billy looked out of the corner of his eye at Slocum. As it was, he kept his legs coiled under him, ready to launch himself into full flight if the need arose.

"Randolph's ma is in jail. She wants me to be sure he's not getting into trouble."

Billy laughed, then fell silent. He cast a sidelong glance at Slocum, then stared straight ahead, as if the two of them locking eyes would be wrong.

"You're different," Billy said. "You don't prance around the truth like most grown-ups."

"Never had much truck with speechifying," Slocum said. "Lying either."

"I ain't a liar!"

"Never said you were. Truth is, the sheriff and others say a good bit about you but never has a one of them called you a liar."

"Good. I tell the truth."

"You know where Randolph is." Slocum made it a flat statement.

"He's not here."

Slocum said nothing. Billy might not lie outright but answers such as that were just as bad.

"You won't lock him up like his ma?"

"Farthest thing from my mind. You know what's happened to me since I got to Silver City. Locking anybody up isn't to my liking."

"You'd kill, though?" Billy sounded eager at the notion.

"I didn't kill Carstairs. Randolph's ma didn't either. You have any notion who might have killed him?"

"Been thinkin' on that. Might be Texas Jack's old partner, name of Jim Frank. He chased me and Randolph off more 'n once for no good reason. Vicious son of a bitch." Billy looked hard at Slocum, who made no sign he'd heard profanity or had any desire to chastise him.

"Frank and Texas Jack had a fallin'-out."

"Know why?"

"They was partners in a mine. Texas Jack sold out. From what Miz Lomax said to Randolph, Texas Jack got rooked. Didn't bother him none, though, since he might have found a bigger strike. Biggest ever since Cap'n Bullard and his brother found silver back in '70. Don't know what his brother's name was. Don't matter."

Slocum thought on this a spell. If Bedrich had made a rich strike, Marianne would have been in clover. He turned over the possibility that she might have killed him for the deed to the claim, then discarded what had to be a busted hand. Women couldn't own real estate, and more than this, Bedrich looked to have been killed in Santa Fe. There hadn't been even a hint that she had left Silver City and gone hunting for him.

"That's easy enough to learn about," Slocum said. "Bedrich would have filed a claim in the land office."

Billy snickered.

"Burned down. Took all the records with it."

"Somebody burn it down or was it an accident?" In a town like Silver City, fire made everyone constantly uneasy. The buildings were constructed poorly, slammed up side by side, so if a fire did start from a kerosene lamp or carelessly emptied stove, the entire town would go up in a flash.

"Hard to say. It was the assay office, too. And the telegraph. I seen how Jerry—he was the clerk and telegrapher and chemist—stored those stinky chemicals of his. Saw him burn up a piece of paper with just a drop of one of them chemicals."

"Where would you go to file a claim? This is the county seat."

Billy shrugged. He worked on the last of his peppermint stick candy and then rubbed his fingers in the dirt to get rid of the stickiness.

"Think Randolph might know?"

"Why him? Oh, you mean Texas Jack might have said something to him? I doubt it. Him and Texas Jack didn't get along too good. Me, I liked Jack. He gave me whiskey when nobody was lookin'." Billy jerked his head around, looking fierce. "He never gave Randolph none. Ever."

"Don't much care," Slocum said. "Bedrich is dead and isn't going to give anybody a free drink. So, where's Randolph?"

"I can give him that candy. The stick you got left."

"You said you'd eat it if I gave it to you. Better for me to eat it myself if Randolph's not getting it." This logic appealed to the boy.

"Randolph was earnin' a dime an hour workin' for Tom. He's the owner of the Lonely Cuss, where Randolph's ma works. Worked."

"The fellow at the store knows you tried to muffle the door bell." With that, Slocum stood, brushed off his pants, and made his way to the crack in the stock pond wall.

He saw how Billy shied away, then relaxed when it became apparent Slocum wasn't trying to nab him. Slocum felt the boy's eyes on him as he returned to town, heading for the saloon. It made sense that Randolph would look for work at a place his ma worked. As much as he tried to distance himself from her, he had to still feel the need to protect her—and be comforted by her when things went wrong. Heaven alone knew how much had gone wrong for the Lomax family, just in the past few days.

Slocum went into the saloon and leaned on the bar. A portly man with a handlebar mustache waddled over.

"Beer? You got the look of a man with a big thirst. Maybe you want a shot of my special whiskey." The man reached for a bottle.

"You're Tom?"

"His brother," the barkeep said, suddenly suspicious. "What's your beef with him?"

"Nothing. I'm looking for Randolph Lomax. His ma told me to fetch him."

"What's that kid up to?"

"What do you mean? I was told he was doing chores here."

"He went off and left the back room needin' to be swept."

Slocum went to the back room, the barkeep shouting at him that he couldn't go there. A quick look around showed that Randolph hadn't simply left. He had put up quite a fight before being dragged out the back door.

"You're gonna pay for that door!" the barkeep shouted.

It had been half ripped off its hinges. Slocum saw a footprint in the middle of the door about the size of a young boy's foot. He had fought, kicking hard as he was dragged away. The knocked-over bottles and the evidence on the unswept floor told Slocum all he needed to know.

Someone had kidnapped Randolph Lomax.

15

"You're gonna pay for all the broken bottles. They cost money, and my brother Tom's not gonna—" The barkeep stopped and turned a few shades whiter under his florid complexion as Slocum whirled on him. He didn't even have to reach for his six-shooter to cow the portly man.

"You see who kidnapped Randolph?"

"Kidnapped? I don't know nuthin' 'bout no—" This was all the farther he got before Slocum wrapped his powerful fingers around a greasy neck just under bouncing dewlaps and started squeezing.

The barkeep kicked and struggled. Slocum ignored the ineffectual blows as he tightened his grip. He leaned forward and pinned the man against the back wall of the saloon.

"You see anything?"

Gurgles came out along with drool. Slocum eased his grip.

"A weasely-lookin' fellow. Don't know him. Don't know nobody in Silver City. I just got in from Mesilla yesterday 'cuz my brother asked me to help out with the Lonely Cuss. I'm Justin Gallifrey. Ask my brother if that's not so!"

133

"What's he look like? Other than a weasel." To Slocum's way of thinking, that described too many miners and prospectors always milling about in town.

"Had ginger hair. A redhead! I swear, didn't see no more."

"Just a kidnapper stealing away a young boy."

"Ain't that young." The barkeep gurgled as Slocum squeezed so hard the tendons stood out on his forearm. Then he released the man, watching with no satisfaction as the barkeep dropped to his hands and knees and puked.

Slocum stepped away, spun, and began tracking the best he could. The thin, dry dust didn't hold footsteps too well in the constant wind blowing through town, but he got a sense of direction. Frank had taken the boy to a spot immediately behind an apothecary. Whether there'd been two horses or Frank had forced Randolph to ride double lay beyond Slocum's skill to tell. The hoofprints were too muddled for anyone to tell, even an Apache tracker.

But of one thing he was sure. Frank had been the kidnapper. There might be dozens of red-haired men in town, but who else was mixed up in Bedrich's murder and matched even this sketchy identification?

He knew he ought to tell the sheriff. Even if Whitehill wasn't likely to go chasing after Jim Frank, Slocum was sure he could convince Dangerous Dan Tucker to join him on the trail. It'd be useful having a lawman at his side. It'd be useful, but it would slow him down. If he told Whitehill, the sheriff would let Marianne know, and she would worry. Penned up in the cell the way she was didn't give her much room to pace about. And Slocum knew this tidbit would be passed along immediately.

If Whitehill was sweet on the woman, he would do whatever he could to put Slocum in a bad light. Slocum got to the stables and slid bareback onto his captured pony. He didn't have money for a saddle and gear, but the horse was strong and would run all day and far into the night if he demanded it.

With a snap of the reins, he started on the trail after Frank.

Slocum about fell from the horse, exhaustion his only companion. For two days he had ridden, trying to find any trace of Randolph Lomax. He was sure Frank had kidnapped the boy, but the pathetic trail had vanished on him only a mile outside Silver City. Giving his pony its head, he had walked along hunting for any hoofprints, any trace. Now and again he found something. His best clue was a piece of cloth that might have been ripped from Randolph's sleeve on a thornbush in a wild tangle of undergrowth.

He couldn't be sure.

Slocum drove himself mercilessly, circling about, using every trick he had ever learned to find the trail. He had finally decided to simply study the terrain and make a guess. His belly growled, his vision blurred, and he lacked sleep from his crazy hunt. There should have been an easier way to proceed, but Slocum couldn't find it. More than one traveler along the roads he crossed furnished information about other riders. None matched Frank's description and no one had seen a boy, much less one that might have been Randolph Lomax.

Finally reaching the end of his rope, Slocum dismounted and gathered some berries. He wanted to hunt, bag a rabbit or squirrel, and get a decent meal. Lacking any supplies but what he carried on his person worked against him staying on the trail much longer. Settling down with his back to a tree as he ate the berries and chewed on some bitter roots, he tried for the hundredth time to make sense out of the kidnapping.

What Billy had said about Texas Jack Bedrich hitting a big vein of silver ore satisfied most of the reasons Frank might have for kidnapping Randolph. He might ransom him off for the mine. If he and Bedrich had a falling-out just before the new strike, he had to feel cheated, no matter how profitable the partners' old mine had proven to be. Slocum had seen this before. It transcended greed and envy. The feeling of being cheated rankled worse than being poor or wasting a life hunting for the elusive precious metal.

Nothing he had heard about Bedrich, save Marianne's account, told him the man would play fair either. Frank might have a legitimate claim to the new silver strike.

With Texas Jack Bedrich dead, stealing away Randolph might be the only way the prospector had of getting his share from Marianne; only the woman had nothing. She had been turning tricks to make ends meet when taking in laundry hadn't been enough.

Slocum's mind wandered when he thought of her sleeping with one miner after another, taking their paltry coins and still not making enough to prevent eviction. Marianne Lomax was a proud woman, and being unable to feed her son would hurt her worse than physical injury ever could.

He spat out seeds and closed his eyes. Sleep eluded him as his memories of him with Marianne back in Georgia poked and prodded at his mind. Realizing the futility of sleep that might be haunted with such memories, he levered himself to his feet and got the lay of the land. He had a powerful thirst. A stream ran a couple dozen yards away, barely audible over the sounds of the woods. Making his way through the trees, he found the small creek tumbling along, clear and pure. Slocum dropped to his belly and began scooping in water.

A sound barely louder than the water slipping over rocks made him freeze. He rolled onto his side to get to his Colt Navy as the rustling noise grew louder. A deer might be coming to drink and hadn't scented him. But Slocum didn't think so. He slipped his six-shooter free and strained to make out anything worth shooting at in the undergrowth. Bushes rustled, then stopped.

Slocum moved fast. He rolled twice more, getting into the creek and causing a curtain of water to splash upward.

Bullets tore through the watery sheet, but Slocum already ran hard for cover. He landed behind a rock and twisted about to get off a shot.

The spot where the rustling had been proved empty. Slocum knew why. He rolled onto his back and fired wildly.

"Damn you, Slocum! You're a cagey one!"

Frank's voice carried no hint of injury, only outrage that he hadn't duped Slocum into looking the wrong direction so he could shoot him in the back. Slocum kept moving, dug in his toes, and found purchase to dive parallel with the ground. He landed hard, but he had let out all the air in his lungs an instant before colliding with the hard ground. Sucking in a new breath proved painful, but Slocum was still in the fight.

"I ain't intendin' to kill you, Slocum. I want you to carry a message back to town."

"You kidnap the boy?"

"Me and Randolph, we been havin' a fine time. The boy's wasted in Silver City. Nuthin' for him to do but get in trouble."

"You teaching him how to steal?"

Frank laughed harshly.

"No call for me to do that. His step-pa was real masterful at that."

"You mean Bedrich?" Slocum hunted for a way to get out of the trap he had blundered into and didn't see it. If he kept Frank occupied by stalling as long as possible, there might be a chance for him to get off a shot or two.

Then he gritted his teeth in frustration. Killing Frank might mean Randolph would never be found alive.

"Reckon they wasn't actually hitched, Texas Jack and his whore. Don't matter a whit to me since the boy doesn't know where Bedrich hid it."

"What are you talking about?"

"You don't know? Of course not. About the only one who does since the kid doesn't have any idea has to be his ma."

Slocum came into a crouch, ready to explode forward, firing as he went. He thought he had spotted Frank. A frontal attack might take him by surprise.

"Don't bother wastin' the effort, Slocum," came the cheery words from behind. "Why don't you drop that hogleg of yours. Never knew you was so good with it, but then I only just met up with you on the trail."

"Did you kill Bedrich?"

"The stupid son of a bitch wouldn't give me what I wanted. But I shot him in self-defense."

"How'd he end up in the ice?"

"I couldn't track him right away after we exchanged a few rounds. The Santa Fe marshal came to see what the ruckus was about. By the time I got free of him, Bedrich had run off."

"To Holst's ice plant?"

"That was the closest building to hide in. I searched the damned place for an hour and never found him."

"How'd he get in the ice?"

"Must have fallen into one of them snow packers Holst uses. Mashes snow down into ice, then he ships the blocks. I searched that place from top to bottom, then asked damned near everyone in Santa Fe if they'd seen him. The only hint I had he was in the ice came from some blood I saw on the equipment."

"So you came after me?"

"I was right. Bedrich was in the ice."

"But he didn't have what you were hunting for? What was it? Silver?"

"You're too curious for your own good. I told you all I'm going to since you can't prove none of it. Tell the sheriff or that deputy friend of yours. Doesn't change things. Your word against mine, and it doesn't look as if you're in good standing with the Silver City law."

"You had more reason to kill your partner than I did. I never met Texas Jack."

"Partner." Frank spat out the word as if it burned his tongue. "Double-crossing son of a bitch is more like it."

"Are you going to shoot me or talk me to death?"

"Killin' you would be a pleasure, like ice cream on a hot Sunday afternoon, Slocum, but you can be useful. You ride on back to Silver City on that Indian pony of yours and tell Marianne Lomax I'll trade her son for . . ."

"For what?"

"She'll know. She don't bring it, her kid's never found again and will die a horrible death. Or maybe I'll cut him up like the Apaches do and send him back to her more dead than alive. Would she tend a boy with his hands and feet cut off and his eyes all poked out the rest of her life?"

"What's to keep you from killing both her and Randolph if she gives you whatever it is you want and think she's got?"

"Not much that I can see, but it's a risk she has to take. If I don't see her ridin' along the road down to Shakespeare in two days, the boy starts losing body parts. Important parts."

"I won't tell her. You'll kill them both."

"Then I ought to kill you and put you out of *my* misery." The six-gun cocked with a peal of doom.

"No promises. She won't be able to make it. She's locked up for killing Carstairs."

"Do tell? He was a clumsy one, Lester Carstairs."

"You killed him, didn't you?"

"He didn't have what I want, so why not? Him and me never got along. Putting a bullet in his belly ought to get me a reward."

"Give me something to convince Whitehill that Marianne isn't his killer so he'll release her."

Frank laughed, and it was an ugly sound.

"Never goin' to happen, Slocum. Never. You figure how to get her on the road, two days from now. It's a hard day's ride back to Silver City, so you better get a move on."

Slocum feinted right, dived left, and scooped up his fallen

six-shooter. As he twisted about hunting for Frank, he knew the effort availed him nothing. Only empty forest stretched as far as he could see. If he hadn't fired a few rounds so the acrid gunpowder stench still hung in the air, he wouldn't have known Frank had even been here.

He scouted the forest a few minutes, but Frank had left no track to follow. The pressure of time crushed him down. Even killing Frank solved nothing. Randolph was a prisoner somewhere only Frank knew. Kill the redheaded varmint and Randolph likely died of thirst or hunger. This was mighty wide-open country, and Frank had had days to find a proper hiding place.

Slocum vaulted onto the horse and headed out in a straight path until he found a broad meadow with an unobstructed view of the sky. He waited until the sun dipped low and the stars came out so he could get a bearing off the North Star and ride straight back to Silver City. He had no idea how he'd get Sheriff Whitehill to release Marianne, but it likely had to do with someone dying.

16

As he rode, Slocum felt eyes watching him. He tried to locate Frank, but the man proved too wily. The red-haired son of a bitch made sure Slocum didn't try finding Randolph or tracking him to his hideout. The thought had crossed Slocum's mind, but nothing had gone right in the days he had been out hunting for Randolph, and he doubted such a trick would work now. Frank had plenty of time to prepare and think through his scheme.

He wanted something, and the best Slocum could think was that Bedrich had found one hell of a big silver strike. If Marianne had a map to the claim, she'd likely fork it over right away to get her son back. What galled Slocum was the unlikely happening.

Give Frank the map and he would kill both the boy and his mother. There wasn't anything for him to lose doing that, and he had already killed Bedrich, though from the man's own mouth he hadn't intended to. The fight had gotten out of hand. All Frank wanted was to rob Texas Jack, not kill him. Or maybe he had planned to kill the silver prospector all the time and had just jumped the gun, pulling the trigger before getting the map.

The road was long and dusty, but Slocum never faltered. The pony maintained a steady pace and got him to town in late afternoon. He looked around and saw miners slowly filtering in from their mines, a powerful thirst needing to be slaked with whiskey and women. Slocum felt guilty about not going straight to the jailhouse to tell the sheriff what had happened. As hard as he had worked on a wide variety of schemes to get Marianne out of jail, none had come to him that Whitehill would agree to. The man was sweet on her and letting her out of his sight wasn't in the cards.

Slocum dismounted and stuck his head into the Lonely Cuss. The portly barkeep shied away, then reached under the bar, probably hunting for a pistol or a sawed-off shotgun. Slocum didn't see Dangerous Dan anywhere and backed out. No one but the barkeep had even noticed him in the doorway. Quick stepping it to the hotel, he spotted Billy McCarty huddled down and doing something secretive. As he walked up, the boy jumped like he'd had a nail driven into his skull.

"Whoa, don't get all spooked," Slocum said. Billy put his hand down and hid whatever he had in the dust. Likely it was something he had stolen. "Have you seen the deputy?"

"Tucker? Yeah, the sheriff sent him out of town this mornin' to serve process on an old coot east of town. Not sure what it's all about. You want me to find out? For a dime I can do that." His dirty fingers closed, and he hid the tiny treasure behind his back, making Slocum surer than ever Billy had stolen something he didn't want seen.

"How long's that likely to take him?"

"Be back tomorrow noon maybe. I know Tucker. If he took a bottle with him, he might not come back to Silver City 'til it's drained dry." Billy laughed, then sobered when he saw the joke didn't set well with Slocum. "What's eatin' you?"

"Tell me more about the assay office burning down."

"Ain't much to tell. It just did. All Jerry's equipment was burnt to cinders. He was gonna teach me code so I could cover for him, but that's not too likely now."

"The deeds for all the silver mines were lost?"

"Reckon so. Might be copies up in Santa Fe but I wouldn't count on that."

Slocum nodded as more pieces fell together for him. Bedrich had gone to Santa Fe to register his claim there, only to run afoul of Frank. Before he could properly authenticate the location of the strike, he had been gut-shot and died in a block of ice. Frank hadn't expected that and had finally tracked Slocum and the body. Bedrich might have hidden the map before he died.

Or Slocum may have been all wet and Frank had killed him for some other reason. Bedrich might have gone to Santa Fe to enlist the aid of a federal marshal or any of a dozen other reasons.

"You look perturbed," Billy said, rolling the big word over on his tongue as if he liked the taste.

"Got bad news to pass along to Randolph's ma, that's all."

"Ain't seen him neither. He was gonna get a job sweepin' up at the Lonely Cuss so he could steal some whiskey for us, but he crapped out on that."

"Yeah, he must have," Slocum said. He started toward the sheriff's office, stopped, and without looking back, said, "You're going to get yourself in a world of trouble stealing." The boy gasped that he had been accused so readily, but to his credit said nothing. A denial would have been worthless—and a lie. Slocum kept walking.

He felt as if he were mounting the thirteen steps of a gallows to his own execution. With Dan Tucker out of town, his best chance for someone helping him evaporated. He paused in front of the door, then went in. Whitehill sat at his desk reading a paper. Marianne had the blanket pulled up along one side of her cell to give herself some privacy. It looked exactly as it had a couple days earlier.

"What brings you by, Slocum?" the sheriff asked. From his tone, he hoped Slocum was going to tell him he'd come down with a bad case of ptomaine.

"John!" Marianne yanked down the blanket and clung fiercely to the bars. "Where's Randolph? I told you to look after him. Why hasn't he come by to see me?"

Slocum looked at her and realized how distraught she had become. A wild look in her eyes turned her into a caged animal rather than the lovely woman he knew. Rather than explaining to her, he turned to the sheriff.

"Jim Frank kidnapped the boy. I tracked him down."

"But?" Whitehill's gimlet stare pierced Slocum's heart. "You got a dead body to explain?"

"He'll trade Randolph for something Marianne has."

Whitehill exploded. He slammed both fists on the desk and sent his newspaper fluttering away.

"Like hell I'll let him have his way with her."

"That's not what he wants. When I caught Carstairs in her hotel room, I thought he wanted her. But it's something else both men are after."

Whitehill blinked. Then he fixed his hard gaze on Slocum as if he could core out the truth.

"What did Bedrich give you?" Slocum called to Marianne. "That's what Frank wants."

"Give me? He didn't give me anything. Not even a ring. He said he'd take care of that later on, maybe after he got back from wherever he was headed."

"He told you about his silver strike, though."

"Well, he was always going on about how good a prospector he was and how he was going to be richer than all the kings of Europe. Believing him took most of my imagination." She swallowed hard, then asked, "What's this got to do with Randolph?"

"Frank will trade the boy for whatever Bedrich had. It must be a map."

"But Jack never gave me anything like that. How can I give Frank something I don't have? How'm I supposed to get Randolph back?" Her voice rose to such a pitch that Slocum flinched. She was approaching hysteria, which would do her no good all locked up in that iron cage.

"I heard tell that the assay office burned down, and all the records were lost. That so, Sheriff?"

"Careless storage of them chemicals, the ones used in telegraphy. Might have been the others Jerry used to assay ore. The whole building went up in less than ten minutes."

"You're sure it was accidental?"

"Sure as I can be. Jerry hightailed it out of town, ashamed as all get-out."

"If Bedrich filed a claim there, it'd be lost."

"Everyone's was. Mostly the miners protect their claims with drawn guns and knives. It's gonna take weeks to have everyone refile their claims, but first the town's got to hire somebody what can read. That might take longer than the actual recordin' of the claims from the miners' copies."

"Bedrich went to Santa Fe to file his claim there rather than wait. That's when Frank killed him. He confessed the murder to me."

"Do tell," Whitehill said. "Don't surprise me none. Frank was always a sneaky cuss."

"Randolph! How do I get my son back?"

Both men glanced at Marianne, then went back to what had become a silent negotiation. Slocum didn't come out and say what was in his head, but Whitehill did.

"No way I'm lettin' her go talk to Frank. From what you said, he's expectin' a lawman to sneak up and try to arrest him. Besides, I can't leave Silver City 'til Dangerous Dan gets back."

"Sometime tomorrow," Slocum said. Nothing worked out right for him. He repeated what Frank had said about Marianne taking the road to Shakespeare so he could watch and avoid anyone trailing her.

"He may be a mean cayuse but he's smart, I'll give him that," Whitehill said. "If he sees a flash of a badge, he never lets her know where the boy is."

"Sheriff, please. You have to let me go. I can talk him into letting Randolph go. I have to!" Seeing the sheriff's reluctance, she began sobbing. "Harvey, I'm begging you. I *have* to try."

"Let her go. I can trail her and nab Frank."

"You're assumin' he'll have the boy with him. That's not smart. He'll ask for the map and examine it, then tell her where her son is. Might even turn the boy over after he's made sure the map's for real." Whitehill scratched his stubbled chin. "Frank's holdin' a royal flush, Slocum. No way I can see to pry that boy loose. Assumin' he's still alive."

This brought a cry of utter, soul-wrenching agony from Marianne. She began sobbing bitterly.

"If I can catch Frank, I can make him talk."

"All I got's your word any of this happened. I don't know that you're not schemin' to get her free and then ride off together."

"The boy's not been seen for a couple days. Ask the fat bastard over at the Lonely Cuss what happened. He saw Frank kidnap Randolph."

"Tom's brother, Justin?" Whitehill scratched vigorously behind his head now, as if following a migrating flea around. "Ain't seen him sober since he came to Silver City. Not what I'd call reliable."

"All right, Sheriff," Slocum said. "Let Marianne out and lock me up in her place. You want a prisoner? This will guarantee that we're not riding off together." Slocum knew he had hit a bull's-eye from the ripples of emotion on the lawman's face.

"You'd do that, John?"

"I don't have any idea how you can convince Frank to let your son go if you don't have the map. It doesn't set well with me that he might kill both of you if you don't hand him something."

"I . . . I'll come up with a plan. Harvey? Please!" She rattled the bars.

"Hand over your piece, Slocum." He took the six-shooter and dropped it into a desk drawer before giving Slocum the keys to Marianne's cell.

Slocum opened the door and found his arms full of a quaking, crying woman. He held her, aware of the sheriff's cold glare.

"You know what Frank said to do. Maybe if you have a gun, you can wing him and drag him back to town," Slocum said. He hadn't heard such a lame idea since Pickett's Charge.

The best idea was to let Dan Tucker ride along. Slocum knew the man was an expert tracker and had a good chance of riding along unseen by Frank, but he was out of town and might as well have been on the other side of the world.

"Lock me up, Sheriff," Slocum said. "And you go along with her."

"Can't rightly abrogate my official duty, Slocum." He rolled the word out like young Billy had "perturbed." This sparked an idea, a desperate one, but Slocum had nothing else.

Slocum pulled Marianne back into his arms and kissed her. She recoiled and tried to push away from such unseemly behavior in front of the sheriff. He held her tightly until Whitehill looked away in disgust. Then he whispered quickly what he wanted her to do.

"Billy? Why?" she whispered back.

"Get on out of here 'fore I change my mind," the sheriff said.

"Go on. Do it," Slocum urged. She gripped his arms fiercely, then gave him another kiss before fleeing the jailhouse.

"Inside, Slocum. Close the door and lock it," Whitehill called from his post behind his desk. Slocum did as he was ordered. "Now toss me the keys."

The sheriff caught them and added the key ring to the Colt Navy and other contents in his desk drawer.

"You ain't spinnin' a tall tale, are you, Slocum?"

"I wish I was," Slocum said, sinking down to the cot where Marianne had slept. He caught her scent on the pillow and blanket.

All he could do was lie back and wait.

Billy McCarty poked his head up to the barred window a bit after sundown. It didn't take Slocum long to explain what he wanted.

17

"Please tell me what to do, John," pleaded Marianne the next morning. "I don't know where any map is!" She brushed away tears as her stomach knotted. It wasn't fair! How could Jack have done this to her? Now she had to lie and cheat and maybe kill to get her son away from a man who had murdered at least twice.

"All you can do is meet Frank and convince him you're telling the truth."

"You don't think I can do it."

"If I thought I had any chance in hell of getting Randolph back, I wouldn't have swapped places with you." He clutched the iron bars that had held her the day before so tightly his knuckles turned white.

"I can shoot him. I can get a gun, and when he rides up, I can shoot him. In the arm or leg. Then I can threaten him until he tells me where Randolph is." Her resolve hardened. This wasn't much of a plan but it was better than none at all. Randolph wouldn't stay in the son of a bitch's grips one instant longer than necessary.

"Be careful trying that. You kill him, you'll never find your son."

"I can give him a fake map. I know how Jack wrote. Small, crabbed little letters nobody but him could read."

"Play for time—and ask for proof that Randolph's still alive," Slocum said.

"I need help, John. I'll get a gun and break you out so you can ride along. You stay out of sight until he shows his ugly face and—"

"Won't work, Marianne," said Sheriff Whitehill. He looked up from his desk. "I didn't let you out so you could spring Slocum. He's my guarantee you'll be back. Way I look at it, you both have done some killin'."

"She hasn't," Slocum said coldly. "Frank's the man you want, and you're letting her do your job for you."

"Evidence doesn't say that. It's your word that Frank confessed to you. No other witnesses, were there?"

As the two men argued, Marianne pressed herself against the cool adobe wall and tried to hold off a bout of hysteria. This wasn't like her. She prided herself on being calm and collected, but too much swirled about in her head for that fiction to last much longer.

A fake map was a good idea. It wouldn't take her long to make one. Getting a gun might be a bit harder, but not that much.

"Sheriff," she said. "Lend me Slocum's gun. It's not going to do him any good."

"Can't do that, Marianne. Folks might think I was helpin' you commit a murder if you up and kill Frank."

"I'll do more than kill him if he won't tell me where he's holding Randolph!"

"Now, Marianne," Whitehill said, "that kind of talk's what got you tossed in the jug before. Les Carstairs was a no-account, but too many in town heard you threaten him. If I had a lick of sense, you'd be in the cell again."

Marianne went numb. Thoughts refused to rise. Her usual

glib tongue was silenced. She left the jailhouse as if both feet were in pails of concrete. She scrounged about town until she found a scrap of paper caught against a wall in the morning breeze. It took another half hour to get a pen and ink to produce her fake treasure map. She drew lines at random and scribbled in directions that likely contradicted each other. The ink took a while to dry but she held the paper out in the wind and sun before folding it up and tucking it into her pocket.

Time forced her to hurry to the stables, where she took Slocum's pony and began the ride along the road south to Shakespeare, though she knew Frank wouldn't let her get that far. He would lie in wait along the road, let her pass, then see if anyone trailed her. An hour later, she realized with a sick feeling that she hadn't brought a pistol. Even her knife had been left behind. Sheriff Whitehill had it in his desk drawer, evidence of the Carstairs killing.

She wished she could appreciate the bright New Mexico day. The sky sported only a few wisps of snowy white clouds. The gentle breeze cooled her, and the road stretched invitingly. Oh, to keep riding! She could be down in the New Mexico boot heel and reach Mexico in a couple days.

But that didn't save Randolph. Thought of her captive son sparked her fiery temper again until she began making the pony uneasy with her grunts and occasional jerks of her knees and tugs on the reins.

To keep her anger in check, she began studying the road ahead for any sign of Frank. The shimmering heat hid anyone lurking beside the road. She concentrated so hard on what lay ahead that the sound of hoofbeats behind her came as a surprise. She craned around and her heart leaped into her throat.

Jim Frank.

He galloped up and then stopped suddenly a few yards behind her.

"Don't turn around," he called. "You got the papers?"

"Where's Randolph? You don't get anything until I'm sure you haven't hurt him."

"I'm holdin' the winnin' hand," he said. "You ever want to see your son again, you give me the papers or I ride off."

"How do I know I can trust you? You're a cold-blooded killer."

"And you're hot-blooded enough to kill a man. I saw the cut you put across Carstairs's gut. Another half inch and you'd have carved his innards out for him."

"I'll do the same to you if you hurt my son."

Frank laughed harshly, then quieted.

"I ain't got time for this. Hand it over."

Fuming, Marianne took out the fake map and held it over her head.

"You come and get it."

"I got a better idea. You dismount and put a rock on top of it, then you walk away so I can look it over. There's no call to trust you."

Marianne did as she was told, beginning to worry. Did Frank know what the map looked like? She could never hope to overtake him if he upped and rode away. Even if she did, how would she ever force him to release Randolph? Tears welled in her eyes, and she balled her hands into fists until she quaked with pent-up fury.

Frank dropped lightly to the ground, keeping a wary eye on her. He kicked away the rock and snared the fake map before it blew away. Holding it up, he frowned when he examined it closely.

"What are you tryin' to pull? This isn't the deed to the claim."

Marianne's mind raced. Frank hadn't wanted a map, he'd wanted the official claim—or Texas Jack's copy. The claims office had burned down and destroyed all the official records. Everything clicked in her head. Jack had gone to Santa Fe to file in the territorial capital. Frank had tried to get the deed from him and had killed him before he stole it.

But if Jack hadn't had it on him when he died, where was his copy of the deed?

"I'm not dumb enough to bring it," she said, lying fast. She needed to spin a yarn Frank would believe. "That's a map to where the deed is hidden. In a bitters jar. In the roots of an oak tree."

Frank looked at the map again, frowning.

"I can't make head nor tail outta this."

"Release Randolph, and I'll explain the map."

"I'll kill him. This is a trick!"

"No, no, you can't. Randolph even knows what that map means. He . . . Jack gave it to him when he rode off to Santa Fe. Randolph had hidden it, but I saw him." Marianne babbled and knew it. She clamped her mouth shut, took a deep breath, then said, "Randolph can tell you what it means. You ask him, then let him go."

"If he don't, he's dead." Frank swung into the saddle and galloped away, heading north.

Everything depended on how expertly she could track Frank. Marianne got onto the pony and set it after Frank, but riding without a saddle proved more difficult than she thought. Letting the pony walk didn't cause her any trouble staying on its back. Galloping caused her to slip and slide. As she slid backward, the horse slowed. By the time she got her seat again, Frank was out of sight.

She let out a cry of rage and frustration. Marianne rode as hard as she could to catch up with Frank, but the man might as well have been swallowed by the earth. An hour of futile searching convinced her she had to return to town. When Frank found out Randolph knew nothing about the map, he would come looking for her. In Silver City she might depend on the sheriff to stop Frank.

Or she could get Slocum out of the lockup. Even if she swapped places again in jail with him, he stood a better chance of freeing Randolph than she had. Tears running down her cheeks as she rode, she cursed herself for a fool thinking the fake map would trick Frank into releasing her son.

She should have brought a gun and shot him dead. Randolph might be dead already or killing Frank might doom him, but she would have had the satisfaction of putting a slug in the kidnapper's foul black heart.

"I tried, John, I really tried to follow him, but I fell off the horse. Why didn't you have a saddle for it?" Marianne fought back tears, sniffling a little.

It irritated her when he didn't answer but gave her an order she found repugnant.

"Tell the sheriff we want to switch places again. You come in and I'll leave."

"No! I have to find Randolph! I can't do that in a jail cell!" Outrage burned away her fear. She had expected more from John Slocum. After all, he was—

"Do it," he said coldly. "There's damned little time after Frank finds out the map's a fake."

"Randolph might stall him, but that's not going to get him free. I have to hunt for him."

"Frank is too good for that. He's clever, and he probably rode into a forest without leaving so much as a bent blade of grass under his horse's hooves. Let me out of here. Tell Whitehill."

"You have a plan?" Marianne barely dared to hope that Slocum did. She sniffed, then wiped her nose with a shaking hand. Her lace handkerchief had disappeared during her ride to free Randolph, and her clothing was a complete mess. Filthy, she needed a bath and a change of clothes.

"Tell the sheriff."

"Let me freshen up and—"

"Tell him!"

The command caused her to jump. Startled at his vehemence, she backed away and half turned to run. Cursing herself for such a reaction, Marianne hardened her resolve.

"Tell me what your plan is. If I don't like it, you can rot in hell for all I care. Getting Randolph back is all I want."

Slocum's face darkened as he leaned forward. She pressed herself back against the far wall if he reached through the bars to grab her. He might try to hold her hostage to force Whitehill to let them both go, but even as that notion came to her, it died. The sheriff might be a bit sweet on her, but he would never allow them both to go. He knew as long as he held one of them, the other would return.

And he was right, Marianne admitted. She might get mad at Slocum, but she wouldn't leave him. Unless saving her son required it.

"Someone trailed you, then waited for Frank to leave you behind. If he's half as good as he claims, he found where Frank is holed up."

"Is Randolph there? Can we get him free?"

"I don't know because I'm in the cell."

"Who is it? The deputy friend of yours? I'll find out and—"

"It wasn't Tucker. He's still out of town. You'll never see Randolph again if you don't get me out of here so I can rescue him."

Dizziness hit her like a blow to the head. She swayed as she wrestled with all the implications of what Slocum said. He had always been truthful with her. Never once had she caught him in a lie, except possibly by omission. The way he had ridden off in Georgia without so much as a fare-thee-well had always cut her to the quick. Even with the Federals calling out their soldiers to hunt him down for killing that carpetbagger judge, he could have stopped on his way west.

What would she have told him if he had? The chance he would have let her ride with him was slim, but he might have. They could have been together all these years.

"I . . ." Marianne stood a little straighter, then called out, "Sheriff, let him out. I'll take his place."

Sheriff Whitehill ambled over, swinging the key ring on

his trigger finger. He looked at her hard, never once glancing at Slocum.

"Now that's what I call a surprise. I thought he was more of a gentleman and would let you stay free, on his bond, so to speak."

"I know you'd prefer me as your overnight guest," Marianne said. She tried not to laugh when she saw the flicker of expression on his face. He *was* sweet on her.

"Into the cell closest to the front," he said. "I ain't lettin' you both out of a cell at the same time."

"Afraid I might overpower you, Sheriff?" she teased.

Again he reacted as if he had a letch for her. Seeing this made her wonder how she could turn it to her benefit. So far, he had been hard-nosed about helping Randolph. As she entered the cell, she brushed past him, touching just enough to let him know she was there.

"The only thing overpowerin' is your smell," he said. "You're sore in need of a bath."

"You're such a charmer, Harvey," she said as he locked the door behind her. He acted gruff, but the flicker in his eyes and a small twitch of a smile told her using his first name had been the right thing to do.

"All right, Slocum. You can go for now. Same as before. You don't leave town."

"Look at it as saving the county some money," she said. "If you only have one prisoner, you only have to feed one of us."

"The slop I get from the restaurant's gonna get tossed to the hogs otherwise. Don't cost the taxpayers nuthin'."

"I thought the food was pretty decent," she said. She looked past the sheriff at Slocum, who now stood free of his cell.

"Sometimes they get the order confused with real food," Whitehill said. Now she knew for a fact he wanted her, just a bit. He paid for her meals rather than relying on whatever leftovers might come his way from the restaurant for

prisoners. Maybe not Slocum's, but he gave her better vict-
uals than something being fed to the pigs.

"I'm going, Sheriff," Slocum said. "Let me get my gun."

Whitehill nodded, then headed for his desk to pull the
six-shooter from the drawer. For a moment Marianne and
Slocum were alone, face to face.

He said, "Don't worry."

Barely daring to speak the words, she said, "Rescue
my son."

Then Slocum retrieved his sidearm and disappeared
through the door into the street. Never had she felt more
hopeless, more helpless. She had to depend on a man who
had been locked up and someone else she didn't even know
to save her Randolph.

18

Slocum hoped to hell he wasn't signing Randolph's death warrant. He looked around but failed to find the face he sought. Walking fast, he went to the stables and peered in. Marianne had left the pony in a stall. Patting his pockets, he found a few small coins in his vest pocket. No one in Silver City was going to sell him a saddle for the few coins he had.

Before the stableman could stop him to take the pitiful amount of money he had for stabling and feeding the horse, Slocum led the pony out and vaulted onto its back. The pony sagged under his weight. It had gotten used to the much lighter Marianne astride it, but the pony righted itself, got its legs under it, and let Slocum trot it from town, heading south along the road Frank had used as a rendezvous.

"Mr. Slocum! Hey, Slocum!"

He perked up when he saw a distant figure waving frantically. Putting his heels to the horse's flanks, he galloped away from the road toward the draw where Billy McCarty waved to him.

"Did you find him?" Slocum's question collided with the

boy's frantic statement. He held up his hand to stop the verbal flood. "Did you find where Frank has Randolph?"

"I did, I did, Mr. Slocum. I done just like you tole me. I kept way back as Miz Lomax rode the trail, then hid so Frank'd never see me. He took a piece o' paper from her, then I waited 'til he rode past me. Followin' him was hard, damned hard, but I did it. Just like you told me. You're quite a trailsman, knowin' tricks like that."

"You know them now, too," Slocum said. "Is Randolph alive?"

"Yeah, he's all trussed up. I was gonna rescue him, but Frank never left. He played with that six-gun of his, spinnin' the cylinder 'round and threatenin' Randolph. I'd have kilt him if I could but you was right about how to track him, so I figgered you was right about me not takin' him."

"We'll do it together," Slocum said, his mind racing. "You've done good, real good."

"This way."

"Not so fast. Did you ride straight here?"

"Like a bee headin' to its hive."

"We'll take a more roundabout trail back. If Frank spots your tracks, he might run smack into us. Or lay an ambush."

"You're all the time thinkin'," Billy said. "That's good. I need to be more like you." He fell silent as they rode for a few minutes, then said, "How many men have you killed?"

"Too many. Maybe one too many." He couldn't help thinking his life would have been different if he hadn't plugged a crooked judge and his gunman. If he'd stayed in Georgia, he'd likely have married up with Marianne. They had certainly been moving in that direction when the war intervened. Once he'd come home, they had picked up where they'd left off, only sharing more adult pursuits.

If he hadn't killed the judge . . .

"What's it like?" Billy sounded way too eager for Slocum.

"It chews away at your soul, gives you nightmares.

I killed enough soldiers during the war to last me a lifetime. Since then, more."

"But you have killed a lot more? They all needed killin', didn't they?"

"I believe so. It doesn't let me sleep any better, even knowing that," Slocum said.

Billy muttered to himself and finally said, "I'm not gonna kill no one what doesn't deserve it either."

"We get to Frank's hideout, you let me do what's necessary. I'll drag that snake all the way back to Silver City behind his own horse so the sheriff can throw him in jail."

"That's mighty fine," Billy said. "Better than killin' him outright. Let him suffer."

"Let him think about ending up in Yuma Penitentiary to pay for all he's done."

"Or hang 'im. I never seen a hangin'. I'd like to see one."

"What happened to your ma and pa?"

"Ma died of consumption not so long back. She's buried outside of town, not far from Mr. Olney's undertakin' parlor. I found her. She'd died in bed over the night, coughin' up a whole lot of blood. Didn't bother me much, seein' so much blood."

Slocum looked hard at the boy, but Billy's head was turned away.

"Where was your pa?"

"Gone. He upped and lit out a year earlier, prospectin' or doin' somethin' like that. It'd been me and ma and—" Billy drew rein and put his finger to his lips, then pointed ahead.

Slocum spotted the curl of smoke rising above the trees before he caught the scent of burning pine. The wall of trees cut off direct view of what had to be a cabin.

"He has his horse 'round back. You go in the front, gun blazin', and I'll steal his horse," Billy said. He looked guiltily at Slocum and added, "For Randolph. He'll need to ride somethin'."

"Stay here," Slocum said, for the first time wondering where Billy had found the horse he rode. The boy was a tad too bloodthirsty for his liking. Slocum would have no problem filling Frank with all six rounds from his Colt Navy, but he didn't intend killing the red-haired man unless he had to.

Slocum approached the side of the cabin. Billy had been right about the horse tethered behind the cabin. Frank was inside—or around somewhere. Rushing in would likely get someone killed, and Slocum didn't want that to be him or Randolph. He crouched and waited to see if Frank was inside the cabin. After five minutes, he heard a twig snap behind him.

"I told you to stay where you were, Billy," he said in a hoarse whisper.

The sound of metal sliding across leather caused him to react instinctively. Slocum drove forward as hard as he could, his toes digging down into the soft dirt. A slug ripped through the air just above him. He hit the ground, rolled onto his back, and dragged his six-shooter out. All he saw was a branch swaying back and forth where someone had retreated.

He found himself tossed on the horns of a dilemma. The question of Frank's location had been decided. He'd crashed around out in the woods and had just failed to back-shoot an inattentive prowler. Slocum didn't much care if Frank knew who had been spying on the cabin. Dead was dead, no matter if the shooter knew the identity of his target.

New worry popped up as Slocum realized Billy might be in danger. He owed the boy for finding Frank, and abandoning him now would be as serious as neglecting Randolph. But Marianne's son might be all trussed up inside the cabin. Slocum found himself torn between entering the cabin to find Randolph, being certain of Billy's safety, and tracking down the man who had just ambushed him. He was sure it had been Frank—or mostly sure. Not getting a look at the shooter caused him to worry that Frank had a partner.

Slocum swung around and studied the front of the cabin for any sign of someone coming out to join the fight. Getting caught between Frank on one side and a possible partner on the other gave a quick path to that cemetery just down the road from Rafe Olney's undertaker's parlor. More likely, his dead body would be left for the scavengers, and nobody would ever think about him again.

When he heard brush rustling to his left, he took a quick look right and behind, then drew a bead on the spot where a man had to come through the thorny undergrowth. His finger tensed, then slid off the trigger when he spotted Billy.

"Get down. Someone's out here and took a potshot at me."

"I tried to get a look 'cuz I wanted to help." Billy drew a knife and flourished it.

"Get down," Slocum shouted. He caught movement out of the corner of his eye and got off two quick shots.

One of his slugs tore away at the cabin door. The other sailed into the crack between door and jamb, ruining the rifleman's aim. The Winchester pointing from the cabin bucked, but the slug went high. If Slocum hadn't fired first, Billy McCarty would have been carrying an extra bit of weight in his chest.

"Thanks, Mr. Slocum. You saved me for sure." Billy was flushed but not from fear.

Slocum had seen men in battle. Most were scared shitless. Others were stoic. A few, a very few, yearned for combat. They lived for bullets singing past them—and sending death back to those they faced. Billy showed no fear, only excitement. He made stabbing motions with his knife, as if he could reach across the dozen yards between him and the gunman in the cabin.

"Watch my back. There's two of them. You ever see Frank with a partner?"

"Not in town. Only partner he ever threw in with was Texas Jack."

"He's got another one now. Good thing he got buck fever and shot too soon or he'd have drilled me in the back," Slocum said, eyes fixed on the cabin.

"Ain't no windows. Just the one door," Billy said. "I scouted it real good when I saw this was where Frank came."

Slocum nodded once, motioned for Billy to move around and take cover on the far side of the cabin. That way, if it was Frank inside, he would have to open the door almost all the way and expose himself to get another shot at Billy. While Billy was moving around, Slocum crept closer. The hair on the back of his neck stood on end. Every sound behind him sent an electric thrill into him. His best way of flushing Frank from the cabin was to get onto the roof.

Billy waved, giving away his position. Slocum shook his head. The boy had a lot to learn, if he lived long enough. With his six-shooter leveled and ready if the door opened again, Slocum edged closer until he pressed against the side of the cabin.

He holstered his Colt, found a handhold on the side of the cabin, and scaled the wall. Flopping belly down on the sloping roof, Slocum inched toward the chimney, where the smoke billowed up. For there to be so much smoke, Frank must have been fixing a meal.

Slocum stood and used the stone chimney as a shield as he took a quick look around the treed area nearest the cabin, hunting for the gunman who had tried to back-shoot him. He whipped out his pistol and steadied it against the rock chimney when he saw a flash of brown about the color of a miner's canvas pants. He squeezed off a round for effect, watched as the bushes began rustling to the left of where his slug had gone. Moving in a smooth arc, he fired to the right. Slocum was savvy enough to recognize a feint.

He heard a loud yelp. He fired twice more but had no sense he had hit the lurking gunman. The cry before had been from surprise, not pain. Slocum had come close, but he had missed. Not by much, but he had missed. As he watched, the brush stopped moving. Straining, he heard heavy footfalls going away.

Frank's partner—or maybe Frank—had decided to cut and run.

Slocum took time to reload, then turned his attention to the chimney and the clouds of wood smoke reaching for the sky. He skinned out of his coat, wadded it up, and stuffed it down a foot to cut off the smoke. Satisfied he had plugged the chimney, Slocum slipped and slid back to a spot at the front of the roof where he could get a decent shot at Frank.

The way he figured it would occur was simple. When Frank started choking on the smoke in a cabin with no windows, he had to come out the front. As he did, Slocum would get the drop on him. Frank was nobody's fool, so he would come out with Randolph as a shield. That made the shot a bit trickier for Slocum, but not impossible. He intended to remove Frank entirely for all he had done to Randolph—and to Marianne.

Choking smoke began seeping from around the door, but Frank didn't come rushing out. Slocum tensed as he heard movement inside the cabin. Somebody coughed. Frank? Then came a second hacking sound joining the first. One of them had to be Randolph Lomax.

Slocum's grip grew sweaty on the ebony handle of his six-gun. The smoke oozed greasy wisps through the roof, out the sides of the cabin.

"Come on out, Frank. Come out and I won't kill you!" Slocum began to worry Frank had passed out from the smoke. His mind raced as he considered what he had to do if this proved the case.

Letting Randolph choke to death wasn't in the cards.

He looked out to see if Billy stood his ground. The damn fool kid waved to let him know all was well.

The smoke coming through cracks in the roof around Slocum reached the level where he couldn't breathe. Inside the cabin had to be impossible.

Slocum waved back to Billy, then dangled his legs over the edge of the roof, turned, gripped the edge of the roof, and dropped. He sank to a crouch, dragging out his pistol. Duck-walking over to the door, he tugged it open a few inches and received a gale of smoke that forced him to look away for a moment. His eyes watered and blurred. In spite of himself, he coughed so hard that he bent double. If Frank had rushed out at that instant, he would have found himself an easy target in the debilitated Slocum.

"Come out, Frank! You can't get away."

Scrapping sounds from inside warned him Frank readied himself for an escape. But when nothing happened, Slocum threw open the door. The billows coming out forced him to look away involuntarily. So much rushed outward that Slocum wondered if Frank had stoked the fire in the fireplace rather than trying to put it out.

Why would he do that if he didn't intend using it to cover an escape attempt?

When the smoke continued to gust out, Slocum knew what had to be done. He pulled up his bandanna so it covered his nose and mouth, wishing he had a bucket of water to soak the cloth first. Squinting hard, he peered around the door jamb. A dark figure slumped in a chair by the fireplace. Slocum tried to locate a second man and couldn't.

He sucked in a deep breath, whipped around the corner, and flopped onto the dirt floor, pistol aimed. The fresh air following him in created an island of better visibility for a split second.

"Randolph!" Marianne's son had been tied to the chair. Slocum couldn't see any movement, even of the boy's chest rising and falling. More than one man had died in a fire, not from the flames but from suffocation.

Slocum wiggled over, grabbed the chair leg with his left hand, and pulled it toward him. Randolph stirred, then choked and began retching.

"Where's Frank?" Slocum tried to get the boy to respond. When Randolph did nothing more than cough in the fresher air, Slocum yanked harder on the chair and scooted it toward the door and fresh air.

He sat up and swung his pistol around, hunting for Frank. The man was nowhere to be seen in the smoke-cloaked room. Deciding quickly, Slocum threw his arms around Randolph and lifted the boy, still tied to the chair, and staggered to the door. With a heave, he tossed him a couple yards. The chair landed on one leg and broke.

"Tend him," Slocum yelled to Billy. The boy had already rushed out to cut his friend free.

Rather than plunging back into the smoke-filled cabin to find Frank, Slocum kicked the door shut. Let it fill, let it kill a man who had murdered two and kidnapped a boy.

Slocum went to where Billy held a convulsing Randolph.

"Breathe out real hard," Slocum ordered. When Randolph only tried to gasp in short breaths, he punched him in the belly.

Billy reacted, his knife coming around.

"Stop that! You can't beat up on him when he cain't defend himself."

"He has to get the smoke out of his lungs," Slocum said to Billy. "Exhale hard, suck in shallow," he told Randolph.

It took a dozen breaths before Randolph began to get color back into his cheeks. His bloodshot eyes opened. His emerald eyes fixed on Slocum.

"You saved me."

"Was it Frank in there with you?"

Randolph nodded, coughed, then worked to clear his throat and lungs the way Slocum had told him.

The boy finally got out, "He went crazy when the smoke started fillin' the cabin. Don't know why he done that."

Slocum didn't either. He stood and surveyed the area, hunting for Frank's partner. Frank must have died inside the cabin, but Slocum was willing to drag his partner back for Sheriff Whitehill to throw into the calaboose.

"You see anyone else with Frank?"

"I heard him talk with somebody outside. Never saw who. They argued over what to do with me. Frank wanted to kill me when I couldn't tell him nuthin' 'bout some dumb map. The other guy wanted to torture me." Randolph coughed again.

Slocum motioned for Billy to get his friend out of the way. He waited for them to reach cover before walking back to the cabin. Getting back to the roof, he plucked his coat from the chimney, releasing a huge gout of smoke. But the open door and the draw up the chimney quickly sucked out the smoke from inside.

Jumping back to the ground, Slocum cautiously went to the cabin door and pushed it all the way open with his six-shooter's barrel.

"You still alive, Frank? You have five seconds to surrender before I come in to get you." He hoped Frank didn't give up. He itched for a reason to shoot the man.

A quick look into the cabin showed how most of the smoke had gathered up near the roof. Slocum looked low. If Frank had been breathing at all, it had to be near the floor where the air wasn't as smoky.

"Damnation," he cried, spinning around and running to the far side of the cabin where a horse had been tethered.

The horse was gone. At ankle level several rough-hewn logs had been pushed away. When Frank had noticed the cabin filling with smoke, he had stoked the fire, then kicked out the lower part of the back wall and escaped on horseback. Slocum had missed the getaway entirely in his rush to save Randolph.

"Where'd the varmint git off to?" Billy asked. He slashed the air with his knife. "I wanted to cut off a piece of 'im. An important piece. Or two."

Slocum slammed his six-gun into his holster, angry at himself for letting not only Frank but Frank's partner get clean away.

"Let's get Randolph back to his ma."

The ride to Silver City stretched for an eternity, Slocum stewing and Billy and Randolph chattering like magpies, working on their tall-tale-telling skills.

19

"If I'd knowed it was gonna be like *that*, I'da left him out there," William McCarty said in disgust. He turned away from where Marianne hugged Randolph so tightly that the boy moaned in consternation at such public affection.

"His ribs are likely sore," Slocum said, but Marianne paid him no heed. She had her son back and nothing else mattered.

"I can always stick her back in the cell," the sheriff said. "I agree with Billy. This is more 'n I can stand." He inclined his head and both Slocum and Billy left the jailhouse, leaving mother and son alone.

"All right, you two, tell me what happened out there," the sheriff said, finding a spot in the shade and sitting down. Slocum heard the man's joints popping and cracking. If he had to stand fast, he wouldn't be able to do it because of the arthritis.

This set off a new line of conjecture. If Slocum signaled to Marianne and Randolph to run, the sheriff would be left in the dust. As appealing as that was, to simply get the both of them out of Silver City and on the road to somewhere else—anywhere else—he wouldn't do it. He had come to a grudging respect for Whitehill.

Billy looked at Slocum, licked his lips, and kept quiet. For once, politeness dictated. He'd let his elders talk first. Slocum almost wished he had blurted everything out. His mouth had sores from too little water out on the trail. Returning had been his primary goal. He had turned a mite nervous knowing both Frank and his partner had gotten away. If he saw Frank, he'd know what to do. His partner remained a mystery and could be anyone.

"You start, Billy, while I get me a dipper of water," Slocum said. He wanted to step back as the verbal dam broke and everything rushed out.

He found a watering trough with enough water in it to give him a drink and to wash the trail dust from his face. He slapped his hat against his thigh a few times and cleaned himself up before returning. Billy had about finished with the recitation.

"Do I have this straight, Slocum? Billy here did ever'thin' he said he did?"

Billy looked defiant, daring Slocum to contradict him.

"That's the gospel truth, Sheriff," he said.

"I don't know if I ought to give you a medal or clap you in jail for bein' such a menace, William McCarty," the marshal said sternly. "That was a brave thing you did, ridin' after Frank and scoutin' for Slocum here."

"You had him locked up. Somebody had to save Randolph." The defiance marking the boy's words would get him in trouble someday, but this wasn't it.

The sheriff clapped him on the shoulder and said, "You done good. When you're older, might be I'll need a deputy."

Billy looked skeptical but accepted the compliment without adding his opinion.

"Don't suppose it'd do any good to ask who's been out of town," Slocum said. "Frank's partner is likely someone from Silver City known to you."

"Hell, even Tucker has been out of town. I'm expectin' him back any time now. No, people go and come in Silver City all the time. Besides, Frank's partner is likely to be a miner. Him and Bedrich knew most all them hard rock–scratchin' bastards. For a dollar and a drink, there's not a man out there in Chloride Flats who wouldn't kill his own granny."

"I don't cotton much to looking over my shoulder all the time I'm in Silver City," Slocum said.

"Well, Slocum, I can solve that problem for you. Let me lock you up. Marianne looks to want time with her son."

"Let 'em both go, Sheriff," Billy piped up. "They ain't gonna run. Give your word, Mr. Slocum, and Sheriff White-hill will let you both out."

Slocum watched the sheriff's reaction and stiffened a mite when the boy's suggestion produced a slow nod. He knew when to speak and when to keep his yap shut. He waited for the sheriff to come to a decision.

"She's been through hell, that I'll guarantee," Whitehill said. He looked up at Slocum. "You done good brining' her boy back, too. But you both got murder charges hangin' over your head."

"Billy will watch us. He's gotten real good at that," Slocum said.

This produced a genuine laugh from the sheriff. He awkwardly climbed to his feet, reminding Slocum of his earlier fleeting scheme to simply walk away. As painful as White-hill's joints appeared, it might be a day before he could get limber enough to mount and chase after them.

"I'm gonna do that very thing. You watch 'em like a hawk, Billy, and if either of 'em tries to leave town, you come tell me straightaway."

"You pay me to be a deputy?" Billy asked.

Again the sheriff surprised Slocum with his reaction. Most lawmen would have blustered and bellowed. Whitehill dug around in his vest pocket and pulled out a nickel.

"This ought to do 'til I get one or both of 'em locked up again."

Slocum didn't listen to any more of the discussion between urchin and lawman. Marianne came from the jailhouse, her arm around Randolph's shoulders. The boy looked like a frightened fawn wanting to bolt and run. He was at an age where having his mother cling so tightly to him would cause taunts for a month. Luckily no one his own age other than Billy saw.

"You two go on," Marianne said to empty air. Randolph and Billy ran off, Billy showing his friend the money he'd gotten from the sheriff.

"He convinced me to let you out, Marianne. You're not free, just not in a cell."

"John, thank you!"

"Not me," Slocum said. "Billy."

Marianne laughed at this, then obviously wondered how true it might be from the way the sheriff nodded.

"I can certainly use a bath," she said. "And maybe a drink."

Whitehill clucked his tongue at that, returning to his jailhouse without a word of approbation that a proper woman publicly spoke of alcohol in such a way.

"It was you that got me free, wasn't it, John?" She slipped her arm through his and steered him from the jailhouse.

"I did what I could, but it *was* Billy that turned the tide."

"Do tell. That boy's going to make a fine lawyer someday."

"Or get himself killed," Slocum said, explaining how the boy had been instrumental in finding and rescuing Randolph.

"You serious about another bath?" Slocum asked, slowing when they passed the barber shop. "Looks like a passel of customers wanting shaves."

"A bath isn't what I want," she said, pulling him closer so her hip bumped his. She contrived to rub against him like a cat greeting a long-lost friend. Her fingers stroked over his forearm.

"What is?" Slocum asked, wanting the same as Marianne but inclined to make her ask.

"What we did before, without the bath."

"Do tell. My memory is a bit hazy," he said. "What might that have been?"

"Do I have to remind you?" She grinned wickedly now.

"Won't do any good unless you show me."

"You were a good enough student in school."

"There were lessons Miss Demetrius could never teach me."

"She was as ugly as a mud fence," Marianne said, leaning closer and putting her head against his upper arm.

"She was as ugly as you are beautiful," Slocum said softly.

"I don't know, she was mighty ugly."

"You're mighty beautiful." Slocum didn't care that they were just off the main street and still in plain view of anyone passing by. He kissed her.

She returned the kiss with ardor. They wrapped their arms around each other and kissed, and time stood still until Marianne broke it off, breathing heavily. He loved the way her breasts rose and fell so fetchingly. Truth was, he loved most everything about her.

"You smell of smoke. We've got to get you out of those clothes."

"And you smell wonderful," he said, burying his nose in her hair. She did. In spite of being locked up for days, her hair carried a faint whiff of violet that sent his heart pounding. Or was it more?

Her body pressing into his accelerated his heart, as did the way her fingers danced over his vest, his shirt, undoing a button here and lingering there to stroke over bare flesh as she probed under his shirt and across his chest. He gasped when she became even bolder and pressed her palm into his crotch.

"It's getting mighty hot in there," she said.

"I can think of somewhere that might just be even hotter—and wetter." He ran his hand down the front of her blouse, pressed into her belly, and worked lower slowly until he could finger her privates through the folds of cloth. "I'm right. You're wet." He nibbled at her ear and whispered, "and hot."

"We have to get off the street, John, or the sheriff will arrest us for indecency."

He looked around and said, "I reckon I'll have to take you to the woodpile."

Several cords of wood had been stacked behind the bakery. The mouth-watering scent of baking bread mingled with sweat and dirt and the exquisite violet in Marianne's hair.

"Are you going to . . . punish me for being a bad girl?"

"Depends," he said. "It wouldn't do any good to spank you through all those layers of clothes you're wearing."

Both of them stared into the other's eyes, then silently rushed to the high stacks of wood. Between two cords was a yard-wide space. If they stayed low and no one walked around the ends of the woodpile, they wouldn't be seen.

Marianne went to the middle of the stacks and began hiking her skirts, showing her ankles, her calves, then more slowly revealing her knees and thighs. When she saw the effect it had on him, she moved even more slowly to reveal she didn't have on any underwear.

Seeing this made Slocum want to erupt. He hung up his gun belt and worked to unfasten the buttons in his fly. He gasped in relief as his erection popped free, but his target had disappeared. Marianne turned slowly, giving him a view of her hip and then the flare of her bare ass cheeks. She bent forward as she lifted her skirts to moon him.

"I'm a *very* bad girl," she said, her voice husky. "What are you going to do about that?"

He stepped forward, half turned, and landed an open-handed swat on her exposed butt. The sound echoed, then was drowned out by her sob.

"That stung," she said. "But I'm not feeling like a good girl yet."

He began spanking her with his open hand, slowly, leaving a red outline of his hand on her snowy white rump. Her knees sagged and then she dropped to hands and knees. He had to hike up her skirt to keep her well-spanked bottom in view.

"I'm on fire, John. All over. On fire. Stoke my fire, I need you to—oh!"

He dropped to his knees behind her, ran one arm around her waist, and pulled her back into the circle of his groin. His meaty shaft parted the rosy ass cheeks and found the dampness leaking from within. He poked a little harder, got the tip just between her pinkly scalloped sex lips, and then arched his back. He could have rammed as hard into her as he wanted. He chose to enter slowly, inch by torturous inch. By the time he was buried balls deep, she quaked in reaction.

"Oh, you're filling me up so much," she said, shuddering with every jerk of his hidden organ.

He pulled her back firmly into the curve of his body and then groped about until he found where he disappeared into her center. His fingers came away oily. He smeared this all around as he explored until he found the tiny bud growing at the top of the nether lips. He pressed his finger into the fleshy button. Marianne cried out and half stood as orgasm crashed through her.

As she settled down, Slocum began to move with methodical strokes, long, deep ones that built the woman's desires to the breaking point again. He tugged gently at the dangling tits, moved his hands around, hunting for new places to excite her. He found one on her hip. Then he reared back and landed another open-handed swat on her curvy rump.

"More, John, do it more. I want you to spank me more!"

He did. His hand turned warm from the spanking. Then more as his hand burned when he felt her constricting around his buried manhood. She sobbed and moaned, then called out his name as she squeezed down all around him. This pushed him to the limits of his endurance. It was as if hidden fingers stroked over him, silky, delicate ones milking him. He began thrusting with more determination.

He had to use both hands to hang on to her hips as she bucked and thrashed about. Then they fell into a motion that drove him wild. She slammed back as he raced forward. Then she rotated her hips in one direction as he circled in the other. The coupled motions robbed him finally of all control, and he spent. He grunted as the warmth in his groin spread throughout his belly and body and exploded in his head.

Finally done, he rocked back to about the sweetest sight ever. She had stayed with her butt up in the air. His red handprints still glowed dully. She waggled her ass a little to tease him, then agilely swung about and sat facing him.

She lifted slightly and rubbed her behind.

"You ever a schoolteacher? You surely do know how to deliver a swat."

"I was inspired," he said, rubbing his hands together. The right palm still tingled from the contact with her snowy white ass flesh.

Marianne sighed, then said, "Thank you. Oh, not for this. This was incredible. Thanks for saving Randolph. That boy knows how to get himself into trouble."

"It wasn't his fault. He was working at the Lonely Cuss when Frank nabbed him."

"What do you mean?" Marianne looked worried.

"The owner's brother gave him a job sweeping up. Randolph was in the back room when Frank spotted him, I reckon, and decided to get Bedrich's map in exchange."

"Tom Gallifrey's brother?"

"Big galoot. Fat as your boss is skinny."

"I don't know him. Tom never mentioned a brother."

"Said he'd come in from Mesilla because his brother'd

asked for help. Without you to charm the customers, the Lonely Cuss is likely losing money every night it's open."

"Not the most prosperous saloon in town, that's for sure." Marianne smiled wickedly. "Except the nights I work. Then the miners are packed in there for some reason." She pushed up her breasts, released them, and let them bob about.

"Yeah, no idea why the miners flock in the nights you work."

Marianne turned dour.

"I need to check with Tom to see if I still have a job. Being locked up or out gallivanting around trying to trap Frank has made me miss a couple nights."

"You wouldn't have to work if Bedrich had given you the map to his claim. From all that Frank said, it might be more than a map he's looking for. Did Bedrich record the deed?"

"The claims office burned down," Marianne said. "But if Jack had his copy of the claim, all duly signed, it would tell where the strike was." She shook her head. "The son of a bitch never gave me anything."

"Frank thought he had it on him when he went to Santa Fe."

"To record the claim with the territorial claims office?"

Slocum agreed. But Texas Jack had either hidden the deed or lost it before Frank ambushed him. Bedrich's body had been searched after it came out of the ice block. With everyone still willing to kidnap and kill, that deed was proving elusive to find.

"I'd better change clothes. And get a real bath," Marianne said. "You could do with following my lead."

"Not what I want to follow of yours," Slocum said.

They laughed. Slocum stood, helped her to her feet, and gave her a satisfying kiss. Then they made sure they were presentable before stepping out from between the stacks of wood. Slocum looked around. Nobody had any idea what had gone on there. That suited him just fine. Marianne's reputation as a harlot was firmly established among those in Silver City. She had to rehabilitate herself. Working in the Lonely Cuss might not be the most respectable job in town, but it was better than being a soiled dove.

Keeping a respectable distance, they went back to the hotel. Marianne paused on the front steps, finally saying softly, "Any way you could sneak up to my room? There's a real bed there."

"There you are," came Mrs. Gruhlkey's shrill voice. "Where is he?"

Marianne rolled her eyes, then turned, her smile benign as she faced the hotel proprietress.

"Who do you mean, Mrs. Gruhlkey?"

"That boy William, that's who. I give him a free room in exchange for chores. He's nowhere to be found, and I need him to clean out the back storeroom right now. Immediately!"

"I have trouble enough keeping up with my own son," she said.

"Well, that's why I asked you. They've gone off together. Find Randolph, find William."

"I'll look for them, Mrs. Gruhlkey. They have to be somewhere. We saw them only a few minutes ago."

"A half hour," Slocum corrected. "I'll look, too."

"If I don't get that room cleaned out by sundown, he's fired!" Mrs. Gruhlkey left in a swirl and hiss of floor-length skirts.

"We were that long? It seemed over so fast," Marianne said softly, looking up at Slocum.

"If she hunted in the hotel, you can bet Billy and Randolph aren't there. I'll ask around. You do the same."

"Very well, John. We can meet back here in a few minutes." She sucked in a deep breath, held it, then let it out in a quick gust that set her breasts bobbing again. "I know Randolph's hiding places. I'll check there first."

Slocum forced his attention back to the chore at hand and away from the delicious sight of the woman's teats. Even encased in a blouse and layers of other material, they captivated him. The idea of sneaking into her room without Mrs. Gruhlkey noticing recommended itself to him more and more.

After he found the boys.

Two hours of searching failed to turn up either Randolph or Billy.

20

"I declare, I've never seen a woman less able to keep her own affairs in order," Sheriff Whitehill said, shaking his head. He worked the tips of his mustache into sharp points, only to have them fluff back out when he quit twirling. "Tell me what you know. Not the guesses, the facts."

Slocum thought Marianne was going to explode. He put his hand on her shoulder, but she angrily shrugged it off, leaned forward, both hands on the sheriff's desk, and moved until her face was only inches from his. Slocum had to give this much to Whitehill. He didn't budge an inch or even blink.

"They were last seen over at the Lonely Cuss. Nobody's spotted either Randolph or Billy since an hour before sundown."

"No way to track them in the dark," Whitehill said, "assumin' there's somewhere to track 'em to. What's your opinion on this affair, Slocum?"

"Randolph was talking with a couple miners. Nobody's seen any of them since the miners left town."

"Now that's peculiar," Whitehill said. "Miners come to

town to whoop and holler and get drunk. Why'd they leave 'fore they got a chance to do any of that?"

"Randolph had a job sweeping up at the saloon," Slocum said. "That might be why they went to the Lonely Cuss. Randolph was overheard saying he needed a lot of money for something." Slocum didn't miss the sudden furtiveness in the sheriff's eyes. Marianne did.

"Find them, Sheriff. That's your job," she demanded.

"Go on back to the hotel, Marianne," Whitehill said. The uneasiness in his voice further alerted Slocum to something being wrong.

"Not until you *do* something. Find them!"

"Go on. I'll be along in a few minutes," Slocum said. He took her arm. She tried to pull free, but his fingers dug in cruelly, getting her attention. She started to turn her wrath on him, then subsided.

She left the jail without another word. Slocum waited until she had gotten out of earshot before accosting the sheriff.

"What'd you tell the boy? Why'd he need so much money?"

"Well, it's like this, Slocum. I didn't actually promise him I'd release his ma for good, but I mentioned bail money. He might have misconstrued what I said."

"So Randolph thought giving you the bail money would free his ma for good?"

"Might have gotten that idea. Didn't intend it to come out the way it did." Whitehill looked away, pointedly avoiding Slocum's cold glare.

"How much? How much did you tell him his ma's bail was?"

"A hunnerd dollars."

Slocum's mind raced. How could a young boy ever hope to raise that much money? Legally? Or had he listened to Billy? That boy's imagination knew no bounds. While Billy had never hinted at larceny, he had shown a mighty big curiosity about killing and what it felt like. Slocum had heard men talk like that before, and they'd all ended up in shallow graves.

Randolph and Billy might have cooked up some scheme that would get them both planted six feet under.

"When's Tucker getting back to town?"

"Eh? Dan? I can't rightly say. Might be sometime tomorrow. But you can't go orderin' him about like he was your deputy, Slocum."

"One of you can stay in town. The other can hit the trail as we track down the boys," Slocum said.

"Now, you listen to me," Whitehill said, getting his dander up finally. "I'm in charge here. I say who rides where. You and Marianne are out of this here jail because *I* said so. For two cents, I'll clap the both of you back in."

"No, you won't," Slocum said. The menace in his voice caused Whitehill to harden and reach for his six-shooter on the desk. "Don't think about trying that, Sheriff. You won't like the way it turns out."

Whitehill froze.

"It might be that Marianne and I leave town for a while. It's to fetch back Randolph, wherever he went. You won't come after us or send Dangerous Dan either, because we'll be back when Randolph's safe."

Slocum turned his back and felt the sheriff measuring him for a shroud. One quick grab of that hogleg on the desk, a close-by shot, and Slocum would be dead on the floor. He walked through the door into the night without taking a .44 slug in his spine. Judging Whitehill meant less to him right now than finding the boy.

Cursing all the way to the hotel, he stopped on the steps and saw Marianne in the sitting room, swaying back and forth furiously in a rocking chair. Rather than go in since he had nothing to tell her yet, he headed for the Lonely Cuss Saloon. The crowd was sparse. Tom Gallifrey's brother worked the bar, idly swiping at the shot glasses and mugs, stacking them in curious piles, then starting all over with the time-killing construction.

Slocum went directly to the bar, leaned over, and grabbed the corpulent man by the front of his shirt. A hard yank sprawled him half over the bar.

"Who was with the boys? Randolph and Billy Mc-Carty? Who?"

The man sputtered.

"Let Justin go."

Slocum looked up to the dirty mirror behind the bar and saw Tom Gallifrey's reflection. The man wasn't armed. At least he hadn't thrown down on Slocum.

When Slocum did as he was told, Justin Gallifrey fell back, caught himself, and started to go for a weapon under the bar. Slocum would be content putting a .36-caliber slug in the man's gut, but quicker than a bullet came Tom's order.

"Don't be more of a jackass than you have to be, Justin. Go fetch some more mugs from the back room."

"But Tom, he—" Justin Gallifrey sputtered, then obeyed with ill grace.

Slocum didn't have to tell his brother he had saved his life.

"You look to be mighty good with that Colt, Slocum," Tom said. He inclined his head toward a table at the far side of the saloon. Slips of paper were scattered on the surface, some held down with empty beer mugs. A tin cashbox stood open and empty.

Gallifrey sank into the chair and leaned forward to cover some of the papers. Slocum read more than one of them marked OVERDUE. Gallifrey wasn't pulling enough business to stay afloat. Slocum reckoned how this took special skill to go bust selling whiskey to thirsty miners in a boomtown.

"Randolph has a job here. A couple folks saw him talking with a miner before he upped and disappeared."

"He don't work any harder than that whore ma of his,"

grumbled Gallifrey. He looked up, eyes wide, when Slocum's hand drifted for his six-shooter. "'Course I know what her problems are, so that's not so bad, her missin' a few shifts forcin' me to call in my no-account brother to work in her stead."

"The boy," Slocum said.

"He was sweepin' up for me. Heard that he got kidnapped, but since he came back real fast, I discounted that."

"It was this afternoon, early evening, when he'd have come by for more work."

"Never laid eyes on him today," Gallifrey said. The man's thin face tightened and his big nose twitched. "Saves me a few pennies, not havin' to pay him." He looked up again, his eyes like chips of ice. "The only customers in here this afternoon were from the Argent Mine. Don't know their names, but they worked for Carstairs 'til she sliced his belly open and killed him."

Slocum knew Gallifrey referred to Marianne. He didn't bother correcting him about how Jim Frank had murdered the mine foreman.

"Anything you know would be a help," Slocum said.

"Smitty. One of them galoots was named Smitty. Leastways, that's what his partner called him. You know how it is with miners. That might be a summer name and—"

Tom Gallifrey spoke to thin air. Slocum ran from the saloon and made a beeline for the hotel and Marianne Lomax. In ten minutes, they were on the road leading to the Argent Mine. By sunrise they had found it.

"What do we do, John?" Marianne shifted uneasily behind him on the Indian pony.

"If Gallifrey wasn't lying, the miner who talked to Randolph is in this camp." He remembered his earlier scouting into this camp, and how he had barely escaped with his life. But Carstairs had been alive then, in command of the entire crew.

Was his replacement any better? For all he knew, the whole damned bunch of miners might have been in on the scheme to steal Bedrich's map with Les Carstairs.

"Let's go."

He started to tell Marianne to stay there, then knew she would never obey. Worse, he would have his attention split in two directions. Finding Randolph was paramount, but if he worried that Marianne would be discovered and captured, too, he couldn't expect to have a good outcome with the miners.

He snapped the reins and got the pony walking slowly into the camp. A couple miners poked at breakfast. The smell of biscuits and frying bacon made his mouth water. It had been a spell since he'd eaten. From the way Marianne leaned toward the cooking fires, he knew this was on her mind as well.

"Who're you?" demanded the miner boiling a large pot of coffee. He didn't seem upset at the sight of Slocum. The question was reflexive.

"We're looking for a miner named Smitty. He's supposed to work for the Argent."

"What'd that scalawag gone an' done now? He sure as hell didn't knock *her* up. He's so damn ugly not even the cows'll let him get that close."

This produced a round of chuckles, but not outright laughter. Slocum took that to mean Smitty fancied himself a ladies' man and likely wasn't too ill-featured.

"Please, we've got to find him. It's important!"

The miner poured himself a cup of the hot coffee, sampled it, and spat it into the fire. He dashed the contents to the ground, then poured himself a new cup and sipped at it before looking up again.

"He got back from town 'fore midnight. That's 'bout the time I dragged my tail into camp, and he was here already." The miner pointed toward a tent.

From astride his horse, Slocum saw only a blanket flat

on the ground. The miner had already left, if he'd even been there at all.

"I . . . I'll serve you all breakfast if you tell us where he is," Marianne said. She kicked free of the horse and landed lightly. Settling her dress and making a point of pressing her hands into her breasts got the miners' attention.

In a few seconds, she had a dozen of them crowding around, holding out cups and tin plates for her to fill.

"Now, boys, don't crowd. I'll be happy to serve Smitty, too."

As a chorus, the other miners declared he had already left to work in the mine. Slocum nodded to Marianne and saw she would be fine. Her work in the Lonely Cuss had inured her to the rough jokes and other antisocial behavior that passed as acceptable among the miners.

He rode in the direction of the mine, then galloped when an explosion shook the ground. A huge gout of dust billowed from the mouth of the mine and covered him with fine rock powder. He hit the ground running, secured the horse, and made his way through the brown cloud to the mine.

"What happened?" He took off his hat and fanned away the choking dust.

A man stumbled out, then dropped to his knees. Bending double, he put his head between his knees and spat blood before looking up.

"Powder went off premature."

"How'd that happen? Why are you blasting by yourself?"

"Got a couple powder monkeys. Might be they screwed it up and detonated early."

"Are they trapped in there?" Slocum demanded. He went to the mouth and peered into the darkness. Whatever damage had occurred to the Argent had been much deeper. This part was shored up well.

Then a coldness settled into his belly. He backed away, drew his pistol, and shoved it into the miner's face.

"You named Smitty?"

"Hell, mister, I'll be whosoever you want me to be. Put that pistol away."

"Those new powder monkeys wouldn't be a pair of kids from town, would it?"

"Offered 'em a dollar a day to be my assistants. The one claimed to know everything there was to know about blasting. Thought he was young, but he sounded real sure of himself."

"Name of Billy?"

"That's him."

This was all the further Smitty got before Slocum swung his pistol. The hard metal barrel crunched into the side of the miner's head, sending him sprawling.

"You stupid bastard," Slocum said. "Billy's fourteen and Randolph's only twelve. What could they know about mining or setting powder charges?"

He plunged into the mine, choking at the dust rising about him. He found the ledge where the miners kept their thick, squat wax candles. It galled him to stop to light one but going deeper without seeing where he stepped amounted to suicide. Suicide like allowing two young boys to set charges and blast.

Candle guttering, Slocum edged forward a dozen yards before he came to the spot where the mine roof had collapsed. Randolph and Billy were on the other side of a solid rock wall.

Trapped.

21

"John, John! They're trapped, aren't they? Randolph and Billy?" Marianne felt sick to her stomach and clung to herself, arms wrapped about her body tightly.

Ahead in the dust Slocum paid her no attention as he moved the feeble candle about, its flickering light hardly enough to see anything. Stumbling over the fallen rocks, she made her way forward until she could touch his shoulder. He jerked in surprise when her fingers gripped down with more force than she intended. One thing that had always drawn her to him was how he could concentrate. Sometimes, she wished he would concentrate more on her and less on everything else in the world.

But now she wanted him to save Randolph.

"Smitty used them to set dangerous charges," Slocum said grimly. "They didn't know what they were doing, and this was the result." He waved the candle around to indicate the destruction.

She reached out to steady his hand. Hot wax trickled over her fingers, making her flinch. She guided his hand back to the spot she wanted lit better.

"See that?" she asked.

"You've got good eyes," Slocum replied. He moved closer to the darkness at the top of the rock fall blocking the mine-shaft. The flame flickered and then moved in the direction of the hole. "They're getting air. The draft is carrying the flame in that direction."

"That means there's a larger air hole on the other side of the rocks, doesn't it?"

"The miners burrowed into the hillside," Slocum said, looking at the layers on the walls, then returning to the hole letting air flow deeper into the mine. "They wouldn't get this deep without ventilation."

"There might be cracks in the rock all the way to the shaft," she said. "Can we reach them that way or will it be easier to remove this rock wall?"

"Ain't no use tryin' to get through that 'less you want to blast some more," Smitty said.

Slocum whirled around and started for the miner. Mari-anne stopped him. She felt Slocum's heart hammering in his chest as she pressed hard to keep him from ripping the miner's head off. It didn't calm her knowing he was so scared. Outwardly, he had a cold anger toward Smitty, but she felt how he was anything but cold inside.

"You mean blasting will only bring down more rock?" she asked, leaning hard against Slocum and not looking at the miner.

"No way of knowin' what the roof looks like deeper in the mine," Smitty said. He spat. "Might take a month to dig out this rock. Might be lucky, and it'd only take a couple days."

"They'll be dead by then," Slocum said.

Marianne pressed harder against him and felt his heart beating even faster.

"We might get water through the air hole to them," she said.

"Ain't nuthin' to tell us they're alive," Smitty said.

Now it was Marianne's turn to want to rip the man's head off. She shoved Slocum back to let him know she'd take care of this. Swallowing her fear and directing it toward the miner, she said, "They're alive. Say anything different and it'll be *you* who's pushing up daisies in some unmarked grave."

"Don't mean nuthin' by it," Smitty said. "Plenny o' miners bought themselves a rock grave. More 'n a half dozen in the Argent, and this is one o' the better mines fer that. Hardly nobody dies."

"And those boys you lured to work for you won't die either," Marianne said. "Come with me, John. I want to find the air holes in the hill and call down to them . . . because they are still alive, dammit!"

She shoved Smitty out of the way and flounced off, head high. She had to duck more than once to avoid rocks jutting down from the roof. What seemed an eternity later, she burst into the open space in front of the mine. Fighting hysteria, she looked around, pushed her matted, dirty hair back out of her eyes, and then started walking to circle the hill where the mine gouged out its load of silver.

"Wait up," Slocum called. "You're going off half-cocked."

"That was never your problem, was it, John?"

"Marianne, use your head. We need to be methodical about how we find the air vents."

"So? How do we do it?" She swept her arm about to take in the entire side of the hill. She paused, swallowed, and then pointed. "Like that? There?"

She didn't wait for Slocum to see what she already had. A fountain of dust had risen from the solid ground—only it couldn't be solid. The funnel of dust had to blow out from the mine. Scrambling up the rocky slope, barely avoiding patches of prickly pear cactus, she found the source of the dust.

"See, John? A crack in the rock. This must go straight down to the mineshaft where Randolph is!"

The boys would get plenty of air this way, but despair hit her like a solid body blow again as she realized the crack in the rock was too narrow for anything else.

"We can dribble water down. If they see it, they can catch it as it drips from the crack. We might stuff down food and—"

"Here, Marianne. I found a bigger vent."

Eyes wide and hope soaring, she went farther up the hill to where Slocum worked to move a large rock. Beside it a large vent still spewed out dust. On the gritty cloud she caught the acrid stench of blasting powder. She remembered how Texas Jack would come to her bed reeking of it. He would always laugh it off and tell her it was the smell of money. Then they'd make love all night long, and she had come to associate the sharp scent with manliness.

Now the smell turned her stomach. Her son might be dead down below.

She dropped to her knees, cupped her hands around her mouth, and shouted, "Randolph! This is Mama. Are you all right?"

She turned and put her ear close to the wide vent. For a moment she heard nothing, then she looked up at Slocum, excited.

"He's alive. That's his voice. Faint, but he said he and Billy are alive. But they're trapped, pinned under rock." She laughed. "Of course they're trapped. They're in the mine that fell in on them. They're safe!" She laughed until she cried. The tears turned to sobs she couldn't control. Slocum took her in his arms, and it felt good, secure and safe again.

She finally pushed him away and asked, "How do we get them free?"

Slocum's reaction did not hearten her. He kicked at the edges of the vent and shook his head after a closer examination.

"We've got to find another way to reach them. This chimney is too small for me to wiggle down."

"I'll go!"

Slocum looked at her as if she had gone crazy. This sparked her anger.

"What's the matter? Don't think I can get down there?"

"What'll you do when you get to them? Dig out?"

"If I have to! What would you do if you went down?"

"Get a rope around them, pull them up. They're likely small enough to fit in the chimney."

"I couldn't pull them up. You're stronger."

"They're buried under rock. There's no telling how injured they are."

"Blood," she said, "doesn't matter to me. I've seen plenty in my day. The boys can't get out from under heaps of debris. I can move rock because I have to."

She wiggled to the vent and put her feet into it, then slid half in before Slocum could stop her. Marianne looked up, daring him to prevent her from saving her son.

"I'll get a rope. Don't go any farther until I tie it to you."

"Good idea, John," she said. "If I get stuck, you can pull me back up." She graced him with a quick smile to speed him on his way. Then she scooted lower, testing the size of the rock chimney. She pushed herself back up and sat on the edge, chafing at the wait for Slocum to get back with a long rope. She had expected miners to come with him.

He answered her unspoken question as he looped one end of the rope around a boulder.

"They're working in the mine. They don't care about the boys."

"I can't fit," she said. "I tried it, and I'm too big." She stood and started stripping off her skirts.

Slocum stared at her and moved to stop her.

"If I have to go down naked, I will, to save them." She finished stripping off her skirts and then shucked her blouse so she stood dressed only in a thin shift.

"Leave your shoes on," he said. "You'll skin up your feet otherwise. You're going to need to dig your toes into crevices on the way back up."

"I'm depending on you, John." She let him wrap one turn of rope around her. If the need to reach her son hadn't been so pressing, she would have enjoyed the feel of Slocum's hands moving over her barely clad breasts as he tied the rope. She gave him a quick kiss that tasted of sweat and grit, then stepped back into the rock chimney.

She almost fell the entire way. If it hadn't been for Slocum's quick jerk, she might have plunged down a full fifteen feet. The rope bit into her ribs, then abraded the skin under her arms.

"Randolph! I'm coming."

"Ma, we can't move. The rock's piled on top of us."

"What about Billy?"

"Dunno. He's still breathin', but he ain't awake. Hurry, Ma, hurry!"

"I'm coming real quick now." She turned her feet sideways and slid down another foot before getting stuck.

Marianne sucked in her breath and held it. She slid over rough rock and then cried out when her feet kicked free. Hands shoved hard against the rough wall, she lowered herself another few inches, then called up to Slocum, "More slack. I'm almost there, but you're holding me back!"

She let out a whoop of glee when she fell the final few feet into the mineshaft. It was too dark to see more than a few inches. The light coming down the narrow chimney afforded little illumination, so she dropped to hands and knees and gingerly felt her way.

"Talk to me, Randolph, so I can find you." Her hand touched hot, sweaty flesh.

She recoiled, then gently reached out and traced over the face. Billy McCarty. She had found Billy, and Randolph was right. The boy was knocked out but still breathed regularly. He couldn't be too severely injured. By feel she started moving the rocks atop him.

"Ma, I can see you silhouetted by the light. Billy's right in front of you."

"I can feel where the rocks are holding him pinned," she said.

Fingers groping, she scraped off skin as she began shoving away rocks covering the boy's lower body.

"Looks like you got him free, Ma."

"I'll see if John can't drag him to the surface."

She dug in her heels, glad that Slocum had suggested keeping her shoes on. She skidded and slid on the rough floor until she found purchase, then scooted Billy to a spot under the rock chimney. She took a quick turn around his body and fastened the rope under his arms with a granny knot.

"Can you pull Billy up?" she called. Her voice echoed and sounded strident. She cleared her throat and tried again, pitching her voice lower. Having Slocum think she was scared bothered her greatly. No matter that she had been through worse, and he had seen her then.

"Pulling. You keep him lined up so he doesn't get caught on any rock, and we'll have him out in a minute," came Slocum's confident words.

She held the boy's feet together as he slumped in the rope sling, then began a jerky, halting rise to the surface. Marianne dropped back to hands and knees and crept forward until she reached her son.

"I been doin' some diggin', Ma," he said. "I got one big rock I can't move. Other 'n that, I'm clear."

"Why'd you do a crazy thing like running off to work in a mine?"

"The money, Ma. I wanted to give the sheriff money so he'd forget about lockin' you up."

"Sheriff Whitehill set bail at one hundred dollars. You and Billy'd have to work for two solid months to get enough." Her fingers slipped under the heavy rock. A quick heave budged it, but not enough. "Or was there more?"

"Well, see, Ma, Billy said there'd be all kinds of silver nuggets in the mine and—"

"You were going to steal the silver, weren't you?"

"It was for *you*, Ma. I had to do somethin' an' what else could I do?"

"Lend a hand. Three, two, one, heave!"

The rock slid away. Randolph cried out in pain.

"I think it's busted. My leg's broke."

"There's no way I can set it here, even if I knew how. I saw your pa set a leg once, but I don't know how to do that. You're going to have to grit your teeth."

Randolph cried out several times, ripping away at her heart. She finally got him to the air vent, where Slocum had dropped the line again. Marianne closed her eyes and steeled her heart against Randolph's piteous moans as Slocum dragged him up to the surface. She sat and shook. She had done it, though. She had rescued the boys.

"Marianne? You ready?"

The rope dangled down. She looped it around her body, made her way up the chimney, and finally popped out onto the rocky ground. She sat up and realized her thin shift had been tattered by the rough chimney walls, leaving her almost naked. Somehow it didn't matter. Slocum had Randolph stretched out on the ground, flat on his back as he examined the leg. Billy lay a few feet away, still unconscious.

"What can I do to help?" she asked.

"This is just like the time I set Joshua Timmins's leg when he busted it falling out of that tree back in Georgia," Slocum said.

"He didn't want his pa to find out he had played hooky," she said, details bursting on her.

"Randolph's leg is about the same. A clean break. You grab hold of him under his arms, and I'll pull his leg."

"Pull my leg," Randolph said weakly. "This is gonna be funny?"

"Keep thinking that," Slocum said.

When they were in position, Marianne looked up. Slocum

nodded once. She leaned back, pulling hard on her son's arms as Slocum applied pressure directly on the leg. There was a grinding sound, then the boy screamed. Slocum sat back, released the leg, and looked satisfied.

"All fixed?" Marianne asked.

"Just like Joshua's, only I didn't have your good help then. He had to hang on to a tree himself while I pulled it back into place."

"Jesus Christ," came the choked exclamation.

She looked over her shoulder. Billy struggled to sit up. He stared at her.

"You're nekkid!"

"Damned near," she said, grinning. Having the boy seeing her so disheveled hardly bothered her. She took more than a little pleasure in the way Slocum looked at her for the same reason now.

There was a big difference between boy and man. And Marianne intended to give Slocum his reward for saving the two from the mine. She seemed to be doing that a lot—and it suited her just fine.

22

"The good thing about Randolph having a broken leg," Marianne Lomax said, "is that he's not likely to go running off with Billy on some crazy adventure."

Slocum had to laugh. The boy sat on the front porch of the hotel, his leg splinted up and a crude crutch beside him on the board floor. The fracture hadn't been bad, and Slocum had done a good job setting it, or at least that's what Doc Fuller said. From what he had seen of the doctor, Slocum doubted Fuller would lie about a medical condition, even to placate a worried mother.

"You think having a busted leg will slow him down if he takes it into his head to listen to Billy?"

"That William McCarty can charm the rattles off a snake," Marianne said.

"Might be why there are sidewinders," Slocum said. He was pleased that this brought not only a smile to her lips but a genuine laugh. She had been too somber since they had returned to Silver City.

"I want to get out of here for a while, John," she said unexpectedly.

"You want to move? Sheriff Whitehill would have something to say about that since we're both suspected of murder."

"That's not what I meant. Besides, the sheriff is out of town now that his deputy got back from serving process."

"Dan said he made close to five dollars evicting a rancher who hadn't paid his taxes." Slocum tried to keep the bitterness from his voice but couldn't. That smacked too much of what had happened to him back in Georgia.

Back in Georgia. He looked at Marianne and saw her in profile. The strong chin, the fine bones, the intelligence and determination in her, all made him remember Georgia. They had been so young then. Time had added more than years to both of them.

He looked from her to the boy, leaning back in the chair and whispering furiously with Billy. What they talked about was something of a mystery. Boy things. Slocum looked back at Marianne. Just as he and Marianne had talked about boy and girl things. Back in Georgia.

"You need to take a break, too. Get away from town."

Slocum blinked. He had been thinking about his past, something he seldom did.

"Jack and I used to go camping up in the hills just to be alone. I want to go there with you, John." She saw his hesitation and misinterpreted his quick look at Randolph. "He'll be fine. As you said, he's not going to run far."

"I suppose I ought to let Dangerous Dan know, or we'll have the law on our trail."

"He's like Harvey. He'll know I wouldn't go anywhere without intending to come back as long as Randolph is here." She paused, then said in a lower voice, "He knows that about you, too."

"I'll talk to Dan. You rustle up some food." Slocum stood and walked away, an uneasy feeling gnawing away at him. He tried to decide what caused it but couldn't. More than once on his way to the jailhouse, he stopped, looked around, but seeing nothing, continued on his way.

In the jail, Dan Tucker sat in the sheriff's chair, but unlike Whitehill, he wasn't poring over a newspaper. He rested his head on crossed arms and snored like he was sawing wood.

Slocum slammed the door and brought the deputy bolt upright, eyes wide. To his credit, he didn't reach for his six-shooter.

"What brings you by? You lookin' for a place to sleep?"

"You already took it," Slocum said.

"Don't let Whitehill know. He gets all riled."

"Where'd he go?"

"North. Maybe to Santa Fe. He didn't tell me. I asked around and that's the only way I found he was out of town. Just tole me to keep the peace."

"Marianne and I'll be leaving town for a spell. Be back before sundown."

"Storm's building up west of town. You go far, you might get caught."

"Would that upset you much if we didn't get back until tomorrow, if the storm breaks?"

"I know you, Slocum. You're 'bout the most honorable man I ever met. You give me your word, and that's all I'll need."

"Done," Slocum said. "And look after the boy."

"Done," Tucker echoed. "I might toss him in the clink, just to be sure I know where he's at."

"Don't let Marianne hear you say that. She's a wildcat when it comes to defending that boy."

Tucker looked at Slocum hard, then said slowly, "You are, too. 'Spect you heard this before, but that boy is your spittin' image."

Slocum laughed it off, shook hands with the deputy, and went to the stables to fetch his horse. Not for the first time, he wished he had money enough to buy some gear. If he

was going to ride all over the New Mexico countryside with
Marianne behind him, a saddle would make the travel easier.
Might be the pony would prefer it, too.

He led the horse back to the hotel, where Marianne was
speaking with Randolph. From the expression on the boy's
face, he was trying to convince his mother he didn't want
her to go and, when she did, would be on his crutch and
hobbling into trouble the instant she was out of sight. When
the cat's away, the mice will play. Billy stood at the end of
the boardwalk, not quite rubbing his hands together in anticipation, but damned close.

"Ready?"

"All ready, John." Marianne looked back quickly at her
son, then jumped onto horseback, letting Slocum ride behind
her this time. She clung to the picnic basket.

As they reached the outskirts of Silver City, Slocum said,
"He'll be all right."

"What? Oh, I wasn't thinking about Randolph at all," she
said. She looked back, twisted about, and gave him an awk-
ward kiss. "*That's* what I was thinking on."

"Only a kiss?" he teased.

"Oh, a bit more."

"Such as?"

"Why, I was wondering if you knew how to pitch a tent."
She reached behind her and pressed her hand into his crotch.
"Well, I have my answer. Can we ride a bit faster?"

"You won't say that when we get to your special camp-
ground."

Her laughter rang true, giving Slocum more pleasure than
he had experienced in a month of Sundays. Making Marianne happy sparked something in him, different from the
way it had been between them in Georgia, but better.

Somehow, words after this weren't necessary. Slocum
was lost in his own memories and thought Marianne was,
too. She didn't have to give directions to her special camp-

ground. All she needed to do was lean this way or that, and once on the trail, they reached the spot quickly.

Slocum spotted a fire pit immediately and stopped beside it. His quick eyes took in the area. A tent had stood nearby, and from the crushed grass now recovering amid the undisturbed, it had been at least a month since anyone had stayed here. He looked around when Marianne lifted her leg high and slipped to the ground with a dull thump. She set down the picnic basket.

"There's the tent Jack brought up here. He said it was a mighty expensive one, though I could never see it."

Slocum took the time to fasten his horse's reins so it could graze but not run off. He went to the pile of canvas and lifted. The tent had a hole or two in it. Most striking was the heavy support pole. He hefted it. His fingers circled it and barely touched. He guessed it was a good four feet long and two inches in diameter.

"Texas Jack didn't want the tent collapsing," he said dryly. "This would hold up a full-sized circus tent."

"Oh," Marianne said, grinning from ear to ear, "that's not far wrong. We had a real three-ring show underneath more than once."

Slocum dropped the pole and stepped over the tent.

"Why do we need a tent when we have the clear blue sky as our roof?"

"Because one of us will get a naked butt roasted in the sun," Marianne said.

"There're trees all around. We don't have to stay in the middle of a meadow."

"Should we have lunch first?" Marianne asked. "Or are you going to pitch your tent?"

She began unfastening the top buttons on her blouse, exposing milky skin. Another couple buttons allowed the swell of her breasts to show and entice him. He began responding.

"I don't mind eating first," he said.

"The tent. *That* tent," she said, pointing to the lump of canvas and wood. "We can decide what to do under it."

Slocum gave in to the inevitable. It took him longer to put up the tent than he expected because of the thick pole. It had been poorly chosen. A sapling half its size would have worked better. A small breeze turned the minor chore into a job that would have had him cursing if Marianne hadn't been discarding a piece of her clothing with every advance he made on pitching the tent. The stakes went into the ground, ropes were pulled, and the huge pole steadied.

"It's roomy inside," she said, pushing past him. She dropped a blanket Slocum had brought onto the ground, but he hardly noticed.

Marianne had shucked off all her clothes except for thin bloomers. The day was warm, and she sweat enough to plaster the cloth against her curves, outlining every turn and swell, every hollow and delightful terrain on her lower body begging to be explored. She turned, causing her breasts to jiggle about slightly.

"We're out of the sun," she said, indicating the canvas above them.

"And I see where I want to be in," he said, moving to her.

He reached down and pressed his palm into her crotch. Sweat had soaked her bloomers but a different sort of moisture dampened his hand here. She moaned softly and reached for him.

They kissed, pressed together, and slowly sank to lie side by side on the blanket. Slocum never noticed the tent above. Sky would have suited him as well because she was what he sought. He peeled the bloomers down, revealing the fragrant thatch between her legs. She propped herself up on her elbows and looked down at him.

"Go on, John. I'd like you to—oh!" Her legs spread wide as he pushed his head between willing thighs.

He lapped at her nether lips, then thrust his tongue out to wrest a new sob of joy from her. Sucking hard at the tender flaps, he lifted her off the ground. She shoved herself down into his face. He began moving his tongue in and out slowly, licking up the juices leaking from her insides.

Then he went blind and deaf. Her legs clamped down on either side of his head, holding him firmly in place. But he had no desire to go anywhere else. Not at the moment. He used his tongue as he might have his other organ until Marianne rocked from side to side, her desires pushed to the breaking point.

And then she cried out, arched her back, and finally sagged down. Her legs released him. She looked down at him, a small smile on her lips.

"You'll get cauliflower ears doing that."

"Are you complaining?"

"Yeah, I am," she said. "Because I want something bigger."

He thrust his middle finger into her. She gasped, closed her eyes, and got her voice back.

"Bigger. I want bigger."

"Greedy bitch," he said. He added a second finger and began moving in and out. His hand was soon drenched in her slippery inner oils.

"S-Still not big enough. Or long enough."

He stared at her. Her chest rose and fell as she sucked in short, quick breaths while her desires mounted. The tiny buttons atop her breasts had turned rock hard and pulsed visibly with every beat of her frenzied heart. He longed to pop them into his mouth, gnaw on them a little, suckle, then move on, but his own needs were intruding.

Reaching around, he grabbed a double handful of ass and used these sexy handles to pull himself up between her wantonly spread legs. She reached between them, captured his manhood, and tugged insistently.

"There, John, there!"

She guided him to the spot where his tongue had already explored. The wetness, the heat, his urgency, all conspired against him. He slid forward quickly, entering her fully. The fast thrust released another flood of sensation in the woman. She clung to him, her fingernails clawing at his back.

He began pistoning in and out until a lewd sucking sound filled the tent, almost drowning out the woman's joyous cries. He thrust into slick, hot, moist female silk that began squeezing down all around his hidden length. Pulling back, never hesitating before he launched into her anew, they quickly found the rhythm that excited them both the most.

As she cried out in a third release, Slocum lost control. He felt the heavy pumping and electric explosion in his body. He slammed forward and remained buried, riding her as she bucked about under him. All too soon, he began to melt in her inner heat.

"I . . . I'm glad I had you put up the tent," she said in a husky voice.

"Why?" A warm afterglow filled him. They lay with their arms circling each other, sweaty bodies close.

"We'd've scared the birds. And the deer. And the mountain lions, and who knows, we might have even scared the earthworms with all our thumping around."

"Were you scared?"

"I was satisfied," she said, snuggling closer. She ran the instep of her foot up and down his leg.

Slocum laughed, but the thought flitted through his brain that it might have been scary for him. He had been with a passel of women, but never had it been quite like this.

"The last thing Jack said before we left here the last time was how rich we'd be because of this tent. That made me wonder. He was like you. Not all that poetic."

"Rich?"

"We had each other. Of course, he had found that rich silver strike but never told me about it. I think he wanted to keep it a surprise. A wedding gift."

Slocum's muzzy feeling evaporated as she talked about

Texas Jack. He rolled over and stared up at the tent. Bright sunlight burned against the outer surface. A few tears let the light through atop bright spires of dancing dust. His mind disconnected from rational thought. Could the holes form a map? If he lined them all up with nighttime stars, could the tent be the map Bedrich had hidden, that Frank sought?

"You went away, John," she said.

"No, I'm still here," he said.

She pushed up, hands on his chest. He tried to read her expression and couldn't.

"I'll fix some food," she said suddenly.

"Don't get dressed just for me," he said. This brought a new smile to her face. She left the tent, and he imagined that the smile melted once she turned away. He lay flat on his back, the heat building inside the tent. Outside it would be cooler, even if he was in the sun.

He worked his way to the mouth of the tent, gripped the huge tent pole, and used it to pull himself to his feet outside. Watching a naked Marianne putting out the food caused a new jumble of thoughts he didn't want to sort through at the moment. He went and sat on a log near the cold fire pit.

"That looks like it's rough," she said. "The grass is better." She patted the patch next to her. Slocum wasn't sure why he found himself reluctant to sit close to her, but he did.

Giving in, he swung his long legs around and stretched out beside her. She handed him a roast beef sandwich on thick bread. There was something about eating naked that pushed away all his earlier worries.

"Pickle?" She teased him with the thick dill pickle, brushing it over his lips. Just when he started to take a bit, she pulled it away, only to drip a bit of brine into his mouth as he pulled back.

He finally got a good chomp, setting free Marianne's bright laughter again.

"I wish this could go on forever," she said. She lay half across him, her cheek on his bare chest.

A cloud passed across the sun, followed quickly by a rising wind that caused the tent to flap and snap loudly.

"At least the tent pole's not going to break," Slocum said. "It'd take a tornado to snap that."

"As much work as Jack put in on it, it ought to support the sky itself."

"What work?" Slocum asked.

"He whittled and carved and shaved it. Took him the better part of three days. Never saw a man so pleased with himself when he finished it." She sighed. "That night in the tent was . . . special. Never saw him so aroused, and Jack was a man of intense passions."

Slocum stared at the tent, wondering what Texas Jack had been doing. The bark had been stripped and the wood polished down a bit. That wouldn't take a man with a dull knife an hour to do. Less. Lots less.

"He was whittling on it?"

"Why the interest? You—oh!" Marianne looked up at the sky as another raindrop smacked her in the eye. She turned her face down and blinked hard. "That blinded me."

The rain began falling heavier. She wanted to retreat to the tent, but Slocum prevailed. They stayed out in the warm shower and made love again. Only when they had finished did he suggest they return to town, using the tent to keep the rain off them. Marianne didn't even think it was odd when he insisted on taking the thick tent pole with them, too.

23

The silence between them had been good as they rode out, but Marianne found it uneasy as they slowly made their way back to Silver City. She still glowed from the lovemaking, but an apprehension built to push it away. Trying to pin down the reason worried her more than anything else. It wasn't anything Slocum had said but more what he hadn't.

And she didn't know what she had wanted. Words came to her lips that might change everything between them, then she bit them back. Right now she felt whatever bond there was between them was too fragile to risk with a truth she had lived with far too long.

"There's Randolph," Slocum said. "See? He hasn't gotten into any trouble while you were gone."

She waved. Her son reluctantly waved back. He was at that age where any attention by his mother in public was a curse worse than anything an Apache medicine man might put on him.

"I'd better go see how he's doing. Since Billy is nowhere to be seen, he might be the one getting into trouble."

"I'll put the tent in the stable with the horse," he said.

She barely noted the way he clung to the tent pole as she dropped off and went to see what Randolph had been up to.

"You're walkin' funny, Ma," he said. "Kinda bowlegged."

She blushed. To cover it, she ran her sleeve over her face to clean off some of the trail dust.

"Riding double on a horse can do that," she said. "What did you do while I was gone?"

"Not a whole bunch." He hiccuped loudly, then covered his mouth guiltily.

She stepped closer and took a deep whiff.

"Randolph Lomax, have you been drinking? That's whiskey I smell on you! Did Billy McCarty give it to you? I'll have his ears on a string for this!"

"Ma, wait, no, don't go blamin' him. Ain't Billy's fault."

"How'd you get *whiskey*? Who gave it to you?"

"I was moanin' and feelin' poorly. My leg was all swole up and felt like somebody was hittin' it with a hammer. Mr. Gallifrey had a pint with him. Carries that silver flask in his coat pocket. He tole me it was medicinal." Randolph hiccuped again. "Did help. Pain went away for a while."

"Tom Gallifrey gave you liquor? You're twelve years old! I swear, I'll start a WCTU chapter here if he really did that."

"He did. Ain't Billy's fault, so don't go blamin' him."

She heard bare feet slapping on the boardwalk. Without turning, she said, "Is that true, Billy? Did Mr. Gallifrey give him whiskey?"

"Yes, ma'am, he did. Wouldn't give me none. Said it was for Randolph's leg. Almost made me want to have a broke leg, too. Only Randolph says it hurts like a million ants are always gnawin' on his flesh."

"When did this happen?" she asked suspiciously.

"Right after you and Mr. Slocum rode out. Gave me the whole danged pint, too. Went down easy, but burned in my gut. Thought I was gonna puke, but he gave me somethin' else."

"Brandy," Billy piped up. "He didn't give me none of that either."

"Gallifrey gave you a pint of whiskey *and* brandy?"

"Didn't like the brandy. Said it was peaches, but it burned like hell all the way to my belly."

"You shoulda seen him, Miz Lomax. He was drunker 'n a lord!" Billy laughed. "He tried to get up and dance on that bum leg."

"I hope Mr. Gallifrey had the good sense not to allow it. Randolph could have hurt himself even worse." She thrust her face within inches of her son's. "You could have. You know better."

"Wanted to dance and not let him keep on with all them questions. Didn't know what he was askin', so I kept drinkin'."

Marianne forced away her anger at the Lonely Cuss's owner. Maybe Gallifrey thought he was doing the boy a favor, but getting him drunk solved nothing. Randolph would be hungover and in pain when the booze wore off. Unlike most of the saloon patrons whose pain came from long hours of work, her son's pain would pass soon enough. He had to learn to tough it out.

"You stay here. I'm going to have words with Mr. Gallifrey."

"Aw, Ma, he didn't mean nuthin' by givin' me the liquor. He was tryin' to help."

She forced herself to calm as she neared the Lonely Cuss. The rush hadn't happened yet, but the silver fields would empty of miners soon enough as they rushed into town. Walking through the swinging doors, she first saw Gallifrey's portly brother, Justin, behind the bar. Then she spotted the owner at his wonted table to the side of the main room. The stacks of paper in front of him had grown into a small mountain range.

"Marianne," he said, looking up at her. His thin face and dark eyes made him look furtive.

Or was it the way he couldn't—quite—look her squarely in the eye?

"I know you were only trying to help, but you shouldn't have given Randolph that whiskey. Not a drop."

"You're no teetotaler. Why deny your son?"

"He—" That argument got her nowhere. She suddenly asked, "What were you asking him?"

"I—" Gallifrey began to sputter. "I don't know what you mean."

"Randolph said you were asking a lot of questions. He didn't want to answer so he kept drinking."

"Well, there you are. He admitted he was the one to blame for getting snockered."

"What questions?"

If Gallifrey could have bolted and run, he would have. She repeated her demand to know what Gallifrey had wanted of Randolph.

"You're talkin' the word of a drunk kid? He got confused. I asked him simple stuff like how he busted that leg. I've heard some wild stories, mostly spread by Billy McCarty. I wanted to know the truth."

"So do I," Marianne said. Whatever Gallifrey had asked, that wasn't even close. She knew when a man lied. Gallifrey did it a little better than most, but not enough to pull the wool over her eyes.

"I wanted to know if you was comin' back to work. My shiftless brother's terrible behind the bar. If it's not beer, he screws it up."

Again she heard an ounce of truth and a ton of lie.

"When he gets over his hangover, I'm sure Randolph will remember everything. He's not like most of the customers who drink 'til oblivion hits them like a sledgehammer."

Gallifrey looked past her toward the back room and made

a shooing gesture. She glanced over her shoulder in time to see the door close.

"Who was that?"

"You want to work here or not? If you do, I can put you to work right now. I'll boot that lazy jackass brother of mine out all the way back to Mesilla."

"I'll let you know," Marianne said. She left before Gallifrey answered. If he had a reply at all.

Curiosity itched at her like a mosquito bite as she went around the side of the saloon hoping to catch sight of whoever had barged into the Lonely Cuss, only to be chased off by its owner. She went to the back door and nudged it open. Whoever had entered the saloon came this way and likely lit out without properly locking it behind him. She looked around the alley, wishing she had Slocum's skill at reading tracks.

The ground was all kicked up and dusty. Making out one footprint from another proved beyond her skill and imagination. Marianne headed back to the hotel to find if her son had even a faint memory of what Gallifrey had been asking. Billy might know, too, since he acted as repository for all rumors and gossip in Silver City. He had to spy on everyone, see everything, think constantly about how to turn it all to his advantage.

As she neared the hotel, she saw Randolph struggling to stand. She walked faster, intending to help him.

The shot came from across the street. For a heart-stopping moment, Marianne thought she had been the one on the receiving end of the bullet. Then she cried out in panic. Randolph tumbled to the boardwalk and lay there kicking feebly. She skidded to a halt on her knees and bent over him, to protect him with her own body.

"Randolph, Randolph! Are you hurt? Where did you get shot?"

"Ain't shot, Ma. Bullet hit my crutch." He held up the

end of the crutch. The slug had blasted the wood into splinters only inches below his hand grip.

She reared up, keeping her body between him and the direction of the shot. It was getting toward late afternoon and twilight hid many doorways. Picking out the gunman's location proved impossible.

"Get into the hotel. Stay away from windows."

"What are you gonna do? You can't go after a sniper by yourself. Get Mr. Slocum. He's real good with that six-shooter of his, I'd wager. Leastways, Billy says it looks that way to him, and he knows."

"Inside," Marianne said, half picking Randolph up and acting as a crutch until he got his good leg under him.

Only when he was in the lobby did she turn and look for the ambusher. It was dangerous. But something felt wrong to her about the shooting. Missing the boy from a few yards away hardly seemed likely.

"Miz Lomax, what happened?" Billy ran up, face flushed, and chest heaving from exertion. "I was down at the bakery and heard the rifle shot."

"Rifle?"

"Sounded like it to me."

"Go tell the sheriff somebody shot at Randolph."

"Where is he? He all right?"

"They missed. Now scat."

"Deputy Tucker's in town. Sheriff Whitehill ain't back from Santa Fe yet."

"Get somebody who wears a badge. Go!"

Billy lit out, gasping from exertion. Marianne stood stock-still, looking at the shadowy doorways. She caught her breath when a man holding a rifle stepped out and revealed himself to her. He carried the rifle so it rested in the crook of his left arm. When he was sure she saw him, he turned his back to her and walked away slowly.

Marianne wanted to cry out in frustration. The gunman would be gone by the time Deputy Tucker got here, no matter how fast Billy was. And she had no idea where Slocum had gotten off to. Although she wasn't armed, she ran after the man. He turned a corner and disappeared. She ran faster, swung around the corner, and crashed headlong into Jim Frank.

The man shoved her back with his rifle. He reeked of gunpowder.

"You tried to kill Randolph!"

"I hit what I aimed at," he said. "From twenty yards away, if I'd wanted to kill him, he'd be dead and on his way to the funeral home."

"Why'd you fire, then?"

"I want it," Frank said. "I wanted you to know I can kill your brat any time with a single shot. Give me the deed and I promise to let you and him go on your way."

"I don't have it."

"Texas Jack didn't have it on him in Santa Fe."

"You killed him."

"I'll kill your boy and you to get that deed. I saw the assay. If it's half as rich as the sample, I'll be richer than anybody in this godforsaken town inside a year. Give me the deed."

"How will it do you any good?"

Frank sneered, then herded her backward until she was pinned against an adobe wall by the rifle barrel. It was still warm from the potshot he'd taken at Randolph.

"The deed's in Bedrich's name, but it gives the location of the mine. With the claims office here in town all burned to the ground and no official record, I can stake it out for my own."

"You'd stop trying to kill Randolph?"

"And I leave you be," he said. He leered. "Then again, you might want to take up with a rich man. After all, that's why you and Texas Jack was together."

Anger flared. She'd loved Jack! He hadn't even told her any details about the silver strike before heading out to Santa

Fe and his death. It wouldn't have mattered to her if Jack had never found so much as a speck of silver, but knowing that he had and that this was his legacy made her stiffen with resolve.

She had never thought much on being rich, but that silver claim was her and Randolph's way out of poverty so grinding she had to turn tricks just to keep food on the table.

"Or maybe I'll be so rich I can buy all the whores in Silver City," Frank said, watching to see how much this riled her. "But I'd have two bits left over to buy your favors."

"You'd leave us alone if I get you the deed?"

Frank's eyes widened in surprise, then narrowed as he studied her carefully for any hint that she'd lied to him.

"That's the deal."

"I have the deed hidden."

"I'll go with you."

"I'll get it myself and meet you tomorrow night. It's not easy to reach, and I . . . I don't want anyone else knowing I'm giving it to you."

"You're cuttin' Slocum out?" This caused Frank to laugh heartily. "That's rich. The only reason he's been bangin' you is to get the deed. You know that, don't you, whore?"

"Tomorrow night. Right here. I'll—"

"I'll let you know where to meet up. It'll be outside town so you won't try settin' no trap for me. And I want—"

The gunshot ripped through the still night air. Frank's eyes widened again in surprise. When they closed, it was in death. He slumped forward, his dead weight forcing Marianne against the wall. She eased him to the ground, but the shot had smashed into the middle of his back, blasting his spine to splinters.

She reached for the rifle to defend herself.

"I don't want to shoot you, Miz Lomax, but I will. Drop the rifle."

Dangerous Dan Tucker had the drop on her. From the expression on his face, it wouldn't take much for him to draw back on the trigger of the six-gun in his steady hand. She dropped the rifle and wrapped her arms around herself, squeezing tightly to keep from crying in frustration.

24

"There's no call to hold her," Slocum said, about ready to throw down on Dan Tucker, take the cell keys from him, and release Marianne. She sat slumped in the back cell. The blanket she had used before to ensure privacy lay on the floor, neatly folded. Slocum wondered who had done that. Probably Sheriff Whitehill, since Dangerous Dan lived up to his name. Getting him to bathe required an act of Congress. Folding a blanket for a prisoner on his own lay far beyond his comprehension.

"Whitehill would skin me alive, Slocum. I can't let her go traipsin' around town, not after I found her with that rifle in her hand. It had been fired, Frank is dead, she was holdin' the weapon. What else can I do?"

"When's the sheriff due back? He'll see what you didn't. Frank was shot from some distance. There wasn't any burn mark on his coat, like there would be if Marianne had jammed the rifle smack dab against his back."

"Might be she was away from him when she shot him," Tucker said doggedly.

"How much time was there between the shot and you finding her with Frank at her feet?"

"A couple seconds," Tucker said. An expression of understanding spread over his face. "I see. Ain't no way she coulda fired into Frank from a ways off, then hustled around to where I'd found 'em."

"You heard what she said. Frank had the rifle and used it to pin her against the wall. Somebody else shot him in the back."

"Who'd do a thing like that?"

Slocum almost volunteered that he would have, given the chance, but managed to hold his tongue. Tucker looked for an easy solution to the crime. He'd found Marianne with a dead man at her feet. After all the logic had been squeezed and pulled and finely presented to the deputy, Slocum wasn't about to give him someone else to blame for the crime. Tucker owed him for getting him out of the deadly jam in Colorado, but Slocum didn't want to push so far that the deputy had to arrest him in spite of the honor debt.

"You know Frank. He had enemies out the ass," Slocum said.

"He admitted to killing Carstairs," Marianne said, coming out of her shock at being locked up once more. "And he killed Jack, too. He was a mean son of a bitch."

"Don't go usin' language like that," Tucker said. "You're a lady."

Marianne laughed harshly. "Folks hereabouts call me a whore to my face."

"Ain't the way Sheriff Whitehill thinks about you."

Slocum swung about when the jailhouse door opened. His hand was halfway to his six-shooter when he checked the move and tried to cover his reaction by hooking his thumb over his belt buckle.

"Evening, Sheriff," he said. "Good to see you back in Silver City."

Whitehill looked past Slocum to the back cell, where

Marianne hung on the bars, looking as forlorn as a lost puppy dog.

"I can't leave this damn town for a day without everythin' comin' unraveled," he said with a heavy sigh. "So tell me what went on."

Between Tucker and Slocum, with choice pleas from Marianne interspersed, the story of Frank's murder came out. Whitehill sat perched on the edge of his desk listening in disbelief.

"Just when I think I've heard it all, you come up with a new wrinkle," Whitehill said. He scratched his chin, then moved around the desk, shooing Tucker away from the chair. He collapsed into it, the vision of exhaustion. Seeing Slocum staring, he said, "I rode straight through from Santa Fe."

"What did you find, Sheriff?" Slocum asked.

"A goddamn wasted trip, that's what it was. I followed the tracks laid down by Bedrich and Frank, put together the evidence, and was comin' back to arrest Frank for Texas Jack's killing. I had witnesses, even got that varmint Holst to explain how them icebergs of his are formed outta snow and ice chips. All for naught."

"Frank's dead," Slocum agreed.

"If you know he killed Jack, does that mean you're letting me out, Harvey?" Marianne sounded eager, yet just a touch wistful. Tears ran down her cheeks.

"Between the two of you, men are dyin' left and right. Texas Jack, Frank, Carstairs, and the only crime I solved was Jim Frank killin' Texas Jack."

"But Frank admitted to me he killed Jack and Carstairs," Marianne cried.

"Real convenient," Whitehill said. "The dead man killed the other two dead men. So who killed Frank?"

"His partner," Slocum said, remembering how he had rescued Randolph after Frank had kidnapped him. "There was another man."

"Why'd he up and kill his partner if this mysterious deed

of Texas Jack's ain't been found yet?" Whitehill looked hard at Marianne, who shrugged.

Slocum was glad he didn't get the same penetrating stare directed at him. Even with his best poker face, he would have betrayed himself as knowing where the deed had been hidden.

"I was going to try again to find the deed," Marianne said, "and give it to Frank so he wouldn't shoot at Randolph anymore. He promised he'd take it and let us be."

"Liar," Whitehill said gruffly. "Once he verified the location of the strike, he would have killed both you and Randolph."

Slocum had come to the same conclusion. Frank had never shown himself to be shy about murdering anyone who got in his way. Marianne and Randolph would have been able to testify against him. It was easier to leave them both in a shallow grave than worry they might cause him legal trouble.

"If you're not going to let me go," Marianne said, "could you look in on Randolph? He's still gimping about on his busted leg."

"How'd that happen?" Whitehill perked up. "Nothing serious, is it?"

"I set his leg," Slocum said. "He and Billy were in a mine explosion."

Whitehill closed his eyes and looked a dozen years older.

"I should never have come back. If I'd kept on ridin', I coulda been in Colorado by now." He opened his eyes and pointed at Slocum. "You come with me. We'll talk this out with the boy. Might be he knows more about the shootin' than he's lettin' on."

Slocum started to protest, but Marianne shook her head and made shooing motions. She wanted him to find her son and be certain he was all right. How many times could a young boy endure having his ma thrown in jail for murder?

"He's over at the hotel," Slocum said.

Whitehill heaved himself to his feet, brushed off some trail dust, and then said to Tucker, "You watch her real good. If she gets outta jail 'fore I get back, I'll have your badge—and your hide."

"Don't worry none, Sheriff," Dangerous Dan said. "She's not goin' nowhere on my watch."

Slocum and Whitehill left, the dark silhouette of the jail at their backs.

Marianne sat on the cot, her legs drawn up so she could rest her head on her knees and shut out the reality of the cell and the whole damned stinking world. Nothing had gone right. She almost wished she had killed Frank. That would have been satisfying after he had kidnapped her son and then taken a shot at him. More than this, it would have been something solid. She felt as if she had turned into a feather caught on the wind, blown this way and that, influencing nothing, a captive of invisible forces beyond her control.

She held back tears. That wouldn't be right to cry.

"What would John do?" she muttered to herself. Somehow it helped her keep calm trying to decide what Slocum would do in a similar situation. He was unflappable and always did the right thing as needed. His honor guided him and made him the bulwark against everything crashing into her. If only she could be more like him . . .

"I want the deed."

She looked up, startled. She peered around the corner of the blanket dangling down to give her some privacy. Dan Tucker sat at the desk, leaning back in the chair and gently snoring. The words must have been part of a dream she was having, though Marianne was certain she hadn't nodded off.

"I got your kid. He dies if you don't hand over the deed."

She jumped to her feet and looked up at the high window. Bars securely set in the adobe prevented even a wisp of hope at escaping that way, but moving outside the jail she saw a shadow.

"I'm locked up, in case you hadn't noticed," she said.

"I got your son, and he'll die a slow death if you don't give me the deed to Bedrich's strike."

She stood on the cot and could barely peer out through the bars. The man outside moved into deeper shadows to keep from being seen.

"You killed Frank," she accused.

"He tried to double-cross me. You know I ain't kiddin' when I say Randolph dies if you don't give me what I want."

"Who are you?"

The muffled laugh mocked her. The man wore a dark canvas duster that erased his body. His face hid behind a bandanna pulled up so only his eyes peered out, but she couldn't get a good look at them. He tugged repeatedly at his hat brim to hide even this small chance for recognition.

"I'm the man with a gallon of blood on my hands. I don't mind addin' to it neither."

"I don't have the deed."

"Randolph dies in one hour. Bring me the deed out at the old stock pond, the one where your kid and that little bastard Billy play."

"I know it," she said, "but that doesn't help me any. I'm locked up!"

"The deed. Inside one hour." The shadowy figure reached into a pocket and pulled out a small pistol, wrapped it in cloth, and tossed it through the bars next to Marianne's face.

In spite of herself, she jumped when it thudded to the cell floor with a sound that had to awaken the dead.

"Wait!"

She called out to the night air and nothing more. The man had hightailed it. She heard the thunder of a galloping horse receding into the still night, going in the direction of the stock tank on the outskirts of Silver City. Futilely, she shook the bars, then looked at her palms. Rust had flaked off and turned her hands brown. Tiny bits of decaying metal had scratched her, causing a pain that was both distant and overwhelming. Marianne stepped back off the cot and dropped to hands and knees on the floor.

She grabbed the cloth-wrapped bundle and opened it to find a derringer inside. The small pistol lay on the cell floor accusingly. Idly wiping the blood beading in her hands on the cloth, she let her mind run wild.

Randolph's life in exchange for the deed. And she had figured out where to find it. Texas Jack hadn't told her, but he might as well have carved it into her back. There had been so many other distractions she hadn't realized he hid it in front of her.

The thought of being rich faded fast as she scooped up the derringer and cocked it. An hour wasn't long, and she didn't doubt the threat was real. Randolph would die if she didn't hand over the deed. Texas Jack had already died, Carstairs and Frank as well. Killing a boy for what had to be a fabulous mother lode of silver was nothing in comparison to the risks already taken.

"Deputy," she called. "There's something wrong back here. A snake! There's a rattler in my cell!" She screeched shrilly as she hid the pistol in the folds of her skirt. "I don't want to get snake bit!"

Dangerous Dan snapped awake, muttered something, then leaped to his feet, hand going to his six-shooter.

"What's that you're sayin'? A snake inside the jail?"

"There, under the cot. Hear it? It's mad and rattling up a storm!"

"I don't hear anything," Tucker said. "Step away from the cell door."

Heart racing, Marianne did as she was ordered. Her chance to escape was slim, but odds turned in her favor as Tucker opened the door, drew his six-shooter, and bent to peer under the cot. She pressed the derringer's cold metal barrel against the back of his neck.

"I don't want to hurt you none," she said, "but the man

who killed Frank has taken Randolph. If I don't go fetch my
son, he's going to die within an hour."

"Marianne, you're makin' a powerful big mistake. If you
don't let the sheriff help you, get Slocum. He's a good man
in a tight spot."

"There's no time." She reached around and plucked the
gun from Dangerous Dan's fingers, then backed from the
cell.

Kicking it shut, she hastily turned the key in the lock and
flung the key ring in the direction of the sheriff's desk. The
metallic clang caused her to jump.

"You can't deal with vermin like this by yourself," Tucker
said. "I'll help you, Whitehill be damned! I know you didn't
shoot Frank, and so does the sheriff."

"Then why'd he lock me up?"

"Haven't you figured out he's got feelings for you? Whoever killed Frank likely wants you dead, too. This is Whitehill's way of protecting you."

She looked at the derringer she held in her hand so tightly
her knuckles turned white. If Frank's killer could pass her
a gun, he could have shot her. But then he wouldn't get the
deed. As long as she held it, both she and Randolph were
safe.

But when she turned it over was another matter. Slocum
would be a help. So would Harvey Whitehill. She had seen
the way the sheriff looked at her and it came as no surprise
what Tucker said. For all that, she thought the deputy
wouldn't mind sidling up to her either.

"I don't have time to leave a note letting the sheriff know
it wasn't your fault that I had a gun and got the drop on you.
You tell him."

"Don't matter a pile of matchsticks to me if he fires me.
You're gonna get yourself killed, Marianne!"

She had no more time to debate her escape. She rushed
out, saw Tucker's horse around at the side of the jailhouse,
and stepped up into the saddle. After riding bareback so

often recently, it felt strange having the curved leather under her. It felt even stranger not having Slocum's arms circling her waist to hold the reins.

Marianne didn't take the road out of town. She headed, instead, for the livery stables where Slocum kept his pony. As she trotted toward the dark, looming barn, apprehension grew. She wanted Slocum to be there, to take the burden from her shoulders. It felt so good, so right, being in his arms all safe and protected. At the same time, Randolph was her son and whatever danger had to be faced was hers and hers alone.

She slid from the saddle and fumbled at the latch on the barn door. So much noise made her close her eyes for a moment to focus. Did she want to get caught and hand over the responsibility for Randolph to someone else? Anyone else? Even Sheriff Whitehill would be a boon right now, even if he hardly believed her stories of not killing Carstairs and Frank.

The latch yielded and allowed her to slip inside. A few horses stirred. A mule kicked at its stall, then sank back into sleep when she didn't make any more commotion. On silent feet she went to the stack of canvas at the far end of the stalls where Slocum had dumped the tent. She picked up the canvas and ran her fingers over it, remembering the times she and Jack had spent under it, making love.

And the most recent time with John Slocum.

She cast it aside and fumbled in the dark until she found the thick tent pole. Holding it up allowed a vagrant beam of light coming through a window to show her the wood plug in the bottom of the pole. Her fingernails broke as she finally found purchase and slowly drew the plug out to reveal a hollowed interior. This was why Jack had been so diligent about carving the tent pole. He had done more than skin off the bark. The cavity whittled out was stuffed with paper. Hardly daring to believe it was this easy, she worked out the roll of paper and examined it.

Her lips moved as she read the names, saw the date, and finally located the description of Texas Jack Bedrich's silver strike. This deed wasn't legal because its original in the assay office had been destroyed, but with it an enterprising thief could register at the land office in Santa Fe as if Bedrich had never found the silver.

Hands shaking a mite, she tucked the deed into her dress pocket. For a moment she touched the cool metal of the derringer alongside it. One way or another she would free her son.

Marianne left the stables and mounted, resolutely riding for the edge of town and the abandoned stock tank.

25

"No question in my mind," Sheriff Whitehill said, raising the beer mug to his lips. He licked off the foam before pouring some of the bitter fluid down his gullet. He made a face, then put the empty mug on the stained table. "I got witnesses comin' out the ass that Frank was stalkin' Texas Jack up in Santa Fe."

"Whoever killed him did you a favor," Slocum said. He leaned back, watching the fat barkeep pace back and forth like he was trapped in a cage. "Think of the expense of a trial, then a hanging."

"Likely he'd have been sent to prison. Yuma's got room right now, or so I hear." Whitehill motioned for another round. Slocum wasn't going to object since the sheriff seemed inclined to pay in return for someone listening to his bragging about good detective work.

"So who killed him?" Whitehill fell silent as the barkeep delivered the beers and then left, walking slow as if he hoped to overhear what the two men were talking about.

"I've got my suspicions. There are a passel of miners out

at the Argent Mine who wouldn't take kindly to anyone killing Carstairs. For all his faults, his crew respected him."

"As a miner, maybe, but he was a son of a bitch. Lost a dozen men in less than three months 'cuz he pushed them to take risks underground." Whitehill took a deep breath, stared at the beer, then downed it in a long gulp. "That's why Smitty bamboozled those two urchins into settin' explosives. He figgered nobody'd notice if they got blowed up. He was right."

"Almost right," Slocum said. He left his beer on the table, watching the bubbles die a rapid death along the rim. "Marianne's not the kind to let her boy risk his skin like that, especially without telling her."

Whitehill laughed and then said, "She's a fine mother. You gonna drink that, Slocum? Can't let a beer go to waste."

Slocum pushed it across to the lawman, who began sipping at it. He made a face at the bitter taste, then upended the mug as he had done before. This kept the taste from gagging him.

"You find anybody in Santa Fe who knew where Bedrich's strike was?"

"He never got to the land office, but I seen a copy of an assay report that should have gone with a formal claim. That's one hell of a strike he found, if the ore's any indication."

"So a man recording that claim is likely to be rich?"

"Filthy rich. I think Texas Jack wanted to get free of Frank to work the claim. That's why he gave up a moderately good mine, but Frank wised up and knew Texas Jack was up to something. Probably thought he was owed half."

"But he tried to take it all," Slocum said. He looked up and motioned.

"Who's that?" Whitehill said. "Son of a bitch, he ain't comin' in here! I—"

"Calm down, Sheriff. He won't be here but a minute." Slocum motioned more decisively. Billy McCarty came in, looking fearfully at the sheriff.

"You're supposed to be watchin' after your friend," Whitehill said.

"Aww, Randolph's all right. He's asleep over in the hotel lobby. I been doin' some, uh, work for Mr. Slocum here."

"What'd you see, Billy?" Slocum took out two bits and spun the coin on the table. The whirling silver mesmerized the boy. As it slowed, he grabbed it faster than a striking snake. Slocum was impressed with the boy's reflexes and good eye.

"He rode on out o' town like the demons of hell was after him. I followed a ways, then came right on back. He went to the old stock tank."

"The one where you and Randolph played?" Slocum asked.

"Played. Hell, Mr. Slocum, we—" Billy looked at Whitehill, more defiant than before. "We hung out there, that's for sure."

"He's out there now?"

"What's this all about?" Whitehill demanded.

"Just cleaning up some unfinished business. No need to get your dander up, Sheriff." Slocum left the Lonely Cuss, but Billy tugged on his sleeve and stopped him when they got outside. Slocum looked at him, then tensed at the expression rippling across the boy's face.

"He tossed somethin' into Miz Lomax's cell. She busted out a few minutes later, then lit out goin' in the same direction."

"You did good not saying anything in front of the sheriff. Did Marianne hurt Dangerous Dan?"

"Locked him in his own cell," Billy said, grinning wickedly. "Where all them lawmen belong, if you ask me."

"You're sure Randolph is still in the hotel?"

"Was not five minutes 'fore I found you in the saloon."

"You stay with Randolph and don't let him out of your sight. You've got that knife of yours? Use it if anybody tries to kidnap him again."

"Yes, *sir!*" Billy flashed his knife and waved it about.

Slocum was glad he wasn't on the receiving end of that sharp-edged weapon. Billy's bloodthirstiness would keep Randolph safe, and woe to anyone trying to harm him.

Marianne Lomax slowed and finally drew rein on Tucker's stolen horse so she could look over the dark earthen bank of the old stock tank. She had no idea why it had been abandoned, but it presented a real threat for her now. The dark walls, broken in places, afforded her mysterious benefactor in escaping jail—and Randolph's kidnapper—any number of places to hide. A single shot would take her from the saddle and doom her son.

She stepped down and used the bulk of the horse as a shield. Not knowing where the kidnapper hid made this futile. For all she knew, she was exposed on the wrong side of the horse's body, but it made her feel a little better. Clutching the derringer hidden in her skirt pocket until her entire arm trembled, she took a step forward.

Aware of any slight noise, she advanced until she reached one breach in the earthen wall. She heard night birds swooping down on small animals trying to sip at the scum-covered water. Tiny death cries mocked her. The wind had died and in the distance a coyote howled mournfully. But she heard nothing of the man who had stolen away her son.

"I have it. Where's Randolph?" Marianne tried to speak up strongly, putting on a brave front. The reality betrayed her emotions. A shrill voice, trembling and unsure, only bolstered her adversary's courage.

For all she knew, he might get off on her fear. The crinkle of paper in her pocket as she pulled the derringer out a small amount so it wouldn't get caught on cloth told her what Frank's partner actually wanted. Torturing her the way he did might be fun, but his greed drove him to kill. The deed Bedrich had hidden away in the hollowed-out tent pole made all this worthwhile for the man.

"You brought it?"

She spun, looked around, then elevated her gaze to the top of a dirt wall. Starlight glinted off the muzzle of a rifle pointed down at her.

"Where's my son?"

"Safe enough. For the moment. He'll die if you don't have the deed and give it to me."

She started to yank out the derringer and fire, but the shot for her was impossible. All the man exposed was an arm, a hand, and the rifle. She could only make him mad. He had her squarely in his sights and held the high ground. She had never understood the advantage before. Now it worked against her, having a sniper able to track her no matter how she ran or hid.

"That's not good enough," she said. Marianne dropped the pistol back into her pocket and clutched the deed, pulling it out to flash whitely in the night as she waved it about. "You don't get this without me getting my son first."

"I can kill you."

"You don't know if this is the deed. It might be a map to where I hid it. A map that's no damned good to you unless I tell you the key."

"You're bluffing."

Marianne wanted to cry out that she wasn't. She knew the pitch of her voice would betray the lie. It took all her self-control to remain silent. Let the son of a bitch find his own answer.

"Don't think you are," he said. "But you spin a good tale. I've heard that."

Marianne tensed. She finally identified the voice.

"Gallifrey!" Marianne tried to hold her tongue, but the revelation that the owner of the Lonely Cuss was Frank's partner stunned her.

"Took you long enough to figger it out."

"You greedy bastard!"

"Greedy? Yeah, maybe, but I ain't makin' a dime off the saloon. Got bills comin' out my ears and bill collectors threatenin' to break my head if I don't pay up." Tom Gallifrey stood, silhouetted against the stars. He still held the rifle pointed down at her.

The shot would still be hard for her to make. And the bluff she ran with Gallifrey might mean her son's death. She hadn't heard a peep out of Randolph. Gallifrey might have him tied up somewhere else. If she killed Gallifrey, she might never find her son before he died of thirst and hunger.

"Put the deed under a rock and ride away. I'll set your boy free when I stake the claim."

"But the map is—"

"You're lyin'. That's the deed. You made that up about this bein' a map to where you hid the deed, didn't you?"

"Yes," she said, slumping.

She bent, put the deed under a rock so a tiny breeze wouldn't carry it off, then looked up. Fingers wrapped tensely around the derringer again. Her finger tapped nervously on the trigger.

"Where's Randolph?"

For a moment, Gallifrey vanished from sight. She heard rock and dirt sliding into the pond, then the saloon owner appeared in the notch in the pond wall. He kept the rifle leveled on her. She would have to distract him, then draw and fire.

When she found out where he had hidden her son.

"Your brat's in town. Go to the Lonely Cuss and ask my brother. He'll tell you."

"Just like that?"

"Tell him the owl's roostin' tonight. That's the code that'll let him know you gave me the deed."

Gallifrey dropped to his knees and snatched up the deed, holding it over his head to get the faint starlight onto the page. Marianne knew this was her only chance. She whipped out the derringer, held it in both hands as she aimed, and pulled the trigger.

The dull metallic click made her cry out in horror.

Gallifrey looked over and laughed harshly.

"You didn't think I'd give you a gun that'd fire so you could use it against me, did you?"

"How'd you know I wouldn't shoot the deputy?"

"Didn't much matter if you tried and nuthin' happened. I know them lawmen too good. Shove a gun under their noses and they'll beg you not to shoot."

Marianne tried to fire the derringer again. Again all she got was the hammer falling on a punk cartridge.

"You get on back to town. But first . . ."

Gallifrey moved fast. He batted her hands holding the tiny pistol out of the way, stepped close, and kissed her hard. The move so took her by surprise she couldn't resist. He pushed her away.

"Maybe when I'm rich I kin pay you to come to my bed."

She went crazy, clawing at Gallifrey's face. He shoved the rifle muzzle into her belly and held her at bay.

"Reckon that means you don't want to see any more o' me. That's fine. You won't. I'll stake the claim and get rich and let you and your guttersnipe starve." He poked harder. Marianne took a step back, stumbled, and fell heavily.

This spooked her horse. It reared, clawed at the air, and then ran off.

Tom Gallifrey laughed and disappeared behind the earthen walls. Before Marianne could get to her feet, she heard his horse galloping away into the night. Tears of frustration ran down her cheeks.

"If you lied about Randolph, so help me, you won't be able to run far enough. I won't care if they hang me. You're going to die if you've hurt him!"

26

"There you are, you flea-bitten, cock-sucking son of a bitch!" Marianne Lomax launched herself from the door leading into the Lonely Cuss Saloon all the way to the bar and across it, her fingers grabbing for the rolls of fat on Justin Gallifrey's neck.

She crashed onto the bar and knocked glasses in all directions. The customers separated and stared. Marianne didn't explode like this, not that they'd seen.

"Wait, stop, you're chokin' me!"

"I mean to do more than that if you've hurt him. I'll rip your balls off and stuff them in your gaping eye sockets!"

Slocum looked at the sheriff, who shrugged. When Whitehill made no move to stop the one-sided fight, Slocum heaved to his feet, went to the bar, and grabbed Marianne around her trim waist. It took two heaves to pry her loose from Gallifrey.

"He's got Randolph. His brother kidnapped Randolph and this one's hiding him out somewhere. I swear by all that's holy, I'll *kill* you if you've harmed one hair on his head."

"I don't know what you're talkin' 'bout," Justin Gallifrey said, rubbing his raw and bleeding throat. Marianne's fingernails had raked along both sides of his fleshy neck. If Slocum hadn't pulled her away when he had, she would have ripped out the man's throat.

Slocum considered letting her go to watch it happen, but he kept a firm grip until she settled down. Then he had to grab for her again as she surged forward, going for Gallifrey's eyes.

"Settle down," Slocum said. "Randolph is fine. Billy's watching over him."

"Where? I want to see him. Where is he?"

"At the hotel, in the lobby, more 'n likely," Whitehill said, sauntering up. "That's where me and Slocum left 'em hours back."

"He wasn't kidnapped?" Marianne's eyes turned into cold pools of death. She started for Justin Gallifrey again, but the barkeep shied away, slamming into the back bar and knocking down a few bottles.

A couple patrons made comment on how that was such a waste of liquor, but nobody crossed to the other side to sop up any of the spilled whiskey. To have done so would put them between Marianne and Gallifrey. Better to try to lasso a Texas tornado.

"I don't know what the bitch's talkin' about! Honest. She's gone plumb crazy from havin' so many men that it's rotted her brain."

Slocum swung Marianne behind him and stepped to the bar. His arms were longer, and he grabbed a handful of canvas apron. He pulled hard, slamming Gallifrey into the far side of the bar and drawing his face so it was within inches of his own.

"You apologize."

"Else?"

"I could beat your face into raw beefsteak for such disrespect, but I'm more inclined to let her do with you what she wants. That's not going to be pretty."

"I don't know what you're talkin' about. I saw that red-headed guy with the boy, like I told you days and days ago. I ain't see either of them, man or boy, since. What's my brother upped and done now?"

The beer hung heavy on Gallifrey's breath. Slocum relaxed his grip and let the barkeep back off a few inches, but he still held his apron. The man was telling the truth, as far as Slocum could tell. He twisted hard, slammed Gallifrey's head into the bar, then released him. The man let out a moan of pain and fell to the floor amid the broken glass and spilled booze.

"Tom's been real busy," Whitehill said. "That one down there, Justin, he don't have the sense God gave a goose."

"He doesn't know anything about this," Slocum agreed.

"He lied? He *lied* about taking Randolph?" Marianne cried.

"Wouldn't be the first time a man's fibbed to a lady," Whitehill said.

"Oh, no," she said, finding a chair and sinking into it.

"Randolph is fine," Slocum assured her.

"But Gallifrey has the deed to Jack's claim. I gave it to him thinking I was ransoming Randolph."

"Ma? What's goin' on?"

Slocum saw the expression of despair vanish from Marianne's face as her son hobbled into the saloon, followed by Billy. The older boy grinned ear to ear.

"Randolph!" Marianne grabbed up her son and whirled him about, to his sharp cry of pain.

"Ma, stop. My leg's hurtin' somethin' fierce."

"You're safe, you're safe. He never kidnapped you?"

"Frank? He's dead. Mr. Slocum got me away just fine. What are you goin' on about?"

"Mr. Slocum's kept you safe. You and Billy go on back to the hotel."

"Do I have to? Miz Gruhlkey is on the warpath. She's orderin' us around like we was hired help. Well, Billy is, but she don't pay him 'til the end of the month and that's—"

"Back," Marianne said firmly, gently pushing her son toward the door.

As soon as the two boys left, Marianne whirled about and pressed close to Slocum, looking up at him.

"You saved him this time, too. You kept him safe as you said you would. But Gallifrey has Jack's deed." She sighed. Slocum liked the sight of her breasts rising and falling. Her lips thinned as she saw his attention. "Don't look so smug. Gallifrey *stole* the deed!"

"Swindled you is more like it, though I likely could make a case for him stealin' it," the sheriff said.

"It's lost for all time," she said. "Jack's legacy is gone since I have no idea where the claim is. Gallifrey can register it as his own, and there's no way I can dispute it."

"You got some spare time now, Sheriff, or should I take Dangerous Dan with me?" Slocum asked.

"Nuthin' of pressin' interest here in Silver City. You got your gear?"

"Don't have a rifle, but I don't think I'll need one if you're along."

"What are you talking about? John? Harvey?" Marianne looked from one to the other but her gaze settled on Slocum for the explanation.

"I know where Gallifrey is going. He has to put down his own markers before registering the claim."

"How do you know?" Marianne stared at him. Slocum tried not to smile too much.

"I figured out where Bedrich had hidden the deed back at the campsite." He glanced sidelong at Whitehill, wondering if the sheriff would ask about this. The lawman seemed oblivious to what Slocum and Marianne had been doing before finding the hollowed-out tent pole.

"You knew it was there, and you let me give it to Gallifrey?" Her mouth opened in surprise, then she clamped it shut. The set to her jaw told Slocum a storm was brewing.

"We got to ride, Slocum. Don't want that varmint to get too far ahead of us."

Slocum touched Marianne on the arm, then rushed from the Lonely Cuss, trailing the lawman. That he had found the deed before her had to rankle, but Slocum would never have let her make the exchange for Randolph if he had known Gallifrey had conspired to get her free of the jailhouse. The saloon owner had been a mite more clever than Slocum had expected.

But it would all work out now. He vaulted onto horseback and trotted after the sheriff, ready to put this to an end.

"You sure this is the place, Slocum?"

"I'm sure," Slocum said. "It took a spell for me to figure out a patch of worthless ground that hadn't been claimed already, yet was likely enough to fool Gallifrey."

"He ain't a prospector. He knows squat about mining. From what Marianne said, he wants Texas Jack's claim so he can sell it and then hightail it."

Slocum wondered at the sheriff's anger. Somehow, it seemed a worse crime to sell the stolen claim than it would have been to work it. If Whitehill thought a minute, he would realize Tom Gallifrey spent all his time avoiding hard work. The Lonely Cuss was a failure in a sea of opportunity because he had no idea how to run a business. His brother, Justin, was clueless and yet did a better job. Marianne could have turned a profit if she had been in charge.

His thoughts turned to her. She was something special in his life then and now. He admired the way she put her life on the line to save Randolph. It wouldn't have been necessary if she'd stayed in jail, all safe and sound, but he couldn't fault her for escaping. Since Whitehill never mentioned the jailbreak, the sheriff wasn't likely to charge her with a crime. Before they had left, Whitehill had let Tucker out of the cell. The embarrassed look on the deputy's face was punishment enough. When word got out in Silver City, Tucker would have a hard time living it down. But he would. He was a hard man and brooked no argument when it came to enforcing the law.

"You coulda picked a better spot to ambush him. He can ride up from any of three directions. No way of being sure we got him in a cross-fire."

"Up on the rise," Slocum said. "We position ourselves there and can get a decent view of all the approaches."

"Not through the trees," Whitehill said, snapping the reins to get his horse moving in the direction Slocum had indicated. He bitched about their post even as he settled down with his rifle, overlooking the likeliest direction Gallifrey would use to stake his claim.

They sat in silence for more than an hour. Slocum's patience had been honed during the war when he was a sniper, but the killer's absence began to wear on him. He doubted Tom Gallifrey had anything up his sleeve, but he'd been smarter than Slocum had expected several times before. It wasn't until he'd figured out Gallifrey was Frank's partner that everything fell into place. Gallifrey had been careful about not being seen at the cabin where Frank had held the boy hostage.

"It don't pay to think too much," Whitehill said softly.

"He'll be here."

"That's not what I meant," the sheriff said. "After we nail this bastard, what are you gonna do?" The way the sheriff fixed him with a hard stare made Slocum uncomfortable.

He wasn't sure what he intended. Duty required him to get some justice for Marianne. Her time in Silver City had been rocky, and the people didn't cotton much to her. They might think better of her if she had the full wealth of a major silver strike in her pocket, but Slocum knew things never changed deep down. Surface politeness peeled away quick unless there was deep-down respect.

"Gallifrey might kill us both. That'll take care of worrying about the future."

Whitehill snorted contemptuously.

"Ain't what I meant and you know it."

"Need a saddle for the pony," Slocum said. "A rifle would be good, too."

"You can prance all around it, but what are your intentions toward—"

Slocum silenced the lawman with a quick gesture. He pointed into a stand of trees where a man appeared as if by magic.

"There's the varmint," Whitehill said. He lifted the rifle to his shoulder, finger tightening on the trigger. Slocum had no doubt the sheriff was going to cut down the claim jumper and murderer.

"I'll fetch him," Slocum said. He slid his six-shooter back into its holster and made his way carefully down the side of the hill overlooking the claim.

He knew how easy it would be to leave Gallifrey's body for the carrion eaters, but he wanted more. He wanted to see the expression on the man's face when he learned how he had been snookered. It gave some payback for his crimes. Not enough, but maybe a noose around his neck would give the best satisfaction. Slocum intended to find out.

Moving like an Apache warrior, Slocum came within a dozen feet of Gallifrey without being detected. The man worked to pencil in descriptions of each cache he left to mark the boundaries of the claim. Now and again, he pulled out the deed he had taken from Marianne and matched the description. As he hummed to himself, he neglected to watch his back.

"You wonder why you don't find any of Bedrich's markers?"

Gallifrey whirled about, hand going for the six-gun tucked into his belt. He froze when he saw that Slocum had the drop on him.

"Slocum," he said, more a snarl than mere recognition. "You figured out where the claim was, too."

"Something like that," Slocum said, going to the saloon owner and plucking the six-gun from his belt. He tossed it away.

"We don't have to fight over this. There's plenty for the both of us. I ain't spendin' my life squeezin' silver from the ground. I'll sell the claim. We can split it. You don't have the look of a miner either."

"I've done some of that in my day," Slocum said, beginning to enjoy watching Gallifrey squirm. The weasely man's eyes darted about like a trapped rat. He ought to suffer a bit more. "Truth is, I worked as a surveyor for damned near six months."

"What's that got to do with anything?" Gallifrey straightened as the truth hit him. "This ain't Bedrich's claim!"

"Sheriff Whitehill came back from Santa Fe with a stack of blank deeds. I spent some time filling in the description of this piece of land."

"It's worthless?"

"Looks like it."

"Then where's the real deed?"

"It was in the tent pole," Slocum said. "I replaced it with the one Marianne gave you to ransom her son."

"You have the real deed? You're gonna steal Texas Jack's claim for yerself!"

Gallifrey feinted toward the spot where Slocum had tossed his six-shooter, but Slocum saw a different scheme in the man's eyes. He half turned and fumbled in his coat pocket. By the time he pulled out a derringer, Slocum had squeezed off a shot that hit a thigh bone and knocked the man to the ground. Gallifrey continued to fumble his small pistol into line with Slocum's chest.

"You'll never make it," Slocum said, taking aim. "It's not like shooting a man in the back, is it? Or killing a partner who doesn't expect you to double-cross him."

"They had it comin'. They'd've done the same to me."

Slocum considered where to put his slug as Gallifrey steadied his derringer with both hands. The report from behind Slocum settled the matter. Whitehill had put his rifle bullet through the top of Gallifrey's head.

"He couldn't have shot me, Sheriff," Slocum said, sliding his pistol into the cross-draw holster.

"Not the way I saw it."

"How did you see it?" Slocum asked, knowing the answer.

"No way of provin' he had anything to do with kidnapping young Randolph that first time. Frank was on the hook for that. Killing Frank? Could have been Marianne what done the deed. A clever prosecutor would make that point in court. With the drunk miners we got for a jury, and how they think about Marianne, they might have believed it."

"And him getting the bogus deed means nothing either, since Randolph was never actually kidnapped the second time," Slocum said.

"Might have tried him on fraud, but in New Mexico Territory who ain't guilty of that?"

"Better get on back to town," Slocum said. "Do we leave him or take him with us?"

It took them the better part of a half hour to tie Tom Gallifrey over his horse since Slocum took his saddle for his own pony.

27

"Good riddance," Marianne said through clenched teeth.

She stood in front of the Lonely Cuss watching the under-taker struggle with Tom Gallifrey's body. He finally released the knots on the rope Slocum and Whitehill had used, only to have the corpse flop over the bare back of the horse and fall into the dust. Gallifrey lay sprawled in such an ungainly fashion that his brother rushed out to help Mr. Olney get the body upright and into a small cart he used to haul bodies around town.

"You can thank Whitehill for that," Slocum said. He almost added that he had considered the shooting all the way back to Silver City and had come to the conclu-sion Whitehill had gunned down Gallifrey to impress Mar-ianne.

"I'll thank him in due time," Marianne said. She stepped closer and pressed into Slocum's side. "It's well past time for you to get your reward for all you've done."

"Not that much," Slocum said. He tried not to respond to the lovely woman's nearness. He failed. She saw the bulge in his jeans and grinned broadly.

"I see something that *is* that much," she said, her fingers threading through his. She squeezed, then tugged him back from the crowd gathered to see Gallifrey carted off to the funeral parlor.

Slocum was glad to leave the buzz of the citizens. Most of them speculated as to what happened, why the sheriff had cut down the saloon owner, what part Marianne Lomax had in it. From the overheard comments, many of them, especially the women, blamed Marianne for an innocent man's death. The truth would percolate about and eventually they'd realize what a snake in the grass Tom Gallifrey had been.

Slocum figured that Justin Gallifrey had nothing to do with his brother's schemes. If anything, he had been used as cruelly as any of the others. But Justin might come out ahead and inherit the Lonely Cuss. The saloon might be knee-deep in unpaid bills, but anyone who couldn't make a success of a gin mill in a mining boomtown was not concentrating on business. That had been Tom Gallifrey's problem, Slocum guessed. He wanted to get rich quick and hadn't tended his bar. The real mother lode had been his for the taking, and he had ignored it in favor of ill-gotten precious metal.

"We can go up to my room," she said in a conspiratorial whisper. "Mrs. Gruhlkey is out for the day, over at the church getting ready for the social this Sunday."

Slocum let her lead him up the stairs.

"What about Randolph?"

"He and Billy are somewhere. I don't know, and the way he's been since that mending leg started itching something fierce, he's not likely to come home 'til sundown."

They went into her small room. She looked around, hands on her hips.

"Hardly seems right to call this home, but maybe home is where the bed is." She turned and shoved Slocum backward. The edge of the bed caught him at the knees so he tumbled back, rocking on the springs.

The springs creaked even more as Marianne added her weight to the bed, straddling his waist and towering above him. Their eyes locked. Her expression softened as she began unbuttoning her blouse. He helped her shuck it off, leaving her naked to the waist. She rose and scooted about, getting her skirts out of the way.

His hand strayed under the piles of cloth, found a warm, bare leg, and worked upward. She wasn't wearing her bloomers.

"No underwear?" he said, grinning. "Is it that hot a day?"

"Not yet. But it will be," she said, leaning forward so her breasts hung just inches above his face.

Straining, he locked his lips around one nipple, teased it to a throbbing hardness, then moved to the other. Supporting her weight on her hands, Marianne threw back her head as she moaned in pleasure at his oral attention.

His tongue laved the tips and then slipped down into the deep canyon between. Salt and woman-taste assaulted his taste buds. She was sweating but there was more, so much more. He loved the way Marianne tasted, every part of her body. He lapped and licked and worked around the base of the cones until she trembled.

She pushed back upright, catching his hands and pressing them into the tits he had just licked so excitingly. As he squeezed the soft, milky globes, she reached down and worked at his belt, his jeans, the buttons on his fly.

Through some passionate wrestling, they rolled over and over, changed positions, and finally both ended up naked as jaybirds on their sides, facing each other. Marianne threw a leg up over Slocum's hip and snuggled closer, his manhood pressing into the thatched triangle between her thighs.

She rocked back and forth until Slocum thought he was going to lose control. The feel of her flesh, flowing under his roving hands, her firm round ass, the sleek thighs, and the tender spot now turning damp with her inner oils all convinced him he needed more.

"Are you ready?" he whispered.

"I've been ready from the instant I saw you back in Calhoun," she said. No further talk was possible.

Their mouths crushed together in a kiss that mixed passion with desperation. They clung to each other as their hips repositioned. The tip of Slocum's erection touched her nether lips, parted them, and then sank in with a single long slick thrust.

The sensation assaulting Slocum caused his body to freeze. She surrounded him with warm and wet female flesh, then began squeezing his hidden length. He felt her belly muscles as she massaged him while so far up into her core. Slocum tried to relax and enjoy the sensations mounting throughout his loins, his belly, his chest.

He saw that she was flushed from her throat down across her breasts and knew she was as aroused as he was. Hips moving in a circular motion, he began stirring about within her. Her leg over his hip tightened, drawing him in even more.

The small movements of their bodies became more pronounced, more powerful, took on the same air of desperation the kiss had enjoyed. The air filled with lewd noises and then Marianne cried out. She tensed, clung fiercely to him, and relaxed. Slocum kept moving, slipping in and out of her well-greased slit with complete abandon now. When he finally got his release, they were both covered in sweat.

They flopped onto their backs, staring not at each other but at the cracked plaster ceiling. Slocum sought words to ask the question that had burned in him for some time.

"Is he?"

"Randolph?" Marianne partly turned away so he couldn't see her face, even if he looked.

"Is he my son?"

Marianne was silent for a spell, then her body began to quake. She sat up, her bare back toward him as she slumped forward. In a tiny voice, she said, "No, he's not."

Slocum sat on the other side of the bed, trying to figure

if she'd lied. Or if it mattered. He put on his clothes and strapped down his gun belt. By the time he tugged on his boots, she had slipped back into her dress. Her eyes were dry, but her face was pale and drawn.

"You're going?"

"I need to talk to the sheriff about a matter."

"But I'll see you . . . later?"

"Later," he said, leaving her room. His footsteps were slow, measured, as if he were marching to the gallows. By the time he reached the street, his pace picked up.

He found Sheriff Whitehill in his office, struggling over a pile of papers. The sheriff looked up with a disgusted expression.

"Should have left the son of a bitch for the buzzards. Olney's convinced the judge that the county's responsible for payin' for Gallifrey's burial. I'm gonna be lucky if it doesn't come out of my pay."

"I wanted to give you something," Slocum said, pulling a couple sheets of paper from his coat pocket. He let them flutter to the desk.

Whitehill didn't even glance at them.

"I wondered where Bedrich's real claim had got off to. Didn't want to rock the boat none on it, not since things look to be workin' themselves out."

"Marianne hasn't asked that question yet. Tell her you discovered the deed, then you give it to her."

"Woman can't own real property."

"Then you should record the deed as her legacy from Texas Jack and help her sell it. From all that's been said, the assay was high enough to have mining companies bidding on it till the cows come home."

"You don't want to give it to her yourself, Slocum?"

He shook his head. He wasn't sure if she had lied and, if she had, why. Or if she had told him the truth. After so many years, she might not want to be tied down to him—or thought he didn't want to be tied down with a family.

"Sheriff, Sheriff Whitehill! Come right now. I caught this sneak thief stealin' a half wheel of cheese from my store!"

Slocum saw the burly owner of the general store with his hand on Billy McCarty's collar. The boy struggled but couldn't get free.

"Are you goin' to arrest him?" the storekeeper demanded.

"A fellow gets mighty hungry, Seth," the lawman said to the store owner. He heaved a sigh, got to his feet, and took Billy by the arm. "Come along, son. I got to lock you up."

"You cain't! Mr. Slocum, you tell him I was only helpin' out Randolph. He was hungry and—"

"Take this to heart," Slocum said. "Don't do anything that'll get yourself locked up again."

He glanced at Texas Jack Bedrich's deed, fought a momentary hesitation, then nodded to the sheriff and stepped into the bright New Mexico sun. He had an Indian pony with a dead man's saddle on it. He mounted and rode away, trotting past the hotel. He looked up at the window of Marianne's room, thought he saw the curtain move. He might have been wrong.

"Later," he said, then put his heels to the horse and galloped east to find somewhere that wasn't Silver City.

GIANT-SIZED ADVENTURE FROM AVENGING ANGEL LONGARM.

BY TABOR EVANS

2006 Giant Edition:

LONGARM AND THE
OUTLAW EMPRESS

2007 Giant Edition:

LONGARM AND
THE GOLDEN EAGLE
SHOOT-OUT

2008 Giant Edition:

LONGARM AND THE
VALLEY OF SKULLS

2009 Giant Edition:

LONGARM AND THE
LONE STAR TRACKDOWN

2010 Giant Edition:

LONGARM AND THE
RAILROAD WAR

2013 Giant Edition:

LONGARM AND
THE AMBUSH AT HOLY
DEFIANCE

penguin.com/actionwesterns

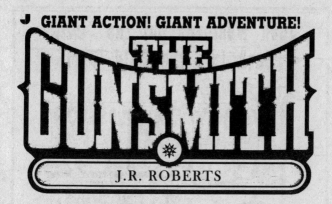

GIANT ACTION! GIANT ADVENTURE!

THE Gunsmith

J.R. ROBERTS

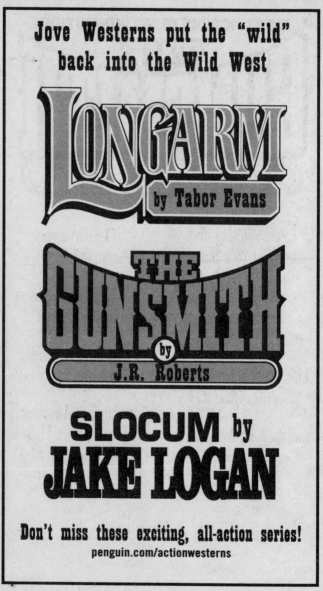